Buds Fore

DESTINY'S ROGUE

LINDA J. PARISI

You are so special!!
So glad you enjoy!!
Huge Hug —

CITY OWL
PRESS

DESTINY'S ROGUE
Blood Rogue, Book 3

CITY OWL PRESS
www.cityowlpress.com

Cover Design by MiblArt. All stock photos licensed appropriately.

Edited by Tee Tate.

For information on subsidiary rights, please contact the publisher at info@cityowlpress.com.

Print Edition ISBN: 978-1-64898-228-6

Digital Edition ISBN: 978-1-64898-227-9

Printed in the United States of America

To my husband John. You are my real-life hero. You are the reason I believe in Romance and HEA's. You will always be the love of my life and I will miss you forever.

Praise for the Works of Linda J. Parisi

"This book hit the mark, amazing characters, suspense, and the mystery behind the rogues. I loved every second of the book and read it in one sitting, now all I have to do is wait for the next book in the series which hopefully won't be too long." – *Paranormal Romance Guild*

"Stacy and Chaz light up the page together and are downright unforgettable. Plenty of steam and just enough danger to keep the plot zipping along at a fast, thrilling clip combine to make this a phenomenal read in the vein of JR Ward that fans of paranormal romance will adore as much as I did." – *April the Book Dragon*

"A charming story that was a nice derivative of a standard vampire story...I loved the drama and danger throughout the book. The insights into vampire politics were fascinating. Well written and very easy to read and understand, it was a great start to the series, and I'm looking forward to what happens next." – *MP Book Reviews*

"The story was well written in a way that the reader could stop after this book and not be disappointed. A great read for a cold weekend." – *Readers Favorite*

"Blood Rogue took me on a journey filled with suspense, danger, humor, and romance." – *Totally Addicted to Reading*

"The debut novel to a new paranormal series, Blood Rogue, is a fast-paced, action-packed fantasy from page one...It is an entertaining story readers can devour in no time." – *InD'tale Magazine*

"With a gritty urban backdrop and plenty of intriguing clan dynamics, Blood Rogue is a perfect vampire romance. Plenty of steam and just enough danger to keep the plot zipping along at a fast,

thrilling clip combine to make this a phenomenal read." – *Kat Turner,*
Author of Hex, Love, and Rock and Roll

"Blood Rogue is a well-crafted, smart adventure of the unlikeliest of
lovers...reminiscent of lore's age-old heartbreak, how can two beings
that belong in separate worlds ever be together? A great read!" – *M.*
Kate Quinn, Author of Endangered Diamond

Chapter One

STARING AT THE BURN MARKS IN THE GRASS, SAMIRA ANAI SE-BAT tried not to draw in the acrid stench of burned flesh as she tasted the terrible finality of death. She clenched her jaw and swept her fingers over the blackened blades. These vampires never should have died. There could not be such a thing as collateral damage.

Funny, in this moment, she felt a well of guilt as she asked the never-ending question. Was fate always the answer?

Sam rose, brushing off her fingers as if such a simple action could remove the blood from her hands. So much pain in the revelations time wrought, so many paths to take, so many more created when a choice had to be made. Why were some called to duty and others to destruction?

The estate seemed as dismal as her thoughts. Barren trees and brown bushes fashioned a picture far from a work of art but very real, as real as what could be a glimpse of their future.

"My lady?"

Lia. Ever faithful and always by her side. When Sam didn't reply right away, Lia didn't continue. Her friend—no, so much more—must have realized Sam was upset but would find out what bothered her in due time.

"Yes?" Sam answered, lifting a single brow.

"We found two vampires hiding in the woods."

Sam's heart sank, fearing the inevitable. Rogue vampires. If Antu had his way, no one would be able to stop Armageddon. "Did they take the Nirvana?"

Lia nodded as she compressed her lips into a thin line. "I can smell the sickness on them, though it is faint."

"Then they have time," Sam murmured. Time, ever a friend and now an enemy. Time had stripped this place of its dignity and its purpose. Had time done the same to her? "Poor fools." She sighed. "Bring them to me."

Lia bowed, slipping away, and all Sam could think of was the waste, just like the home in front of her. Left to rot with white paint peeling from the stately walls and tiles missing like rotted teeth from the roof, Antu always dropped his toys when he finished with them.

Lia returned with two ordinary looking young men, both sharing nondescript brown hair and eyes and common features. Their similarities ended with their outward appearance. One quaked with fear while the other stood shoulders back and chin lifted. Not with pride but anger, waves of which washed over Sam as she waited.

"Who are you?" the arrogant one asked.

"Jake Sully," she murmured, feeling like the movie character, belonging in her skin but not belonging in her world anymore.

"What's that?"

"Never mind." She drew herself up to her full height and answered, "I am Samira Anai Se-Bat, high priestess of the Temple, guardian of our race, keeper of the true light by which we live."

The fearful one clutched his head in his hands and chanted, "We're dead. We're dead."

Sam needed answers so she turned to the one who could at least speak. "You were made without sanction."

This one frowned as if not understanding her while the other continued to whisper the same two words.

"Casperian made you?" she asked.

"Past tense?" the braver vampire asked.

She inclined her head toward the funeral pyre behind the house.

The quivering one started to screech. "We're dead. We're dead."

Sam nearly rolled her eyes. Instead, she lifted her hand, and he froze. Silence at last. "You were created without just cause," Sam answered with a frown. "Vampires are not made lightly, and the consequences of such an act can affect all of us."

His sideways glance told her he didn't care. He looked down on her, obviously not caring about titles or status. "I exist. I am immortal."

"Not true. Casperian lied," she told him, not liking his arrogance. "Eventually vampires age, and then they go rogue, which is what you are doing right now."

"Rogue?"

"Soon the need for blood will destroy all other thoughts. You will want to feed from every human you encounter. Animals as well."

If he seemed surprised, he didn't show it, which made her wonder if his posture showed arrogance or bravado. She'd been forced to tune out the other one's thoughts so she couldn't hear. "I don't believe you."

Denial. Of course. "What you wish to believe or not believe doesn't change the truth. Both of you are aging at an accelerated rate, which will eventually make you crave blood above all else."

She watched him trying to understand. "Like rabies?"

Sam knew of the disease. But those were animals. Then she thought of an out-of-control rogue. Not much difference. "I suppose."

"Then we're dead."

His response sent a quick shiver up her spine. With her age, came the ability to communicate with other vampire minds. These two wouldn't stop shouting at her. Sam refused to allow their thoughts to bombard her. "I've given no such order. Perhaps someone else?"

She unfroze the frightened one, and he began to blubber. "We're dead. We're dead."

"Why does he keep saying this?" she asked the other vampire.

He swallowed hard before answering. "The other. He'll kill us."

Finally. As she thought. "Then you know of whom I speak."

He shuddered. "Yes."

Sam turned to catch Lia's gaze, her worst fears confirmed. Lia paled, if that were possible.

Her eyes widened as she whispered, "Can this be true?"

Sorrow filled Sam. Secrets never remain secret forever. She nodded, blowing out a deep breath. "He escaped."

"How long?" Lia choked out.

"He made Casperian." In light of what had happened, there could be no more lies, certainly no more omissions. "And Hunter Pierce. So at least two thousand years."

"Hunter?" Lia's lips parted as she digested this information. "And he has waited all these years?" Sam could only nod. "His wrath will be—"

"Unimaginable," Sam finished for her.

"Why did you not tell me?"

"So that you would not panic as you are doing now. Besides, I wasn't completely certain. I sensed him in Hunter, but he remained quiet. I hoped a false hope that he would remain that way."

"False hope indeed," Lia bit out. "More like the serpent Apep lying in wait."

"Yes."

Sam turned back to the two vampires. "Your maker lied to you, and he betrayed you. Nirvana isn't just a drug, it's a poison. The Nirvana has caused your cells to age at an accelerated rate. You are already dying."

The frightened one began to weave and moan, crouched almost to the point of curling in upon himself. The other fisted his fingers and locked his jaw, a tic vibrating in his cheek. "We were cheated."

"Yes. There is no such thing as eternal life. Even vampires die."

A picture of Mikhail, the leader of the Paladin, so ravaged that he no longer looked human, filled her mind. As a Paladin, Mikhail had sworn to protect human and vampire alike from the very thing he'd become, a rogue. In the end, as a rogue, he simply wanted to kill them all. Death became his answer. Then she realized Hunter wasn't among the dead, just Casperian. Hope seared through her. Had Tori been able to find a cure using her blood? The possibility stayed Sam's hand.

"I didn't find Hunter's body among the dead," she told Lia. "If he still lives, then perhaps there's hope for these two." She motioned to her soldiers. "Take them back to Hunter's cell. Guard them well."

"Yes, my lady," one replied.

After her soldiers left, Lia remained with the reminder of her failure floating through the air.

Sam said, "We have much to atone for."

"We?" Lia asked. "I do not understand. How could *we* have anything to atone for?"

Sam reached out and squeezed Lia's shoulder. "You are too good to me." Lia shook her head. "We never should have run from the temple that day."

Lia's gasp warmed her heart. "How can you say that? You were already wounded and no match for him. What purpose would your death have served?"

A question that still haunted her. "One less foil for his games."

Lia shook her head. "No, one less protector to keep him in check."

Yes, Lia spoke the truth. But afterwards? "As soon as I knew there existed even the slightest possibility that he lived, I should have sought him out and challenged him. He would have been weak—"

"He would not have let you find him," Lia scoffed. "If he did, it would be to set a trap as he is doing right now. Besides, death is not your way and never has been. All you've ever done is protect."

Sam grimaced. "Which I've obviously failed to do now."

Lia shook her head. "No. He cares for nothing. You care for everything. This caring is why you let me take you away and why you did not hunt him down once you were aware of the truth."

"No Lia, you're wrong."

Lia simply stared, her loyalty a beacon in her gaze.

"I was afraid."

"Afraid of what?" Lia spat out the words as if they burned her tongue.

"Failing. Weakness. This."

"You think caring is weakness? You think staying your hand and not killing is failing? I do not understand. Your heart is why your people love and respect you. It is why they fought for you then and why they fight for you now."

"Steadfast friend," Sam told Lia as her heart warmed. "Thank you." She stared deep into Lia's gaze, finding the rock Sam desperately needed to steady her soul. "But we both know how this will end. He will stop at nothing until I am on bended knee and groveling at his feet." She reached out and squeezed Lia's shoulder. "He wants my head."

Lia's lips tightened into a thin line. Her cheek muscles clenched. "That cannot be allowed."

"I know. For if he succeeds in defeating me, will he be happy? For a time, perhaps. And then what? He will grow tired of his toys and what I once thought impossible will become possible. He'll want all living souls to join him in his death."

Lia's back locked, and her hand gripped the hilt of her knife in the holder beneath the flap of her jacket. "He is chaos, my lady, and we must fight him until our last breath."

Sam sighed. "Then we will fight."

"We will defeat him," Lia answered, conviction ringing through her words.

She sounded so confident. Sam wished she could be as certain. She turned to leave, and a picture flooded her mind of glass doors and a logo with a name beneath. CoRRStar Laboratories. For the first time in over two thousand years, Sam felt his presence. She drew in a swift breath as icy tendrils snaked around her heart. There was a difference between believing a thing within one's mind and knowing the truth.

She faltered, and Lia stopped beside her. Lia felt him too. "My lady?"

"I must go. I am being summoned."

Lia stilled, her eyes widened, and then her brows drew together. "I must go with you."

"No." She smiled. Sam tried to be honest with herself. She feared the extent of Antu's capabilities, the turmoil he could create. She feared her own failure and weakness, but she wasn't frightened of the man. She understood him too well and without her, his games became meaningless. "He doesn't want an ending, he wants a beginning. He won't try to harm me—yet. You must go back to New Jersey. If you can't warn Hunter, then you need to warn Mercy. When I return, I will warn The Council."

Lia made to argue then snapped her mouth closed. Her fist kept clasping and unclasping the hilt of her sword. She withdrew her arm slowly and nodded. "You will do what you must. And so will I."

"Yes," Sam muttered, not liking her choices at all. "Let the games begin."

Chapter Two

SAM PACED THE SMALL CONFINES OF THE ELEVATOR, FEELING EVERY movement of her steel prison. Her hand pressed against the wall as the man-made cage lurched between floors. Swallowing hard, she pictured a cable snapping and the helpless free-fall. She imagined never being able to escape, the walls closing in on her bit by bit. Breathing deeply, she shook her head, angry with herself for being fearful.

Had Antu felt the same in his self-made prison?

Metal clanged on metal, and Sam grabbed the elevator wall again. She braced her legs and sank her weight into her feet. Thirty-four floors in an enclosed box made her yearn for a breath of fresh air. The car slowed, and she whispered a blessing of thanks in her native tongue. The elevator doors opened into a hallway right in front of plate glass doors bearing the CoRRStar name and logo. She reached out, fingers splayed against the cool glass, and the hairs on the back of her neck rose.

Blood.

No human sat behind the massive, curved reception desk. Sam pushed open the door and breathed deeply as she rushed around the lacquered wood. She looked down and found a woman, still alive from the sound of her fluttering heartbeat. Thank the Gods.

Then she caught the scent she dreaded. He was here.

A low moan echoed down a long corridor to her left. Sam bent down and let her incisors grow. She placed them in the same holes on the woman's neck, shuddering at the taste, and gave the woman Lethe, the drug that would make her forget this day. A quick swipe of Sam's tongue closed the holes as she withdrew.

She reared back acknowledging the taste of him, the reality as sickening as the memory was enticing. Her brother in blood, Antu Si-Tayat, toyed with her, for he knew her every move.

We'll see about that.

She flashed down the hallway. Just about to throw open the doors to the office at the end, Sam whirled, sensing another presence. There could be but one other, Bahir, Antu's manservant, who had been with Antu since the beginning. And there could be nothing but death. A man lay on the floor of the office where she stood before. When she didn't hear a heartbeat, sadness filled her.

She ran to the next office to find Antu holding Cordell Stuart in his arms like a child. She'd seen his picture on her computer and had wondered at his likeness to another.

Sam's shoulders lifted. Her back straightened. She drew herself up to her regal height. "Brother."

"Sister."

She slammed her brows together, staring at Antu long and hard. He seemed unfazed by her rebuke. "You have no right to play with them."

Tiny red threads dripped down Stuart's neck, staining the pristine white of his shirt collar. She licked her lips. Antu merely smiled.

There would always be the blood.

His posture defied his actions, at ease, almost carefree. He bore the same bronze skin and midnight hair, falling loose to his shoulders. His black eyes seemed opaque, but they were rimmed with orange, a fire ready to rage out of control at any moment. He wore the colors of the temple, a black tunic with red lettering, a reminder of a past he had no business flaunting.

"Would you like some? In the past we would have shared in joy."

Memories flooded her brain. Blood sweeter than the ripest, most perfect peach. Arms and legs entwined as they coupled with such intense ecstasy. He saw each picture in her mind. Had she glimpsed a moment of regret in his gaze before mockery took its place?

"You destroyed that joy when you chose this path," Sam told him. "End this madness now."

He scrunched his face up at the word madness.

"You have no right to play with their lives," she repeated.

His brows shot up into his forehead. "Surely you jest."

Sam shook her head sadly. "I find no humor in what you are doing. Nor do I share your enjoyment in the games you continue to play."

"Games?" He quirked his mouth, and the blackness of his gaze deepened. He caressed Cordell Stuart's cheek with his fingers like a lover. "Very well. If you wish to call them games, so be it. Let's play. Beg for his life."

Sam curled her fingers as they tried to become fists. She breathed in and out to slow the beating of her heart. He'd been waiting for this day, this moment when their paths would cross again, and the perfect storm he created to force her to face an impossible situation.

Antu shifted, settling Stuart's weight in one arm as he lifted the man's head. "Does he remind you of anyone, sweet sister?"

Yes. Sam stared. *Nuya!* She'd seen the resemblance to the one she lost immediately. Her heart constricted as an old familiar pain knifed her gut. She lifted her gaze to find Antu reveling in her quandary. "You know I won't beg for his life. I cannot and will never be beholden to you again."

"So you've told me. But I wonder. One more minute, perhaps one more draw on his neck? Two at most?" Antu teased. He curled his upper lip, part anticipation, part sneer.

No matter what Antu chose to feel, if Sam gave in now, every being on the planet would be at risk.

She shook her head with the intention of trying to brazen her way out of this insanity. "You used an inferior being, brother. Casperian bore little strength and less intelligence."

"Stupid has its uses," he defended but she heard a hint of exasperation in his tone.

"Of that I'm quite certain. But why go to all the trouble if you were aware you were going to fail?"

"To vex you." His lips thinned. "And to rid myself of that annoying flea. Two thousand years of listening to him whine. You can't imagine."

"Then why bother?"

Antu lifted the corner of his mouth. "He allowed much."

Sam clucked her tongue. "Such behavior is beneath you."

"Is it?"

"I wouldn't know," she answered with disdain. "The Mother and Father gave you their gift. I don't understand why you abuse it so."

"You don't?"

She could feel her guts churn with anger and regret. She wanted to reach out and snatch Stuart from his grasp, but Antu might snap the man's neck before she could reach him. "Remember, brother, everything you do must be paid for. There are consequences to every action. Our parents taught us that."

"Yes, they did," he answered with a soft laugh. "What do humans call them these days? Ah, yes, they're called banks, and they have a word I'm looking for, yes that's it. They call it collateral. Year upon year upon year, asleep yet not asleep. I have gathered enough collateral, wouldn't you say?"

Sam decided not answer and inched closer.

Antu shook his head, brows drawing together in a straight black line. "I wouldn't."

"You're wrong," she countered, choosing caution over action. "What you did to our brothers and sisters can never be expunged. The punishment for murder is still death."

His entire face suffused red then darkened to near black. "Ahh, but you see? I didn't die."

Sam tried to stop the word before it escaped her lips. She failed. "Pity."

Antu's answer? To hoist Cordell Stuart higher in his arms and lower his head so that his lips grazed the man's neck. Sam lurched forward.

"Unh-unh-unh," Antu admonished.

Five thousand years ago, Samira Anai Se-Bat had entered the temple feeling the same hole grow inside her gut. Completely helpless, now as she had been then, Sam stared and begged. "In the name of whatever goodness is still inside you, do not do this. You will never be redeemed."

Antu ignored her words. "Do you want to know how I got out?"

Sam inclined her head, knowing she had to play Antu's game, but her guts clenched. She breathed deeply, not daring to let Antu know. "If you insist."

"A simple force of nature, a shift in the earth. My escape path became unsealed. The Father did not mean for me to die."

"Really? Believe what you will, what you must. You understood then just as you understand now, what you did was wrong. That's why you built the route in the first place. You're a coward."

"Coward?" He smiled. "No. I am a ruler. We were created to rule the earth, and we will do so again."

"We?" she asked, lifting her brow. She'd managed to inch closer while Antu spoke.

"Slip of the tongue." Antu bent his head again and lapped at Cordell Stuart's neck. "When you are dead, there will be no one left to oppose me."

Sam feared those words more than anything. Her mind whirled, and Antu took advantage of her weakness. He bit down on Cordell Stuart's neck again, and this time he didn't stop.

A second at most slipped by. Sam charged. By the time she reached them, Stuart had already begun falling to the floor, and Antu had slipped around her and fled out the door. Sam caught the dying man in her arms.

She'd called it the perfect storm. Antu planned them well. He knew her oath, was keenly aware of the dilemma she now faced. *Mother! Father! Why have you done this?*

She rocked the man in her arms. It would be so easy to end this farce right now and let Cordell Stuart slip to the floor. Easier still to bend down and finish what Antu started and turn the man into a vampire.

By the Gods! He looked so like Nuya up close. Sweet, shy, Nuya. The worshiper of the sun, the boy she grew up with and came to love for his integrity, his quiet strength. The boy who died to give her eternal life. By The Mother and The Father! Once was not enough?

Damn Antu to hell and back again. She faced the same choice now as she did then. Break her oath and turn Cordell Stuart into a vampire or be the cause of all-out war. For now, she realized Antu's exact actions. He planned to take Nirvana and create his army of rogues. Antu didn't care who died in the process for he wanted one thing. Power.

And only one man could stop him, the man who had created Nirvana in the first place. Cordell Stuart.

Sam trailed her fingertips down Cordell's pale cheek. The man gasped shallow breaths, desperate for air. Her heart shattered as the realization pounded away at her, for she would have to kill Nuya all over again.

She gazed down at the man as her heart turned over. For over five thousand years, she'd accepted her duty with the same vigor, the same determination, as she did the first day of her new life. The creators, The Mother and The Father, gave the chosen a gift and a curse. Time. The passage of which could be both at any given moment.

There were ten, five males and five females, chosen as mates for an eternity. Did their creators know the evil they'd spawned? Were they aware? Even when the moon filled the night sky, and she felt alone and overwhelmed, Sam knew there had to be balance. They'd been taught about balance from the beginning. The price of reverence? Duty, the duty to protect all living beings, human and vampire. She'd seen so much, lived through the wonder of discovery, and suffered through the atrocities of war. But love? Once she broke the bond, Sam doomed herself to a life without love.

So be it. And yet, she'd watched the incredible intimacy between Stacy and Charles. She understood the depth of feeling between

Victoria and Hunter. Was she wallowing in a simple case of jealousy because she'd destroyed her own heart?

No. She had no choice. The Ancient's had mated her to a monster. Who'd have thought?

Sam turned and looked down at the face she remembered, so beautiful. How she longed to curl up next to him simply for the closeness he could give. But he wasn't the one she lost, and now she had to separate the two. Cordell Stuart wanted to die. He'd accepted his fate even though he had a daughter, Kayla, who needed him quite desperately. Sam could hear him calling to her. And still, she discerned he wanted to let go.

I can't let him. I must give him life. I must.

He will hate me when he awakens.

The creators explained many times and gave them their most sacred law not to create vampires without reason. The gift could not be given to all, only a chosen few. In the wrong hands the gift became a curse.

Oh my! Didn't Sam know that all too well? For the creators made a terrible mistake. They had made an error in judgment by giving the gift to Antu, and if she didn't tread carefully, both their races, human and vampire, would pay the price.

Sam drew in a deep breath, letting the air out slowly. She lifted her gaze and thought about her home. Sanctuary. Sanctuary, the place for those about to die, the place for those who could no longer cope and saw time as their enemy. She'd searched the world until she found them—naturally made caves against the sea—accessible by a vampire at low tide. No humans allowed.

She'd created her own temple of sorts, and she gave the gift of the temple. Peace. Death wasn't to be feared but embraced, simply another passage on another path. At times she wished she could choose that next path, but fate decreed otherwise. She couldn't, not until she destroyed the monster.

Antu Si-Tayat. Brother in blood, ex-lover and mate, the one ready to kill everyone and destroy everything to take his revenge.

That simply won't happen. End of discussion.

Human technology and advancements put vampires at risk. Cordell Stuart proved that point. So had her brother made his move out of fear or because the timing couldn't be more perfect?

Her eyes narrowed. Antu knew how to wound with deft precision. She bent her head.

Chapter Three

IN THE HAZE OF HIS MIND, CORDELL STUART DREAMED. THE MOST beautiful woman he'd ever seen, and he'd seen plenty, stared down at him with incredible pity in her golden yellow eyes. His heart turned over in his chest. "Give me a kiss, and I'll follow you anywhere."

She frowned. "A kiss will not cure you, Dr. Stuart. But I can."

"Am I dying?"

"Yes." He stared up at her, not comprehending. A haze, a sense of detachment covered everything. As if he'd become a long-distance camera or walked through a long tunnel without end.

"Do you want to live? Think hard but be quick. Are you willing to accept another way of life? Any kind of life?"

"Not...sure what you mean."

"I think you do, Dr. Stuart. I think you know who and what I am."

"Vampire," he whispered. But again, the word held little meaning. It drifted off into a gray fog and then disappeared.

She nodded and he tried to focus. "Your life force is fading. You must make your decision. Life or death."

Reality sank in. Fear scalded, threading through his veins like molten metal. She could feel his emotions.

"Do not make your decision out of fear," she said. "What awaits us is simply another door we must pass through. Make your decision because of good and evil. Your life has been dedicated to helping people, saving lives, making life more bearable."

But that wasn't exactly true. "Kayla."

"Your daughter. Yes, I know. Look deep inside your soul, Dr. Stuart. For once this is done, it cannot be undone."

Another sear of fear shot through him. His fingertips tingled. He began to shake but not from the terror swirling in his veins. He shivered from cold and the lack of blood that should have been flowing through his arteries.

Cord looked up into her face. He swallowed. "Cold."

"Yes. I know."

In the moment it took for Cord to draw his next ragged breath, he observed a vignette of pictures tumble on top of one another. His life truly passed before his eyes. And he watched as his beautiful fifteen-year-old daughter as fought for every breath, every movement, every joy. Peace descended upon his soul. He accepted death. But a flickering spark wouldn't let him go.

Cord swallowed again. He nodded and said, "Not right. Can't fight nature."

"Are you certain?"

"Very."

And Cordell Stuart died. Or so he thought.

"Drink."

Sharp, tangy, thick yet smooth. He didn't mind the taste. Indeed, a craving took hold. He wanted more. He kept sucking. More. He had to have more.

"You must stop now."

He ignored the voice, kept on swallowing and sucking.

"I said, you must stop now."

Not used to being ordered, Cord lifted his head. He'd never seen such perfection. Not one line, not one wrinkle, not one blemish. Not even around eyes that reminded him of a cat. Her gaze was extraordinarily intelligent and shrewd, also patient and just. "I must?"

"Only you can break the chain, Dr. Stuart."

A strange metallic taste filled his mouth. He lifted his head and looked around. Blood. Everywhere. "Wait a minute. Are you saying—?"

"Yes," she sighed.

"No. No. Not possible. I died. I know I died."

Did he? "Yes and no," she answered.

He widened his eyes. Every muscle constricted with the action. His skin rippled, his cells rearrange. How could this be possible? And the truth crashed in on him. "Vampire."

"Yes." She sighed again, her face haggard, her cheeks sunken in. But she looked no less regal. "You did something you shouldn't have done, Cordell. You created Nirvana and because of it, all beings, human and vampire, are in jeopardy. You need to undo what you have done. Show us how to create an antidote, and your wish will become reality. I will even take responsibility for your daughter."

He'd told her about Kayla? "You know about Kay?"

"We found out about you," she explained.

How? No one knew about Kayla except her nursing staff.

"I have sworn never to be beholden to anyone ever again. Help us and I will give you everything you desire. I will take care of Kayla and see she wants for nothing until the end of her life. And then I will give you what you asked for."

Confused, Cord had no idea what she was talking about. "What did I ask for?"

"Death."

CORD AWOKE TO THE SOUND OF WATER LAPPING AGAINST SOMETHING solid. He didn't want to get up, he rather enjoyed floating in a place of peace.

Am I dead?

A sheet covered his body, scratching his legs almost to the point of pain. The sound of the slapping water assaulted his ears, making him want to cover them.

Cord sank down into the float again. There. *Ah, that's nice.* But something wouldn't let go, a hunger clawed deep inside his belly, biting and clamoring to be set free.

Heartbeats. What the hell? He could hear them pounding and pumping. Who did they belong to? And what was that sound? Sort of like when he sank his head underwater, and he could hear his own heart work inside his chest. He could hear the rush of fluid through veins, sounding like a fierce-flowing stream. Did that hand belong to him? Did those fingers? He rubbed them together feeling every crack, every ridge.

Cord opened his eyes to find the room pitch black. Yet he could see every detail of the sanded rock walls, tiny stones glittering but no burrs, no crevices. A question rose from a great distance. How could this be possible? Then he settled back into the float again. But this time he noticed his cheek rested on a satin pillowcase and damn, the fragrance of Channel was hard to miss, even that hint.

His ear scraped against the fabric, the sound loud. The sound too loud, and then he realized he wasn't alone. He turned his head and spied an opening in the wall, cut from the natural slope of the rock. Like a doorway. A figure stood inside the opening.

A thousand nights in a thousand beds paled in comparison to this one moment. Cord stared, the English language utterly lacking when he needed words the most. What he saw constituted a simple silhouette framed by moonlight. And yet....

Small, no petite actually, he could feel the strength flowing from her body in raw power, innate and undeniable power carried as effortlessly as a shawl over ramrod straight shoulders. And he knew deep inside his soul that nothing, nothing, would ever defeat this woman.

Dumbstruck, Cord watched her hand fall away from the rock wall as she turned. He damned his lack of words again for he had no way to actually describe her. A queen? Truly. For she looked as though she carried the weight of the world upon her shoulders. No fluff or soft edges, but every centimeter a woman.

Cord felt his heart turn over in his chest. So beautiful, so sad, carrying the mantle of the world so readily. He'd known so many women but never one like this. Each feature became part of a perfect design. She had straight midnight black hair so dark and shiny it tinged blue in places. She had high cheekbones and a pointed chin, but her face looked more round than long, heart-shaped almost. And those eyes. Cat's eyes. Mesmerizing golden yellow irises rimmed in black, reminding him of a panther he'd seen once, for they were filled with the wisdom of the ages, and they carried no fear, only power. Her eyes were lined with black to accent their almond shape. Mixed in with all the other emotions he recognized, he found them filled with awareness and something Cord found very troubling. Guilt.

Still no words passed his lips.

"Good evening," she said.

The salutation boomed in his ears, and he blocked the sound. Okay. Something here seemed off. Very off.

He rolled his tongue around his mouth, jumping as he crossed paths with an incisor. A long incisor. "Where am I?"

"Sanctuary."

"Who are you?"

"My name is Samira. Samira Anai Se-Bat. Do you remember what happened to you?"

Did he? Cord wasn't sure. "I'd been working in my office. I heard a commotion. Then a man came in. After that, things are a bit hazy."

"That man was my brother, Antu Si-Tayat. I'm afraid you weren't working for Casperian. You were working for him."

"Brother?"

"In blood, Dr. Stuart."

Blood? Yes, he remembered. "Vampires."

"Yes."

Casperian? Cord tried to compartmentalize. The man from V3 Diagnostics. The face behind the front men. The other? So cold and unfeeling. Not an ounce of caring. Now he understood why. "He drained me. Yes, it's coming back now. You asked if I wanted to die. I told you yes. Why am I still alive?"

She turned to face him. "Because you created something you shouldn't have created. Nirvana."

Cord scowled. His heart leaped. Several moments passed before he realized the sound of the rushing fluid came from inside his own body, and as he concentrated, the roar got louder and louder. He denied it all. "I don't know what you're talking about."

"I think you do. Casperian paid you a great deal of money to continue your research."

Cord blanched. No one knew. No one. Except… He caught her gaze filled with truth and a tinge of sadness. "My funding dried up. I was bankrupt."

She nodded. "I have no right to judge. I know about your daughter. However, every action has a consequence, doctor."

His heart sank. "Is this my consequence?"

She didn't seem happy as she answered, "I'm afraid so."

"I should have died," he whispered, wishing the float would swallow him whole. When his wish didn't come true, Cord realized he might have to face reality.

"You did. And you didn't."

"What did you do to me?" Panic set in. A wave of fear started low in his belly and blossomed through his body.

"Control your breathing," she commanded. "Slow your heart." She waited, head cocked as if listening. "There." She waited again. "Good."

Still, he could feel his hands tremble as he asked, "What am I?"

"A vampire."

Impossible. And yet? Seeing in the dark. Heightened senses. Strength. Power flowing though his muscles. He could feel each one bunch and gather with every movement he made.

Cord laughed. The sound grated. He stopped.

You must learn to control your universe from the center of your being.

"Wait a minute. I heard you. Inside my head. But your lips didn't move. You didn't speak."

I didn't?

"I'm sure you suspected Casperian's true nature," she continued out loud. "Then you denied it as you're denying the truth right now. You made a very bad mistake. Casperian is dead. And so will the rest of our race if you don't come up with a cure."

"*Our* race?"

"Yes." She sighed and walked toward him. "I'm willing to make you a bargain. Help my friends find a cure for Nirvana, and I will grant you that which I could not before. Death. Your daughter will be cared for, no expense spared, until the end of her life. She will be cared for as if she were my own. Anything that you require will be provided."

"Can you turn back time?" he asked, his voice tinged with bitterness.

Air shuddered from her lungs. "I'm afraid not."

Anger welled at her answer. "Too bad." God, what the hell was going on? There couldn't be such thing as vampires. Or could there?

"Shall I continue?" She seemed to be waiting for him to catch up. "Equipment. Help. One of my friends is a pathologist, the other a forensic chemist and blood banker. They know what's at stake here."

"And what, exactly, is at stake?"

She didn't answer right away. She lifted her gaze to a place he couldn't see. "Armageddon."

Had he really caused such a catastrophe? Had the process of trying to save his daughter become the key to that kind of destruction? Cord felt his belly hollow again, his lungs pushed and pulled but there wasn't enough air. His hands began trembling. "What have I done?"

She steeled her body, becoming a warrior, grim and determined as she bit out her orders. "Control your breathing! In. Out. In. Out."

Her words mesmerized and he concentrated, following her instructions until the shaking subsided. He made his world shrink until he could deal with the reality she presented. "I never wanted to work for V3. I never even knew his name until a couple of days ago. You have to believe that," he choked out. The full import of his actions became a picture far away as if taken by a long-distance camera. And yet his fear. So very, very real. "My research. So close to the edge of a breakthrough."

"I do understand. But you were dealing with a being far beyond your comprehension. Did you know he scared off your investors? All he had to do was plant suggestions and let them do the rest."

"You can control minds?"

Her tone gentled. "Not control, suggest. In time, you'll be able to do so as well."

A hole formed in his gut. Not just any kind of hole, a gnawing, clawing well of need. He felt hot saliva fill his mouth, and he swallowed several times.

"What you are experiencing right now is hunger. Your need for blood."

Cord doubled over as pain radiated through his mid-section. "Oh, God," he moaned. He clambered to his knees, one arm braced against the mattress, head hanging. "Make it go away."

"I cannot."

Cord looked up. Although he caught a hint of pity, he recognized the steely resolve in her gaze.

"You must make your own decisions now. I cannot fight this fight for you. I can tell you that you have a choice. Give in to the need and let it control you or fight the hardest fight of your life. But if you win, you can control the desire. We all feel it, every second of every day, the wanting and the yearning, the terrible need that fills your belly."

He swallowed and swallowed. Never before had he ever felt...even a man dying of starvation wouldn't come close. What he felt...a hunger the likes of which, perhaps, even an addict wouldn't understand.

Cord heard every heartbeat. Hers, and yes, others, and he could hear the rush of fluid in her veins as well as his own, so very tantalizing. He dug his fingers into the sheet. So easy to give in, all he had to do was let go. And then he realized what he really wanted. He wanted the float, the complete sense of peace. He climbed toward it, crawling on all fours until he reached the edge of the bed.

"Every action has a consequence. I created you because I had no choice. I will put you down for the same reason."

Affronted, he stopped to stare. "Put me down?"

"If you cannot control the hunger, then yes, you're an animal, a rabid animal and a danger to everyone and everything that lives. You will need to be destroyed."

Over the absolute ball of misery worming its way through his guts, Cord felt insulted. Pride rose. "I. Am. Not. An. Animal."

Lifting his head, he stared.

A sardonic sneer crossed her features. "We are all animals in this respect, even down to the lowliest of microorganisms. Surely you know that, doctor. Surely you understand the strong will always survive. Surely you believe in nature."

Cord laughed softly in spite of everything. "You picked a helluva time," he told her, using his hands and knees to slip over the edge of the bed. "To have a philosophical discussion."

He doubled over again.

"Really," she drawled.

He planted his palms on the floor, slipped down slowly, and sat back, rocking on his heels to get enough momentum to lift his torso and stand. He rose, swaying back and forth, his arm cradling his belly. Only then did he realize he had no clothes on. And that he didn't care. He took a step forward and towered over her. He smiled.

She looked up at him and with some trick of the darkness drew herself up until they were nearly eye to eye.

He shook his head. "Who are you?"

"I am a queen."

"What are you?

She fired back. "A vampire. What are you? Say it!"

Every moment came back to him. Antu. Dying. Being reborn. Need blossomed anew. "Say it!"

Cord's world imploded. Everything he thought he had simply ended.

"Say it!" she commanded.

He lifted his shoulders. The pain in his guts receded. Filled with a different fire he bit out, "I should have died. You did this to me."

"You did this to yourself."

To be examined later. He staggered past her, stopped in the doorway, and turned. "I am a vampire."

Then he jumped.

Chapter Four

SAM STARED OUT AT THE OCEAN FOR THE TENTH TIME, THEN SHE turned and walked into her office. She contacted every member of the Council. Once she had all of them on her computer screen she said, "I have not been completely honest with the Council, but I feel I have done so with the best of intentions."

Miklos, in Athens, didn't seem surprised, and Sam tucked that information in the back of her mind to be examined later. Hiroki, in Kyoto, masked his curiosity well, and Jason in California seemed thoughtful.

"The one I thought dead, my brother in blood and high priest of the Temple Antu-Si-Tyat, still walks this earth."

Danika, in Helsinki, gasped. "We thought you were the last Priestess left."

"So did I, I'm afraid. A mistake that has put you all in grave danger. As a Priest of the Temple, it is possible Antu is more powerful than me. I have never challenged him, so I do not know. What I do know is, he is the one who has been creating the rogues."

Hunter Pierce sat next to Mercy in New Jersey, his face grim with resolve. "We can defeat him."

"Yes, we can," Sam told them. "We can use his one weakness

against him, his love of games, and his innate desire to create chaos. Antu loves chaos."

"How? How can we defeat him?" Hiroki asked. "You say he may be more powerful than you."

"Maybe, I don't know," she reiterated. "But my prowess as a warrior isn't important right now. We need to destroy the rogues he's creating, and I have the man who made Nirvana here at Sanctuary. His name is Cordell Stuart. Dr. Stuart has agreed to help fix the mistake he's made."

They all seemed surprised and more than a bit skeptical.

"Can he?" Jason asked.

"Yes, I believe he can. And then we can turn our attention to my brother. Just remember,

you all need to understand. Death follows Antu. Always."

She watched each of their reactions carefully. Miklos appeared to take her words to be a challenge, but not Hiroki. Concern marred Hiroki's features for a moment before he hid his fear. Jason and Danika were frightened but as leaders, hid their fear as well. Hunter and Mercy simply turned stoic, and determination flashed in Hunter's gaze.

"Comments?"

When there were none, Sam closed the call and sat rubbing the bridge of her nose with her fingertips. How had events gotten so out of control? Why? When she found no answers, Sam came out of her office to find Lia waiting for her.

"My Queen? He's been in the ocean for a long time. Shall I follow Dr. Stuart?"

Sam put her arm out to stop her friend. "Let him go, Lia. He won't drown. If he gets tired or tries to kill himself, I'll know. He's simply running away."

"We all have at one point or another, haven't we?"

"Yes." She could feel him now. The ocean like a blanket, no a cocoon. Floating. Giving succor. "But I think he'll manage. He's already gotten over the first hurdle."

"Dr. Roberts called. And there is an encrypted message from New Jersey waiting for you from Hunter Pierce."

Funny, she understood the urgency of both yet wanted to share the peace Cord enjoyed more. Strange. She shared a connection with Lia and the others she had created, even with Hunter, for although Antu had created him, Hunter now had more of her blood than Antu's running through his veins. But nothing like the bond already forming with Cordell Stuart. She wanted more than anything to join him in the sea, to lick the salty brine from his skin, to...

And yet he reminded her so much of the one man she wanted to forget. Her mind drifted into the past with ease.

"Nuya! Nuya! Look!"

Samira became so excited as she ran, she didn't even notice the clip-clap of her sandals on the hard packed sand and stone.

"Slowly, little flower."

Dismissing the concern in his voice, Samira wove her way through the brightly colored robes of the people crowding the street to catch a glimpse of the procession. Today, a child would be chosen from their small town to enter the temple.

"Careful, little flower. Should you hurt yourself, I will have to explain to your father."

Samira shook her head and tilted her chin to the sky. Egg-shell blue. Not a cloud. Ra sent down his blessings, happy this day, and the breeze wafted gentle and cooling. How could anyone not feel their heart swell on such a perfect day, such an important day?

As the bodies pressed tighter together, they became a wall. Nuya caught up to her and she begged, "Please. Lift me up so I might see. Please."

Nuya relented and bent down on one knee. "You know I will do anything for you, little flower. But we cannot stay long. Your father will be very angry if he finds out."

Samira didn't care. What was her father's wrath compared to the spectacle that awaited? She clambered up onto Nuya's shoulders feeling an invisible hand push her up. She watched banners flutter in the wind, gold and silver marking the royal house; blues, greens, and yellows marking other noble houses. Then the red and black of the temple—red banner with black letters for The Mother, black banner with red letters for The Father.

So much gold! The metal glinted from headbands and spears, swords and chariots and bridles. And the horses. Such magnificent beasts sparkling beneath the rays of Ra in their browns, whites, and tans. Only the blacks were reserved for the temple.

The litter seemed smaller than Samira imagined it would be but looked so much grander with pure white linens bordered in gold thread that sparkled in the light. White represented the purity of the chosen, for they had to be pure of body and soul to enter the temple. The gold reminded everyone that the temple bore just as much royalty as those who ruled.

Samira smiled as one of the horses nickered, tossing his great head. He looked impatient, ready to gallop at a moment's notice, neck arched with pride. As the procession came to a halt in front of the house of the second basket weaver, Samira knew who had been chosen. Menet. Their oldest girl. Would she show as much pride as the horse?

Dressed in black, Menet walked out of their house, half crouched in fright as she approached the priest. Even from this distance, Samira could see the trail of tears on her cheeks. Unable to understand, for being chosen to the temple was the highest of honors, Samira thought Menet should be proud. She brought great status to their town and to her family, not to mention the riches they would receive.

Samira found the girl hard to watch as she clung to her mother and father. Perhaps she would redeem herself by lifting her shoulders and chin, accepting her destiny with dignity.

Exult in your fate, she told the young girl.

Menet cringed instead. And so, sitting atop Nuya's shoulders, Samira straightened for her.

With eyes still filled with tears, Menet climbed into the litter, and a wave of something strange filled Samira's belly. She felt sorry for Menet, for even at her young age, Samira understood no one should be forced to do that which they could not. Why, it would be akin to being caged all day long, every day, and become a fate equal to death.

The emissary of the temple lifted his hand to start the procession again, then he turned and called out a halt. His head turned in Samira's direction. Perhaps she'd been unfair or jealous of all the attention Menet received, so she tried to understand Menet's sacrifice. Still, the honor carried greatness. So Samira's shoulders reared back, her muscles tightened, and her head cocked in question just as the man caught her gaze.

Samira shivered.

She watched as a soldier helped the emissary down. This was no ordinary *emissary but a priest, denoted by the gold markings on his black robes. Indeed, gold gleamed everywhere, from the band around his head to the rings on his fingers, seen for a moment before his hand retreated beneath the cloth.*

Samira barely noticed the guards clear a path through the crowd. Pale white skin surrounded his eyes, deep dark orbs that held her and she couldn't turn away. Then she noticed the silence, the complete and utter silence, and she looked down to find everyone kneeling. No one moved.

"Nuya, the priest."

The muscles beneath her legs locked, and the fingers around her ankles trembled. Samira's heart raced inside her chest. She twisted and turned, excitement threatening to topple them both.

Not just a priest, but a high priest, stopped a few feet away. Nuya began to kneel, gripping Samira's legs tight so she wouldn't fall. "Hold," Menet said.

Nuya straightened.

Then Samira heard a voice inside her head. "Do not be afraid."

She wasn't. Merely curious. For it must've been stifling to wear such long robes on such a cloudless day. "You must be hot."

The high priest's eyes widened. The cloth covering his face shifted. Samira told herself he smiled.

"Not really," he answered, as his brows drew together. "Your name?"

"Samira. Samira Anai Se-Bat."

"How old are you Samira Anai Se-Bat?"

"Six. Well, almost six. Father said just the other day that I have grown like a weed."

"Did he?"

"Yes." Samira cocked her head. "Do you get tired of living in the temple? You must get lonely. Are you allowed out?"

He seemed quite taken aback by her questions. "You are a curious little bird, aren't you?

"Flower," she corrected. "Nuya calls me his little flower."

The high priest laughed. "Does he?" More laughter. "And brazen, I see. So, I will answer your question, little flower. Sometimes, I get lonely. Then I meet a soul such as yours and I am refreshed."

"Then I am happy," Samira answered with childish innocence. "You give life to the people. You should get some back."

"Indeed." The priest turned his attention to Nuya. "Where do you live?"

"The—the street of the carpenters," he stammered.

"An emissary will visit soon to meet with your Elder."

Nuya swayed, nearly letting go. Samira wondered why. Then she realized Father wouldn't be happy. But what was meant to be, was meant to be.

The priest looked back up at her. He reached out, his hand pale, and touched her face. Samira started, stunned by his cold touch. She shivered, and the priest turned back to his chariot with regal dignity. Trumpets blared. Horses stamped and pulled. The procession started to move.

And she heard the voice inside her head again. The voice with no sound. "I will see you again, little flower."

Nuya bent down, and Samira clambered onto the ground. "I am dead."

Even at six years old, Samira understood what had just happened. When she received the call, just as Menet had been called today, she would never see her mother and father or Nuya or her sister Hessup again. But that would be in ten years. Ten whole years. A lifetime to an almost six-year-old.

Nuya cowered as he told the tale, crying and begging for mercy. Samira kept insisting she created the issue and the fault, that she ran ahead to watch the procession. Father ranted and raved and muttered over and over again, "You are gone. You are gone."

And when the emissary left that afternoon, Father approached, his gaze broken. "You have been chosen."

Samira felt torn in two. Her heart broke with her father's, but her bones told her where she belonged. "We have been honored, father. Hessup will have enough dowry to marry a merchant. You will have a fine house to live in."

"Is that all you believe I wish for?"

Samira bowed, almost touching the floor. "Forgive me, Father. But I cannot explain. A hand, a hand kept pushing and guiding me there."

Her father lifted her into his arms, his gaze sad. "My pain is because you are my little flower, and you will never be that again."

Samira hugged her father hard. "Of course I will. Forever and ever." But even as she spoke, she felt a wall grow between them, a wall that would allow her to leave when the time came.

"You will regret this day."

Little did Sam know how true those words would become. Poor Nuya. Not once but twice. In the name of The Mother and The Father.

Chapter Five

CORD SLICED THROUGH THE SEA, THE TANG OF BRINE BITING HIS tongue. *Vampire!*

She called her home Sanctuary. But Cord thought for sure he'd end up calling the rocky fortress a prison.

What he'd wanted most frightened him. So he swam and thought about what he'd done. Mitochondria were the little engine that could. Mitochondria were the pistons that sparked the fuel, the bodies that enabled the cell to use the fuel—when they worked right and the body functioned normally.

When they didn't?

Cord sliced through the water like a hot knife through butter. He used such effortless strength. How? What had happened to his body to allow such energy? His mind ranged over the possibilities until reality punched him in the gut.

Kayla.

Kayla, his beautiful dying daughter, a young girl trying to continue on supplements and hope, hope for a cure he'd promised to give her. Mitochondrial disease meant his daughter wasted away, bit by bit, and he could only stand by and watch.

Cord kept swimming. Kay hadn't been out of the house in over a year because he'd failed her. He hadn't found a cure simply failure and failure meant death. Kay would never live long enough to receive the gift of …he wasn't even sure…were vampires' immortal? Whatever they were, he wanted their eternity, a price he hoped he wouldn't have to pay for.

Cord pulled the water with his cupped hand and reached out with other to do the same, letting himself wallow in desperation and foolishness. He'd let the possibility of a cure entice him into believing his actions were justified. The end never justified the means.

Cord fought the water, trying to tire himself out. He let his arms slap at the surface, each stroke angrier than the last. When he finally lifted his head, he couldn't see the rock formation any longer.

"Follow the sound of my voice."

"No."

"I said, 'follow the sound of my voice.'"

"What if I don't want to?"

A pause. Oh, how full of emotion the silence could become. "Free will is always yours."

"Fine. I think I'll stay here a while."

"You didn't let me finish. After that much exertion, let's say I think you're going to be a bit hungry."

The word ignited an ache of emptiness in his gut. His insides clenched and expanded with an almost suction-like motion. He wanted to swallow fluid whole. He wanted to drink and suck and drink and suck. Need clawed its way up his throat. He wanted blood.

Bags filled with the rich red life-giving sustenance filled his mind. He doubled over, sinking beneath the waves. He could stay in this place. He could float forever. This could be his eternity. But Kayla drew him back.

In the recesses of his brain, Cord registered the sound of an engine. As soon as he let go of the cloak he hid beneath, the need for blood pierced with the agony of a thousand needles. Ants marched up and down his arms and legs. His belly continued the suction motion even more violently than before.

He barely registered being lifted out of the water, hardly noticed the chains about his wrists. His mind recognized nothing but the terrible sickness inside, and how the bounce and roll of the boat made him even sicker. All his thoughts centered on the need consuming his every cell.

The vampires who brought him back to Sanctuary were none too gentle. They marched him through the maze of hallways like a prisoner. They threw him into her chamber as if he was her slave. He landed on his face.

"In a way," Sam said. "You are. I am your maker. Your first draught must be of my blood to seal our bond."

"I don't want blood," he gasped. "I certainly don't want *your* bond. You can go take your—unh…" He groaned, agony ripping through his muscles and the ants beginning their indomitable march again.

Her tone, although stern, carried a hint of sympathy. "You're behaving like a child, Cord. You're angry with me. I understand. I asked permission but under untenable circumstances. But now you must face your reality. You're delaying the inevitable. The need will grow worse."

Worse? Dear Lord, really? Cord curled into the fetal position, hoping the knives in his gut would stop slicing away at his insides. "What if, what if I don't want your blood? What if I want hers?" he choked out, pointing at the other woman standing in the room. "Or a blood bag?"

She smiled, the movement seeming bitter and sweet. "You do. All of it. But I am your maker. I am the nectar. I am the honey."

Hot saliva flooded his mouth as her words filled him with excruciating hunger. He planted his palm on the stone floor. He forced his other hand down beside it. Rolling onto his knees, he moaned. "Oh, God."

"You show great promise, incredible fortitude. Not many can withstand the need you feel. But you will lose your mind and your will soon, and I don't want to destroy you."

He hung his head between his arms, his forehead almost touching the floor. "Even if that's what I want?" he bit out.

"Even so. However, I will make a bargain. I will grant this death wish of yours. After you pay your debt."

"What debt?" Stunned, he lifted his head, almost forgetting his misery for a nanosecond. "I think you have that backwards, don't you? I don't owe you anything. You owe me my death."

"Which I promise to give you. I will give you a clean and peaceful death. But not until you pay you debt," she repeated.

His belly heaved in and out. He searched for oxygen with every breath. "What debt, damn you?"

"You created Nirvana. Now you must destroy it."

Cord sat back upon his heels and doubled over. His head moved up and down acknowledging her words. Consequences. There were always consequences. He'd known his actions would require payment. Just not now, certainly not like this.

"I understand." He swallowed, pain and need and craving making him groan again. "On one condition." He pictured his daughter with the strength of ten men, her body whole, trim and fit.

"I cannot," she replied with sadness. "The Council will never allow it. She's too young. Even now you can barely withstand the need. Think of a child who only wants it all to go away. Surely you can see the logic?"

The pain in his gut filled his heart. "Then you will care for her. The very best conditions for what is left of her life after I am gone. And should she, by some miracle, manage to live to an acceptable age?"

"That I cannot promise for even I am bound by rules. I cannot create a vampire without just cause. None of us can. So if I cannot promise, I can try to persuade. Are we agreed?

"Done."

She approached but turned to the other vampire. "Lia. You'll need to pull him away."

"Yes, my lady."

Sam held out her wrist. Cord clamped his jaw around her skin and sank his teeth into her rich red pool of life. What had she called her blood? The sweetest nectar? Oh, so much more. Funny, he hadn't really created Nirvana, but right now, he drowned in it.

"Slowly, young one. Slowly," Lia cautioned.

More. No. He had to have more. Draw in. Let go. Draw in. Let go. Never enough.

A montage filled his head. A picture of the desert, mud or clay buildings, a street lined with stalls bearing clay jugs and brightly colored cloths. Then the vision changed to a young man in a white cloth headdress with a gold band around the crown of his head. The young man looked at him with soulful, deep dark eyes and such sadness in his gaze. The eyes, the pain in the gaze reminded him of the eyes that stared back every day in the mirror. His eyes? Someone else's? If so, whose?

The montage shifted, and he climbed inside her head. Her soul filled with the agony of lost love, and he stared at a distant dusk wondering if eternal life was worth the pain. Seemed he wasn't alone in his wish to end his life.

Lia clamped an arm around his neck and yanked back. She held him as he flailed and grabbed, snarling and biting. However, after a few moments the excruciating desire subsided into a hot burn and realization dawned. The burn, the need, the desire would never ever go away. There existed something now that he'd want even more than saving Kayla's life. Blood.

Chapter Six

"My lady?"

Sam turned. She'd been staring at him lying in her bed. "He is not the one you lost."

The sadness never truly went away, it simply scabbed over by time. "No."

"You must feed." Ever practical, ever faithful Lia. "Please. He took so much."

Sam held Cord immobile with her mind even though his body craved movement. Soon the night faded, and his energy ebbed. Sam could've put him in chains since she had other matters requiring her attention. Instead, she wanted to hold him, soothe him, even though he didn't deserve such care.

Or did he? Sam struggled with herself. Was she feeling guilty? Indeed. For which act, she asked herself, the past or present? Both, she surmised. By the Gods! If Antu's strength of character could have been combined with Nuya's gentleness, what a magnificent leader he could have been. What a Golden Age they could've created. Instead, they lost Paradise and the right to it.

Lia waited beside her. She took the outstretched wrist with gratitude but drank just enough to sustain.

"No, my lady," Lia insisted. "You must take more."

Sam smiled, her heart turning over in her chest. "Why do you stay with me, Lia?"

"Your pardon, lady?"

"Just a simple question. You've served me faithfully for so many ages. Why don't you make a life of your own somewhere else?"

Lia's gaze darkened. "You know why."

"And you know I cannot love you as you love me," Sam answered, her heart constricting.

Lia's gaze filled with pain for a split second and then she shook her head. "The love you give me is enough."

"Is it? I wonder. You deserve more."

Lia laughed, the sound harsh. "Now I know you need more sustenance."

Sam lifted a brow.

"Come now, lady. A beggar girl destined for a whorehouse? Forced to spread my legs for my, what do they call them now?"

"Pimps," Sam muttered.

"Surely, you can understand what that life would've been like for me? Shuddering beneath every man's touch, wishing only for death?"

"And yet..." Sam sighed. "Did I not give you death? Have I not enslaved you in another way?

"Enslaved, lady? Again, I am confused. I served you, well I hope, and then you gave me a choice. I chose this life, this service."

"Did you? Or was I not the lesser of the two evils you faced?"

Lia clutched her hands together as she always did when upset. "Evils? By The Mother and The Father, I do not understand. You took in a starving beggar girl and gave her a home, a purpose. You allowed her to grow and then you allowed her to choose. How can such a life be evil?"

"Because you didn't really have a choice. The alternative was worse."

"Not my choice?" Lia's face cleared, and she laughed. "Yes, my lady." She threw Sam a look, bowed, and left.

"I don't deserve adoration," she muttered.

"You're right. You don't."

Sam swung around. His eyes were closed, and he graced her bed as if he owned the damned thing. "How are you awake? The sun has already risen."

"I don't know," he replied in wonder. "I can't seem to move, don't seem to want to. But for the life of me, I'm not sleepy."

Sam nodded. "You drank too much of my blood." She let go of her hold on him, but he didn't stir. Interesting.

He lay motionless for a moment and then said, "Ah, metabolism on overdrive."

"Something like that but coupled with the vampiric sleep. Your mind is alive, but your body rests."

"Well then, if I can't sleep, and neither can you, perhaps now would be a good time to tell me more about what I am."

Sam smiled softly. "Biologically, you know more than me."

"Not very reassuring," he answered after a long moment. "Please continue."

"Very well, I am over five thousand years old."

"Fascinating."

Through his eyes, perhaps. He would find that time dulled expectation. "We were created by The Mother and The Father."

He didn't answer right away. "Some kind of alien race, I'm assuming?"

"Yes, although we didn't know it at the time."

"You've done a good job of hiding," he replied, his tone filled with awe. "I mean, wow, all this time. You're stronger, faster, and you have psychic abilities. You could take over, could have taken over the world anytime you wished. Why haven't you?"

"It is forbidden."

He paused for a few moments. Would he ever understand the importance of those words? "Why do you hide?"

Vampires simply wanted the right to survive and live in peace. Sam had a good idea of what would happen if humans became aware of their existence. They would try to use their powers, probably abuse them, all for their own gain.

"Hiding doesn't make sense," Cord continued. "You're more than capable of protecting yourselves."

Ourselves. "So we're very clear on this, axes, spears, knives, and now bullets can kill you—us. Up until the last millennium or so, the lack of a steady food supply has been our major problem," she answered. "But there's a second part to the problem. Using vampiric abilities for personal gain."

Do you understand?

"Yes, I do, so let's get to the second part of this problem," he continued. "Antu doesn't seem to agree with hiding, and he certainly doesn't agree with not taking over the earth."

Her heart clenched. "A mistake. The Mother and The Father gave us miracles. Antu brings death. He's using your Nirvana to create rogue vampires, turning newly made vampires old. When a vampire ages, we get what we call blood fever. This blood fever eventually turns into a sickness. We go rogue. A rogue simply can't drink enough because a rogue is already dying. Usually, the sleep replenishes the system but not with a rogue, and the need for blood grows exponentially. Each rogue vampire he creates can drain thousands of humans."

Cord didn't answer right away, and as a scientist, seemed to like considering the words of others before answering. She found his silence annoying, but she did applaud the reason to do so. "Sounds counterproductive."

"Antu doesn't care. He'll destroy us all. He must be stopped."

"You're afraid of him."

Sam drew herself up, but pride had no place in this—war. "You're right. I am. He's capable of anything and twice as unpredictable."

"He's more powerful than you."

Did she answer that statement honestly, even to herself? "I don't know. I was made from The Mother, Antu was made from The Father. We will find out soon enough."

"Gotcha." He paused. "Something happened, didn't it?"

Sam thought back to the stories of the temple. "To understand, I must begin at the beginning. The Mother and The Father came to us in the night. People were nomads back then. Perhaps they found humans amusing, like children. One thing is for certain, human blood sustained them. So they stayed."

Sam still wondered about so many things. "They could have enslaved us. Perhaps, in a way, they did because we worshipped them. And yet they gave us so much in return. They taught us to farm, not gather. They taught us to breed animals, not simply hunt them. They taught us language, mathematics, engineering. They forced us to use our brains to make our lives better, and we learned."

"Something tells me all was not golden," he replied.

She felt pleased that he could sense the discord in her voice. "In the beginning, I'm sure our lives were simple and pleasant. Then they began creating images of themselves. We called them Priests and Priestesses. But the problem with creating an image out of a human is that human traits remain. Where The Mother and The Father seemed above petty emotions, the priests and priestesses retained them, like greed and envy, tenderness and honesty." Sam inclined her head though his eyes were closed. "Arrogance. Some priests were warm and forgiving, others were cold and cruel, and as time continued, the essence of life shifted."

"You mean, like lack of respect?"

"Deeper," she sighed. "Life became power, not love. I guess The Mother and The Father didn't like what happened, so they decided to leave."

"They dropped their toys."

Sam didn't like how his words made her feel, but he spoke the truth. "Before they left, they destroyed all the temples and their inhabitants except one."

"Not very warm or forgiving, eh?"

What could she say? That it had taken her five thousand years to understand that they'd created beings in their own image and didn't like them? "Perhaps. But they did leave one. Then they chose the best of their servants to continue. Antu murdered them all."

The pain of that day never left her. Nor did the difference between brother and sister. Antu would never feel remorse. Tears filled her eyes, tears that could never be shed. Not even she could cry.

"Except you."

"Yes."

"Why?"

She sighed. In this, she never had a choice, and there were so many choices she regretted. "I was his mate."

Long moments stretched out in silence. "Was?"

"I needed to protect the people, all people, human and vampire. When power corrupts, it does corrupt absolutely." Always straight and proud, Sam faltered. Over the millennia she'd come to understand that being right carried a price. "Antu created a monument to himself, believed he'd become a god. I sealed him inside, or so I thought."

"Whoa. No wonder he's mad."

Sam tried to put herself in her brother's place, but she kept ramming into the wall of his betrayal. "Antu will stop at nothing to make me pay for my crime." She huffed her disbelief. "He still refuses to believe that what he did *was* a crime."

"I'm sorry."

Startled, she pulled her gaze back from the past to the man in the bed. "For what?"

"I've been blaming you for not caring."

She quirked her mouth. "Ahh. But not for your predicament."

"We've got a long way to go on that one."

Funny, but talking with him made the eternal hurt easier to bear. "You'll need to come to terms with many things."

"Will I?"

The picture of Nuya kneeling before her, taking his last breaths upon this earth, his heart hammering in her ears but his gaze filled with peace, would never let her go.

Cord lifted his head slightly. As impossible as she knew that to be, what happened next startled her. He opened his eyes in spite of the sleep to stare at her and asked, "Or will you?"

Chapter Seven

CORD AWOKE AFTER SUNSET. HE JERKED UP IN BED WITH MUSCLES simmering to bunch and gather, ready to move mountains. He clenched his fists, feeling their raw power. Then the last forty-eight hours hit him like a ton of bricks. Like a soldier awaiting his first battle or a driver awaiting the inevitable impact of an oncoming car, Cord asked himself a question.

What have I done?

Panic filled his belly. He squeezed his eyes shut and breathed deeply. He donned his proverbial lab coat and put on his scientist, not allowing the fuse of all-out fear to light. Time to admit he'd made a mistake, played with fire, and gotten burned.

The end can never justify the means. Desperation and science can never go together.

Cord turned to find Samira had joined him in the bed. Focusing on her became infinitely more appealing than focusing on his mistakes. With her eyes closed and her midnight black hair strewn all about the pillow, she could've been another conquest. One he would shout about to the world for sure.

"You're incredibly arrogant," she murmured.

He thought about getting insulted and then decided she was right.

But not quite in the way she imagined. "To be a scientist, arrogance is implied. Each step has to follow the next so the one before has to be correct."

"What if one isn't?"

"We go back and dismantle each step, examining every piece until we find out what went wrong."

"And if you don't find the problem?"

"The experiment fails."

She settled deeper into the bed, the movement reminding him of a cat stretching with contentment, at odds with her contentious behavior. "How clinical of you."

What else could he say? "Yes."

He watched as she propped her head on her hand, resting her elbow on the mattress. He'd be a complete eunuch not to notice the sheet dip and rustle against her breasts. She seemed—unconcerned. Her next words showed him exactly where her priorities rested.

"I don't have the time, nor do I have the patience for failure."

Kay's face filled his vision. "I never have."

"Hello, sweetheart." Cord kissed his daughter on the cheek. So cold. "How's my favorite girl today?"

"All right, Dad." They were both aware she lied. She would never be all right. "Can we go outside, please? Just for a little while. I want to sit in the sun."

Cord lifted Kay out of bed and settled her inside her motorized wheelchair. Maria came in, but he smiled and shook his head. "I've got her. We're going for some fresh air."

"An excellent idea," the nurse agreed. She handed him a blanket for Kay's legs. "Enjoy."

Of course, Cord understood his daughter all too well. Once they were outside on the patio, she wheedled, "Can we go down to the stables? Please?"

How could he refuse her request? His heart melted every time she smiled. Every damned time.

She knew every moment she taxed her body brought her that much closer to death. And yet, how could he deny her even one ounce of joy? What was worse? Freedom and death or chains and a fraction of extra life?

He guided the wheelchair down a paved walkway to a huge, whitewashed barn with green trim. "It's beautiful outside, isn't it?"

A huge smile lit her face. "Indeed, it is, my darling," he said.

He stopped the chair at the entrance to the barn, the sun warm upon his skin. She slid her fingers over his on the handle.

He shivered. So cold. "I suppose you're going to ask for more, yes?"

"Oh please. Can we?"

Cord sighed. "Not too long."

Although most of the stalls were empty, three weren't. "Thank you, Dad. Thank you."

He pulled a ramp against the stall door and wheeled her up so Kay could reach the nose peeking out. She maneuvered her chair to reach the opening. Then he grabbed a handful of baby carrots from a bucket nearby. His horse, Perfect Gentleman, reached out as his name implied and nibbled the carrots from her hand. They repeated with her horse, Charismatic, who true to form made a great show of enjoying his treat.

Then Cord took Sadie out of her stall and put her on crossties. He lifted Kay onto the horse's back. Kay straightened immediately. She had an excellent seat. "I'm flying over the oxer." Kay lifted onto her knee. "Now the water jump. Uh-oh, we came really close. Nearly tapped the tape with his hind foot. Char is feeling good today. He wants to fly."

Cord grinned, enjoying the game with her. "The triple is coming. Remember. Three strides, one, and one."

As usual, Kay timed them perfectly. "Well done, darling. And you finished the course under the time limit too," Cord said.

She sat back and grinned but already he could see the lines of strain about her eyes. "That's all for today, young lady."

She threw him a look which he gave right back. "Oh, all right," she groused. "Thank you."

Cord came back to the present to find empathy in Samira's gaze. "Yes. Your daughter." She rose, unconcerned by her nudity. He admired the long lean line of her from shoulder to hip to the perfect rounding of her buttocks. She had pert, upturned breasts just right to fill a man's hands.

"She will be cared for as promised. But right now, we're needed in New Jersey. And you haven't got the luxury of time."

"Luxury of time?" he asked. How could time be a problem when he was as close to immortal as a being could get.

"You need to learn how to feed."

"Learn how to feed?" he repeated. Bite, suck, and swallow, he thought. Not exactly rocket science.

She must've heard because she sighed. "I cannot let you leave here until you can master your thirst. You must learn how much is enough to satisfy your hunger but not take so much as to kill."

Hot saliva flooded his mouth. He swallowed hard and acknowledged his need. "I—I understand."

"No, you don't, for many have drained humans dry with their first feedings. If Lia hadn't pulled you away?"

His belly cramped. "I said, I understand."

"Perhaps."

In spite of the incredible energy singing in his veins, Cord's insides contracted. His fists bunched in the covers "Did you?"

He lifted his gaze to find her taken aback by the question. "You dare a great deal. And I do not have to answer. But again, I feel compelled. So that you truly understand, the answer is yes, I did. And he was the one true love of my life."

She left the room and Cord realized he pressed her too far. She would never forgive him her confession. But as a scientist, his need to know outweighed the consequences.

The one called Lia entered a short while later. She showed him to a natural spring pool where he could bathe. She didn't say a word, and he could feel her anger.

"You don't like me very much. Why?"

"You remind my lady of the past. You look just like him."

Cord floated in the pool trying to tamp down the never ending. "The one she killed?"

Lia flashed him an ugly look, but she answered with an even tone. "Yes."

His stomach cramped. God, did he call his hunger an itch that wouldn't quit, a burn never to be put out? He did, right in the middle of the back where nothing but a backscratcher would suffice, and a place where buckets of water wouldn't be enough to wash the sensation away. "Why didn't she just say no and choose another?"

And once scratched, the skin would itch more. "So one would have been more acceptable than the other?" Lia shot back.

Yes, he understood. "You have a point."

She didn't approve. "You must dress now. And feed."

Cord toweled off and put on a pair of soft silk pants and shirt that did not heighten sensation, and yet did. He clamped down hard on his thoughts, unwilling to walk around with a permanent hard-on.

"There is no shame in the actions of the body," Lia told him. "Only in the deeds of men."

Indeed, he thought. Then he realized. "How did you know what I was thinking?"

"We are born of the same mother," she answered, the anger in her gaze lifting.

"Then you would call yourself my sister?"

She frowned and hesitated as she answered. "You would have to earn that right."

Lia brought him to a small chamber, and he noticed the chains embedded in the wall. "I managed to pull you away the first time. They are simply a precaution."

He expected Sam to feed him. Surprise filled him as Lia remained. "You are too, umm, how did you put it? Jazzed up, that's it," Lia continued. "You cannot drink from her again for a while."

She shrugged and held out her wrist. He hesitated and lifted his gaze to hers in respect. She nodded. "Perhaps there is hope for you yet. At least you have manners."

Cord approached, want, need, and hunger filling his guts. Being kind, behaving with propriety, these weren't terms he'd have used to describe his reaction to the craving deep inside his belly. Lia understood. "If you think of the other, the one who gives you the gift of life, if you can focus on them, you can separate yourself from yourself and stem the tide of your need."

He pulled her arm toward his lips but took her advice. By caring about what would happen to her if he lost control, he found the will to temper the indescribable.

He bit down, felt her wince, and watched her face turn stoic. Then the blood took over. There were no words to describe the ecstasy, and he sucked and swallowed and sucked and swallowed, the river of life sweeter than the water of a desert oasis. His gaze never left her face. Her mouth pinched and her jaw clenched. Remorse filled his mind, so he drew in one last gulp and pushed her arm away, instantly regretting the decision.

All of a sudden, he realized they weren't alone. Other vampires stood ready to chain him should he lose control and attack Lia. Lord have mercy. He wanted to scramble to his knees and beg for one more draught, but he wouldn't.

He shuddered. He lifted his shoulders and straightened, his fists tight. "You won't need to bring me here again."

She smirked. "You say that now but when the real thirst begins, when you haven't fed for a long time, you'll change your mind."

She held no ill will against him. How did he know that?

"There are rules vampires are sworn to follow. The first is not to kill a human when you feed. You must take just enough to sustain. The second is never allow a human to know you are a vampire. When you feed, you will give that human a drug, the Lethe. The Lethe will make them forget you ever existed. The third is to never feed from another vampire. Feeding between us creates a connection that can never be broken."

"We're connected now, aren't we?" he asked slowly. "Your mistress didn't trust me, so she asked you to bind me to you, didn't she?"

He watched Lia try to hide the guilt in her gaze. "That would be quite devious of her, wouldn't it?"

Then he realized Sam had no clue as to Lia's actions. "Ahh. I get it. *You* don't trust me."

She smiled. "I serve my lady in all things." She paused. "Brother."

Brother. Hmmm. He had no siblings and didn't think he wanted any. "Understood."

Cord left Sanctuary to swim and burn off more of the energy driving his body. As he swam, he thought about this new world he'd entered. Not much different from the old, perhaps.

Cord thought about his promise and the intricacies of vampire life. If he looked hard, beyond the lies he'd been fed by Casperian, vampires were a race of beings much like any other race. They simply wanted to survive as best they could, surprisingly enough without causing harm. His experiments, instead of creating a cure, had become a weapon.

Cord didn't like being a puppet. He liked being a murderer even less.

Are you going to renege on your promise already?

Sam again. What was it with these people? Everyone had an agenda. He scowled, his brows drawing together as he tread water. Hadn't he had one? Didn't he still have an agenda now?

"No." He watched her cut through the water, swimming toward him with a natural grace a human couldn't match. Talk about control. She seemed to have control of every cell of her body. "But I'm tired of being used."

She stopped in front of him, as naked as he was, a thought capable of taking over his mind at any time. Talk about weapons.

"I have never, and would never, be so deceitful," she replied to the thoughts in his head.

"Why not? Lia is."

She cocked her head. "What do you mean?"

"She fed me."

Her face fell and she swam in a circle before facing him again. "Sometimes Lia is…over- protective. I would have cautioned against such an act."

"Why?"

"I don't believe she needed to protect me."

He swam closer to her, any nearer and they would certainly brush each other's limbs. "Ah, but you see, she was right." He reached out and grasped her arm to pull her into his embrace. His body heated. He cupped his palm under one of her breasts floating in the water and gave a quick flick of his thumb on her nipple.

Her eyes widened, acknowledging her interest, but she pulled away. "I'm not above using any means to gain the upper hand. Scientists are all control freaks, you know."

"So are certain vampires."

Cord inclined his head. Sam didn't like Lia's actions. Good.

"I should be mad. I'm not." He swam toward her to judge her

reaction. She held her ground but not before she shifted her weight, ready to swim away if necessary. "I make you uncomfortable, don't I?"

She laughed, long and loud and held up her hand. "Not possible."

A strange sensation came over him, making his limbs feel like they weighed thousands of pounds.

Cord shook his head and kept moving, not wanting to sink like a stone. It wasn't easy, but he kept kicking and trying to swim until he could keep his head above the water. He'd be damned if he'd let some spoiled-assed vampire queen best him.

Her brows drew together. Her lips pursed and her gaze darkened. "You broke the command."

"Not sure how I did," he replied, although he figured getting angry helped. "Not nice of you to try and drown me."

"You wouldn't have. You can hold your breath for a long time. Besides, I need you."

What a strange game. No, power trip. "Yeah. You've told me."

She didn't answer, she simply swam away, leaving Cord with a bad taste in his mouth. Casperian may have been dangerous and a liar and a cheat and even a snake in the grass, but these other vampires? More like serpents, and he'd better keep his guard up. Who knew what would happen next?

Chapter Eight

HUNTER PIERCE STARED BACK AT SAM FROM HER COMPUTER SCREEN, looking drawn and grim. Were those lines in his face? Considering what had happened, anything became possible, and she wondered for a moment what it would feel like to begin aging. A slight tick of fear slithered through her. Even after all these years, she mused. So did she fear aging more than death? An interesting question.

"We could use you back here and soon," Hunter said.

Sam turned away from the screen for a moment to gather herself. Her gaze lit on a mix of artifacts and papers strewn about her office. "Cord needs to come to terms with who and what he is now."

"Cord?" Hunter asked her, lifting a brow.

She raised the corner of her mouth. Such irony, so impossible to separate the past from the present. "I am his maker."

Hunter rubbed his chin with his hand. "You feel guilty."

"Yes and no. He brought this upon himself."

Did she recognize compassion in Hunter's gaze? From the Roman gladiator without a heart? Yes, for he was the same man who finally allowed himself to love. "Cord had no way of knowing," Hunter defended. She watched Hunter shudder with the memory of how sick he'd become. "About Antu or his plans."

"True." She held up her hand. "Nor does the end justify the means for either of us. He had his plans, now we have ours."

"And Antu has us all trumped, I'm afraid. We could use your help. Charles and Vanessa tracked down and killed two more rogues while you've been gone. Tori believes they were barely six months old."

Sam didn't feel surprise. "The estate in New York must not be his only property."

"Agreed." Hunter grimaced. "He's hidden himself well, but we're trying to find him."

She sighed. "I know. But if we are to win, then we must catch him before he's able to wage all-out war. We both know war is where all of this is headed."

Sam heard the slight hiss of Hunter's indrawn breath. He had much to lose, more now with Tori. But he gathered himself instantly, and his face steeled, determination filling his cool gray eyes. "We will fight to the death."

My lady. Cord has fed. With restraint and respect.

The tension in her body eased. *You sound disappointed, Lia.*

"You have no idea, Hunter, how much I wish it won't come to bloodshed."

I cannot lie. I am, a bit. And I have another confession. I fed him.

After thousands of years together, Sam knew her friend and confidante would always tell the truth. She wanted to get angry but couldn't. Lia's reason for existence was to protect her. But she did withhold their meeting in the sea. Some things needed to be private.

A thousand pardons, my lady.

Already forgiven, as always. Ready the boat. We need to take him to the mainland.

She watched Hunter nod. They felt the same. There would be no winners in a war. "And you know how foolish," he replied. "It is to believe otherwise."

It is too soon, my lady.

"Yes," she said out loud. Then with a wave of her hand, she changed the subject. "Your wedding?" she asked Hunter.

"Tori wants a small affair, something intimate."

Sam saw flashes of a stone bench and wondered why. Then the

image became self-explanatory. Hiding a smile she answered, "She understands the need for safety?"

"We'll have the ceremony here. Her sorority sisters, her boss Frank, and her colleagues from work, some of the humans who work for us would feel slighted if they weren't invited."

"A wedding would be the perfect place for him to attack. Listen. My soldiers are useless here. There's no need for Sanctuary right now. Any and all rogues must be destroyed immediately and without question. We will all come."

My lady?

"Thank you," Hunter said.

Sam inclined her head and closed her laptop. *I'm sorry Lia. I fear we have no choice. War is coming.*

Antu will stop at nothing.

That's what I'm afraid of.

Sam rose and quit her office. She found Cord standing in the doorway of her bedroom, looking out at the moonlight and the sea. How he reminded her of the one she lost.

"I broke free of your…did you put me under some kind of spell?"

"A power of the mind. A gift, in a way."

He shook his head. He didn't seem angry, simply sad. "Was breaking free some kind of test I had to pass?"

"There's another I'm afraid," she told him, expelling a deep breath.

"If I didn't know better, I'd say you sounded concerned." She watched him swallow to tamp down on his hunger even though he'd just fed. His gaze narrowed and his lip curled. "I can take anything you dish out."

Annoyed with him and herself, Sam shot back, "This isn't a punishment or a contest."

"It isn't? You could have fooled me."

She reigned in her temper. "I'm sorry. I had to gauge your strength. Now I must know if you can control yourself. You need to be able to get on a plane to go back to New Jersey where Hunter's cell is located. I'm needed there and so are my soldiers." He seemed surprised. "Although the flight will be by private jet, there are airports and customs inspections to get through. And though we will fly by day, you'll be very hungry when you wake. I can't have you fighting my soldiers in such tight quarters, nor can I put chains on an airplane."

"I just broke your spell. How many times do I have to tell you? You won't need them."

"So you say. But there's another part of your education missing."

"What's that?"

"You need to learn how to feed from humans without killing them."

He pounded a fist into the wall. "Damn you. When will you listen? I can take anything you can come up with. You won't need chains or soldiers or Lia."

Sam pictured his daughter lying on the ground, tiny rivulets dripping down her neck and Cord standing over her body, his stare completely blank. As much as she hated doing so, she planted the picture in his mind.

He gasped, his face turning white as a sheet. The skin stretched over his cheekbones, turning his features into a mask of horror. "Are you certain?"

SANCTUARY SAT INSIDE A MOUNTAIN OF ROCK IN THE MIDDLE OF THE Mediterranean Sea, far away from any shipping lanes. The nearest landfall was the island of Cyprus. When they stepped off the boat onto the rocky shore, Sam stepped in front of Cord. "It's going to get very noisy soon."

A car waited for them to take them to Paphos Airport. However, Cord had to take his last test first. They headed toward a small marina. As they drew closer, she watched Cord try to cover his ears to no avail. Heartbeats. Beating like drums. Cord crouched in his seat as if he were being pummeled.

"Listen to the sound of my voice. Find the silence you found inside the sea." She paused, a swell of pride filling her. "Yes, that's it. Well done."

He rose in his seat. Although pale and shaken, he answered, "I'm a scientist. We're good at compartmentalizing." He rolled down his window as if seeking fresh air, and his face scrunched up. As he wrinkled his nose he said, "Too many smells and some that aren't very pleasant."

"Breathe through your mouth. Good." Pleased, Sam continued. "Now you must focus. Find the one heartbeat that calls to you."

His eyes widened. "Yes, I hear it. The deep base, the rushing of blood through the veins."

They stopped the car, and Cord started walking. Sam followed with Lia and two of her best soldiers. A young man sat on a stone sea wall fixing a thick rope net. She watched Cord walk up to the young man and start a conversation.

"Can you show me where to go please?" She watched Cord lift his shoulders and arms. "I am lost. Hotel?" He lifted his arms, palms up, and then dropped them to his sides.

The young man nodded and rose. "Little English," he said, walking across the street. There were buildings that looked like the main part of the town. They kept walking, and then Cord pulled the man into an alleyway. Gently, she was pleased to see.

Cord sank his incisors into the young man's neck, and as his maker, Sam swallowed every draught with him. Suck and swallow. Suck and swallow.

Lia started to move forward, but Sam held her back with her arm. *He takes too much my lady.*

Sam's insides tightened. *Cord. You must listen to me. You must stop now.*

So sweet. I want more. More.

Yes. But if you kill him, his death will remain with you for the rest of your eternity.

Sam felt him still. Just as his fingers trembled with the battle raging inside him, so did hers. But the one true gift The Mother and The Father gave them was free will. He had to make his own decisions now.

I killed someone I loved very much. You don't ever want to carry that kind of burden.

You're right. I don't. But the blood tastes so good.

You have a choice to decide who you are and what you will be, Cord. I cannot make that decision for you.

I'm not sure I'm strong enough.

He'd stopped drinking, but he could become feral at any moment. Sam felt Lia tense beside her. She sensed her soldiers moving closer. Unable to stop her feet, she walked toward both men, man and vampire, but motioned everyone else to remain where they were.

You will always remember this day, for this day teaches you the true nature of who and what you are. So, I ask you, Cordell Stuart. What are you?

A vampire.

Sam gave Cord a respectful space, but the next question had to be asked. *Will you let the blood rule you or will you rule the blood?*

I will rule.

Very well. Then I ask. Who are you?

She watched him give the young man the Lethe, lap at the holes he'd created to close them, and swing the young man into his arms. A maker's pride stirred in her heart. Cord carried the sleeping figure back to where he'd been sitting and then set him down gently, propping him up against the wall.

Cord looked up at her with complete and utter understanding as she joined him. Her heart filled with sadness that meshed with the pride. At last, he understood the terrible yet beautiful truth of their race.

"I am a man."

Chapter Nine

HIGH ATOP THE CLIFFS OF THE PALISADES AND ACROSS FROM NEW York, the greatest city in the world, lived a vampire cell. Sam felt a sense of peace wrap around her as their car entered the gates. She glanced at Cord, his apprehension apparent from more than his thoughts. Because of his actions, he feared he wouldn't be welcome. She feared the same. However, apart from Sanctuary, Hunter's cell felt most like home to her. Once the vehicle stopped, she stepped out of the car into a well of warmth. Both Tori and Stacy welcomed her with open arms, while their mates Hunter and Charles hovered nearby.

Tori cocked her head. She must have sensed Cord was no longer human. Her eyes widened, her gaze flying to Sam. Sam nodded. Tori's brows drew together. *Not by choice, I gather.*

A tale for another time.

"Dr. Stuart," Tori said, holding out her hand. "I'm Tori Roberts. This is my fiancée, Hunter Pierce."

Hunter stared, his usual taciturn self, and Charles stood with a slight smile on his face. He walked up to Cord. "Charles Tower." He held out his arm. "My friends call me Chaz. My wife, Stacy."

If Cord seemed surprised, he didn't show it. And by blocking out the cacophony of human voices, he'd blocked hers as well. Cord shook hands with both men and their mates. "A pleasure."

Sam sensed none of this was a pleasure for Cord. She didn't have to be a rocket scientist to know he wanted to get home to see his daughter. Would he break their law and turn her anyway, in spite of their bargain?

"Stacy? Tori? Perhaps you'd like to show Cord around the estate?"

Hunter stiffened. She watched his fingers curl into fists, so Sam cautioned both vampires. *Lia watches from close by.* Chaz felt just as tense. *She won't let anything happen to them.*

Tori grinned. She nodded to tell Sam that she and Stacy would give her a little private time with Hunter and Chaz. "Sure thing. This way, may I call you Cord?"

Cord frowned but let himself be led away. Charles' lips quirked and then he moved to follow. Sam wondered why. Her intent was to speak to both of them.

With a shrug, she asked, "How do you feel, Hunter?"

He appeared to consider his words before answering. "Strange. Almost as if I don't belong to my own body anymore."

"Would it help to drink more of my blood?"

"I don't know. Part of me would like that very much. The other part, not so much. I'm part vampire, part human now."

Sam reached out to squeeze his shoulder. She motioned for them to walk down the driveway and then onto the front lawn for privacy. Her soldiers remained nearby. "Then feeling strange is to be expected. What does Tori say?"

"My reflexes are slower. I can't run as fast as I used to. I certainly couldn't wrestle with Mercy anymore. Or you." He tried to grin and failed. "Where I used to be able to ignore it, the smell of human food makes my mouth water. But I cannot eat. Tori believes my body has already begun to age."

"Really." The same strange feeling from before slithered down her back because she found the concept both repulsive and intriguing. She forgotten time in that way a long while ago.

"We'll see," he sighed.

"And Tori?"

"She's amazing. She's human in most respects. She still craves food, her coffee," he answered, a half-smile lifting the corner of his mouth. "She's stronger, fitter, faster, and more agile than a human. She believes she'll age slower. Although I'm not sure what either one of us is, I'm grateful we're both alive."

"And to keep you alive, I believe you need this." Sam held out her wrist.

Hunter cocked his head. "Are you sure?"

Sam nodded and winced as he bit down. Hunter was a leader. She needed his heart and his skill to face what lay ahead.

When he finished, Sam sighed. No man, or vampire, should be responsible for another's actions and yet she couldn't help herself. "This is our fault, Hunter. Antu's and mine. We let a long-standing disagreement spill into vampire, and now, human lives." She turned from the mansion to look out over the Hudson River at the lights of New York City. Such a wondrous sight and so hard to fathom when she first took her vows. She could never have foreseen such a future. "I should have stopped him a long time ago."

Hunter turned to her, already stronger, shaking his head. "Do you think you could have? Didn't you still have feelings for him, feelings that would have stayed your hand?"

Sam drew in a deep breath, once again amazed at the workings of fate. Antu had created Hunter expecting a champion who would serve him without question, yet Sam had won Hunter's allegiance. She released the breath she'd been holding with a single word. "Yes."

Hunter's gaze softened. "You gave me nearly two thousand years to find the rest of my soul. Are you going to feel guilty about that as well?"

Sam knew the answer to that question. "You wouldn't let me. Nor would Charles, Stacy, or your beautiful fiancée who is returning to us as we speak."

"I know." Hunter blushed. "She's been speaking with me." He dipped his head.

Sam's heart swelled. But so many things were about to get complicated. "There has to be balance, Hunter. I've feared this moment for a long time. Now I must embrace it." She turned to survey the mansion and then turned back to take one last look at New York. So beautiful.

"Perhaps," she continued. "It's time to embrace change. The world has changed. Maybe we should as well. Starting with a select few, I believe it's time to show humans who we really are."

"Human's fear what they don't understand. Then they try to control that fear by controlling the cause."

"Very true," she answered. "So we must teach them not to fear."

Hunter didn't seem so sure. "There will be those vampires who wish to meddle in human affairs."

"And you know that direct involvement cannot be allowed. Our laws cannot be broken. Chaos would reign."

"Agreed. Still, they'll want us to become their soldiers or their police. Their scientists will want our blood, even our bodies, to study so they can become like Tori."

"Any number of things can happen. Including hordes of unhappy humans wishing to become vampires, thinking they'll be happier this way. I understand many of the consequences, Hunter. But we must do something to stop the cycle of hate and fear among our own."

"Yes, we do." He paused, and Sam waited. A decision like this couldn't be made in haste. "Small steps?"

She nodded. "Small steps." In the meantime, Hunter needed to remain strong. "I will feed you again later. No argument."

"Thank you." Hunter smiled as he turned to his fiancée. "There you are."

"I figured you'd go back to your office," Tori told Hunter. "Stacy and Chaz have taken Cord inside so he can feed, then we'll meet at the lab."

Sam opened her arms to give her friend a hug. She still marveled at the warmth and kindness humans displayed. At the end of the day, being worshiped left a body feeling cold, but a friendship never did. "Hello, my friend."

A last squeeze and then Tori let go. "Good to see you. We've missed you."

As soon as Tori stepped back, Hunter slid closer to his mate as if drawn by an unseen magnet. Sam was glad they'd found each other.

They'd both been hurt terribly by the actions of others. Hunter's slavery left physical and emotional scars. Tori's loss made living unbearable. Yet both had managed to survive and even thrive.

"And I both of you," Sam said. I know you both feel as though I deserted you when I left, but now you know why. Antu nearly killed him. I had no choice. We need his help."

"Tying up loose ends," Tori murmured.

"His *help* nearly got me killed, not to mention what's happened to Tori," Hunter bit out.

"I know. And I know that no end justifies any means. But he'd been trying to save his daughter. She's dying. She has mitochondrial disease." Both Hunter and Tori started. "A well-kept secret and one we should divulge to Chaz, Stacy, and Mercy. No one else. Agreed?"

They both nodded, so she continued. "Hunter, listen to me. Cord couldn't possibly have known what Casperian was doing. Casperian hid behind the layers of a diagnostics company. He certainly couldn't have known Antu even existed. If you want to blame anyone, blame my brother for being a game-maker and then blame me for not being able to end his life."

Hunter scowled, and Tori's mouth quirked. She used her finger to turn his head until their gazes locked. Sam was about to look away, feeling like she intruded.

Finally, Hunter laughed softly. "She does that now."

"Frankly, I'm glad. There have been times when I thought we'd have to go a round or two." She turned to Tori. "I must ask a favor."

"Sure. Shoot."

"You won't want to agree to this." A single brow lifted. "I don't think we should let Cord know about your abilities, at least not yet."

"Why not?" Hunter asked.

At times, Sam hated having to be a queen. "Because he'll take the cells and use them on his daughter, and we need his help first."

"Wow," Tori retorted. "That's cruel."

"Yes. I know." Tori hadn't said the rest of the words. She didn't have to. *Even for you.* And they hurt. Sam, the woman, needed her friend.

"You don't trust him. Why?" Tori asked. She reached out to reassure Sam. No matter what actions were taken, they were still friends.

"I would think the reason self-explanatory, no? He made a very bad bargain."

Hunter seemed to agree but not his fiancée. "He had a good reason," Tori answered.

"And I'm trying not to judge," Sam continued. But he created Nirvana, now he needs to destroy it."

Tori sighed, her brows drawing together. "He's going to find out anyway. Those cells are our starting point."

"I understand. The cells not your abilities. Please."

Tori frowned and Hunter simply straightened like a soldier. "I don't like lying, Sam," Tori answered.

"Your choice is your own. You will do what you feel is right."

"Thanks." Tori grinned. "You do realize that by giving me the choice, you've made me not want to use it."

Playing these kinds of games wasn't Sam's style. Her brother managed to be far more adept. But she needed Cord's abilities. "Forgive me?"

"Already done."

Sam hugged both Hunter and Tori and then stepped back. "Cord has finished feeding, and Stacy has shown him to his room instead of the lab. I'd better remain close. He might decide he wants the real thing and use force. My guards aren't known for being gentle."

Hunter nodded. "I'll make sure Mercy understands."

"Thank you."

Sam walked inside the mansion, through the main floor, and down a long hallway. She knocked lightly on the door to the guestroom they'd put Cord in. "Come in."

A slight look of distaste filled his gaze as he sat on the bed. "Not exactly the Ritz," she agreed. "How do you feel?"

"I could use a swim," he replied, his tone rueful.

Sam smiled. "I wouldn't recommend it in the Hudson."

"I wouldn't catch anything, right?"

"No," she agreed. "But you'd have to deal with the police, curious bystanders, and of course, the media. That cannot be allowed."

"First law. No, second law. Humans can't know about us."

"Exactly. Starting with the ones right here. Try to allow some sound to come through your block. Listen."

Sam watched his face.

"Heartbeats." He swallowed several times but held himself in check.

"Again, well done."

Sam knew she needed to explain. "This is Hunter Pierce's cell. We call it the New York cell. He supplies blood to the entire East Coast from this donation center. His lieutenant, Mercy, runs it."

"Donation Center? You're kidding me." Sam simply stared. "When Stacy brought me inside, she gave me a couple of units. But wait a minute. The vibrations."

"Refrigerators."

"Hunh," Cord muttered. The look on his face told Sam he continued to process. "That's pretty incredible."

"Cord you need to remember," Sam added. "You cannot drink from anyone here. Everyone in this cell takes an oath. They abide by it, or they die," she warned. "You cannot be an exception."

He seemed not to want to ask. "And if I can't control myself?"

"Then you're dead, and I can't help you. Oaths and laws are sacred. They cannot be broken."

"Wow." He rose, slapping his hands on his knees. "Then I'm guessing all I get from now on is plastic."

Sam nodded. "Until you can control yourself enough to…hunt."

"Hunt?" He frowned. *I am not an animal. I am a man.* "Gotcha."

"I'm sure you'd like to freshen up," she said, guilt souring her stomach. Now would be the perfect time to tell him the truth of Tori's abilities. Sam hated deceit. "Then Mercedes will show you the rest of the mansion."

Sam was about to quit the room when a vision of them naked and sharing a shower popped into her head. She started.

"My desire makes you nervous," he told her.

"You are a memory, nothing more."

"Whatever you say, great Queen," he mocked as he bowed.

Sam didn't appreciate the humor. "Someday you'll find not everything is a joke."

A tiny sizzle, almost a whisper, snaked down her back. She wondered at its cause. But the urge to go outside filled her, and Sam knew not to disregard her intuition. "Follow me."

They walked down the hallway back into the large open cafeteria. The sizzle turned to a sear of fear as mocking laughter shivered through her brain. *Lia?*

Don't, my lady. I beg of you. He's using me to get to you.

Hide, Lia. Hide. Please.

Lia didn't answer. Instead, another voice filled her mind. *Hail and well met, sister.*

Chapter Ten

CORD FROZE. SAM TURNED PALER THAN PORCELAIN. SHE FLEW through the room and slammed open a door that led to a patio. Cord followed. Several vampires caught up to them, including the ones she'd introduced before, Hunter and Chaz. They carried wicked looking blades. And then a flaming redhead joined them, carrying a knife he'd rather not meet.

They ran through the grounds he'd been shown before and into the woods beyond. He could smell something strange in the air, a sickly-sweet smell, the kind you'd find in a hospital where they tried to cover the smell of death with deodorizer. Deep inside, he understood. These were rogue vampires, ones who'd taken Nirvana.

Lia. Please. There are too many. You must run. Break free.

Sam, begging inside his head. The queen he figured would never beg.

Cord skidded to a stop in a small clearing filled with dead leaves. He had no weapon and with his connection to Lia, he discerned they were too late. Yet his rage knew no bounds. Four vampires crouched over Lia, and he could smell her blood on them, in them. They were frozen in mid-act, a grotesque caricature of feeding. With a roar, Cord ran to them and yanked one of the rogues off his sister. Just as the rogue fell toward the ground, Hunter cleaved its head from its body. Chaz lifted the second, flipped him backwards onto the ground, and did the same.

Stunned, he hesitated and almost missed the extent of Sam's wrath. He watched as Sam leaped toward the fallen body of his sister. She caught the redhead's knife in midair and decapitated the third rogue just as her feet hit the ground.

The last rogue seemed to shrink back into the earth. The redhead lifted the rogue so that his feet hung off the ground. Sam grew before his eyes, no longer petite but tall and statuesque, regal, and very much the queen. Cord straightened and because part of him was deeply connected to Lia by the blood bond, he wanted vengeance for her murder. But his head told him to be cautious. Antu kept doing everything in his power to get Sam to attack and even Cord appreciated how grave a mistake that would be.

Sam stepped in front of the rogue. "I do not understand why you continue to try and provoke me brother," she growled, staring at the vampire. "Some acts can never be forgiven. This time you've stepped over a line. That which has been done cannot be undone."

The rogue laughed, the sound eerily mocking, the voice dancing down Cord's spine. "You do not scare me sister." This voice sounded familiar. In his office. Antu. "Nor do your pitiful friends. I will create an army and rule as I was meant to rule so long ago."

Had a gauntlet just been thrown?

Cord took a deep breath to tamp down the anger burning inside. Sam continued to stare at the rogue, making him wonder if brother and sister were communicating without the rest of their knowledge. Then Sam's face cleared. In the softest of tones she said, "And I will stop you."

With that, Sam walked away from the rogue. She threw the knife back to the redhead and walked into the woods. The redhead did what Sam did not, destroy the last rogue. Cord wanted to follow Sam, but Hunter Pierce held him back. He stared into gray storm clouds as the vampire shook his head. "Don't. She needs to be alone."

Cord nodded and walked to the edge of the clearing feeling terribly alone. He wished he could cry. Seemed vampires couldn't. As he stood, he thought back to his last conversation with Lia. He'd been walking down the hallway with Sam, and Lia chided.

"You should not play with my mistress."

Had Lia been jealous?

"Well, hello sis. How are you doing today?"

Lia let the snark slide. "You would do well to remember your place little brother. My lady is a queen."

"And I don't measure up, do I?"

"You have answered your own question."

"I don't really care. What I do is my business. And hers."

"Are you so sure? Those that play with fire…"

"End up getting burned. I know the drill, sis."

"Do you? I wonder. Hasn't your arrogance already gotten you into trouble?"

He wondered about an even more important question. When would it stop?

Cord lifted his head to watch a group of vampires begin clearing the bodies. The rogue bodies and heads were piled onto a tarp. A military vanguard of Sam's soldiers marched up to surround Lia's body. They straightened her and lifted her, and he joined the solemn procession back to a small house on the grounds. When they arrived, he walked up to Hunter and Chaz who were talking.

"Excuse me. I still don't know what's happened to Sam. She's blocking me."

Hunter answered. "She's performing the death chant of her people. She wishes to be alone."

Did she? He wasn't sure. He nodded and said, "Thank you." Then he walked down to the edge of the woods. He opened his mind and found the one heartbeat he wanted to hear. Hers.

He followed the sound over the high walls of the compound and across the highway and through the woods to the edge of the cliffs. Below him the Hudson River flowed down to the Atlantic. But across from him sat the sight he never appreciated as a human, the skyline of New York City.

Cord wasn't interested in bright lights and false stars. He approached quietly. Sam sat on a rock with her knees drawn up under her chin. She looked so young and vulnerable. "I'm so, so sorry," he said. "This is all my fault. Lia would never have been here, you wouldn't have been here, if I hadn't let my personal needs rule my reason."

She turned her head toward him, resting her cheek on her kneecap. He recognized the sadness in her gaze. "Antu would have found someone else. If not now, then twenty or fifty years from now."

"I could have said no. I should have said no."

She sighed and shuddered, and he felt every ounce of pain inside her. "Choices. Perhaps the cruelest jest of all. The Mother and Father gave us free will. We make decisions based on the import of the moment. Once you have lived a while, you will find that those decisions become superfluous after time passes because circumstances change. Indeed, sometimes they even seem stupid. But you must remember, they weren't at the time you made them."

"So what you're telling me is that I shouldn't live my life in the past but look to the future."

"Yes. Lia sacrificed herself for me. Or did she? Could it have been possible that she had also grown tired of life? She'd been in my service for so long. I begged her to leave and go find another reason for living. She laughed at me. And now I wonder about another possibility. Perhaps, she wanted a way to die that would give her the satisfaction of knowing her death would be her last great statement. I'll never know. What she did was her choice."

Cord slipped a little closer and drew Sam into his side. She let her head rest against his shoulder. "I miss her so much already."

"I miss her, too." He lifted her hand to place it inside his palm. His thumb stroked the back.

He wished he could do more to comfort her, but grieving was about as singular an emotion as they came. Still, he used his body to shield her and found his own comfort beside her. "Yes, although new, you shared a bond as Lia and I did."

He shook his head. "No. Yours was thousands of years stronger." He quirked his mouth. "But I can be your blood bag if you wish."

"My what?" she asked, lifting her head.

Cord urged her to put it back down. "Blood bag. I can't replace the real thing, though."

"Lia." She paused, and Cord figured Sam had gone back in time, awash in memories. "She been born on the streets. She had a whore for a mother, and her father could have been anyone. Lia learned not to trust at an early age."

That information brought a few of the pieces of the puzzle together. "She kept looking for a parent. Someone who cared."

"She called out to me with a prayer so intense, I simply had to save her. Mensah wasn't pleased."

"Mensah?"

"My mentor. The high priest who chose me for the temple." She sighed. "He wanted me to become his 'Lia.' The night of Antu's great betrayal, Lia and I fought his soldiers, but we were surrounded. I drained her to the brink of death, and they thought she was dead. Later soldiers loyal to the true temple rescued her. She felt she owed me her life."

Cord stroked the back of her hand with his thumb, the motion soothing. "You owed her yours."

She lifted her head and this time Cord relented. "You understand me too well."

"And yet you seem frightened. Are you?"

She pulled her hand away. "I'm not frightened of anyone." She drew herself up. "I am a queen."

"Then be a queen."

Cheeky bastard.

Cord nodded. He'd accomplished what he'd come here to do, help her rebuild her walls. The well of hurt he sensed inside her seemed to have diminished. Outside, she had friends to help her win this war. Now she had the strength inside to do what must be done.

She didn't say anything for a long while. "Antu's playing his greatest game. He's stripping away all of the beings I hold dear just as he would strip away the layers of my skin to cause the greatest pain. He thinks this tactic will cripple me. Over the years, I'm afraid, I've grown soft. I won't let my guard down again."

"He's a fool then," Cord answered, turning his head to look deep into her eyes. "Even I know he's done just the opposite."

"Yes. But we can play a little game of our own and let him think his plan is working."

Cord let the silence dictate and finally rose. He held out his hand to her. When she took it, he lifted her to her feet. Perhaps now wasn't the time but then again, maybe it was.

"Sam, I—" Cord swallowed and straightened. "Samira Anai Se-Bat, I swear to you I will do everything in my power to bring Antu to justice."

She didn't smile, she simply lifted her chin and nodded. "I accept your offer. Thank you."

Memories. Hundreds and hundreds of lifetimes. Lia had sustained her for so long, been her bedrock. Feeling the gaping maw, needing to fill it, Sam almost opened her mind to her brother for Antu was the only other being on the planet who could understand her loss.

Instead, she let those memories stitch closed the hole in the fabric of her heart. The robes had long since melted back into the earth. The banners were simply a picture inside her mind. But several items still remained from the temple. A gold circlet, a gift from Mensah. Her knife and sword, the handles bearing a single ruby, red for The Mother, who gave her the priceless gift. Antu had a matched set. His were onyx, black for The Father. The handles were made of solid gold that fit each bearer perfectly, slightly curved for a better grip. The blades were made of a metal not known to man, carved with symbols no human could read. Roughly translated they read, "A gift given can easily be taken back."

Sam stared down at the box Lia had so lovingly carved for her treasures wondering if The Father had told Antu to destroy those that served. Antu had never disputed her belief that he alone had been the instigator of that terrible night. She wondered now if he'd been able to hide such a possibility from her. He'd been able to hide his existence, so anything seemed possible.

Sam dressed in silence, waiting at times for Lia's hand to tuck in a fold or straighten a crease, a hand that would never help her dress again. She walked through the mansion and the grounds to the edge of the cliffs of the Palisades, feeling empty inside.

At the bottom of the cliffs, by the edge of the Hudson River and between two great bridges, they'd built a pyre. Although a challenge for a vampire, Hunter and Chaz had carried their mates down on their backs for she saw them looking up at her. Funny how beings can grow. Vampire and human now waited together to pay their respects to Lia.

They built the pyre next to the water's edge and used accelerant, for they would have to be gone without a trace by daybreak. Flaming torches surrounded the pyre. She held the circlet up to the sky in supplication and then placed the band on her head. She did not speak out loud.

Great Mother, we give back the one you made so that she might live again. Take this soul that has served you so well, give her peace, let her rest, and then let her choose her next path.

Sam paused and then began the death chant of her people. "Death is not an ending but a beginning. The cycle of life continues. The soul never dies even though the body ceases to exist. All life is precious, all souls cleansed when they are released. The Mother and The Father say it is so."

Sam jumped down from the cliff. She landed on the sand on bended knee not far from the pyre. The ground shook as she landed. She walked up to the pyre.

Lia stood by my side ready to fight for that which is good and just in this world. She gave yet asked for nothing in return. She protected, willing to sacrifice her life in return. She has earned rewards greater than all the riches in this world. May they be hers in her next life.

Sam withdrew her knife. Hunter, Chaz, and Mercy stood at the corners and raised the torches. "Farewell my friend, blood of my blood. I loved you then, I love you now. May The Mother welcome you with open arms."

Sam cut off Lia's head with a single stroke and laid it next to her body. A whispered sigh floated upwards through the air. A moment later, Hunter, Chaz, and Mercy shoved their torches into the pyre and jumped back.

Sam welcomed the heat. They all watched the flames, and time did what time does best, it continued on. One by one, the vampires of the New York cell paid their respects and made their way back up the cliff until only her soldiers and those closest to her remained. Each of her soldiers saluted, forearm to chest, before leaving. Mercy and her men were next, then Chaz and Stacy. Hunter and Tori lingered a while longer. Each of them had reached out with a touch of solace until they were alone and Cord remained.

Cord reached out and turned her face from the flames. He enveloped her with his body, and Sam let go, sinking into his chest. Now would be the perfect time to cry, but she couldn't.

Curse or gift. Sam would never know.

Chapter Eleven

CORD WONDERED HOW LONG THEY'D BEEN STANDING THERE. LIA'S funeral pyre still burned hot and bright. The woman in his arms remained every inch the queen yet so much more.

I am a coward.

Cord rested his cheek against her midnight hair. He banded his arms around her, pulling her close. "You're human."

"I'm weak."

"Yes, my Queen."

Her breath hitched and then whooshed out in a sigh. "You sound like Lia."

Cord lifted the corner of his mouth. "Thank you. I'll take that as a compliment." He tightened his hold on her, mesmerized by the flames, feeling the heat between them more than from the fire. "You feel as if you belong here."

She lifted her head. Her eyes seemed to change color with her mood. When she got angry, they could darken to near black. When she was amused, they could lighten to near yellow. Right now, they were rich and warm and golden reminding him of honey. Her eyelids lowered, and her skin warmed. He could use his body to make the world right for her again.

"What you're thinking would be a very bad idea. My promise to end your life still stands between us."

"I'd almost forgotten."

She trembled. Tears that could never be shed filled her eyes. He sensed the walls inside her crumbling. "Don't do this."

"Samira."

She slid her arms around his back, any space between them obliterated. Heat radiated through his body, awakening his senses as they never had before. He bent his head and their breaths mingled until nothing but that last barrier remained. Embers forged to life, pooling in the pit of his belly. Her gaze flared with the life of the pyre in response to the rising of his flesh. He wanted her. God, he wanted her.

"We could both let go and burn up in a fire hotter than the one before us."

"We could."

He rested his forehead against hers and swallowed hard. "But we'd both know the truth."

She lifted back, her brows drawn together, desire simmering in her gaze. "What truth?"

"That I'm not the one you lost." She began to protest, and he placed his forefinger on her lips. "That I make love to women, not with them, which I realize now is kind of cruel, but not completely when they were simply asking for satisfaction." He smiled and cocked his head. "I'm good at satisfaction. One hundred percent guaranteed."

This time she said the words out loud. "Cheeky bastard."

"Yes." He broadened his smile so his eyes crinkled and ran a gentle thumb down her cheek. "And if you want that kind of solace, I'm yours for the taking."

She huffed. "You dare much."

He lifted a single brow, lips lowering. "Do I?"

"Yes. And what you dare comes from the bond between us, nothing more."

He'd known she wouldn't take him up on his offer, so he urged her back against his body and pressed her head into his chest. He couldn't get over how right she felt. "Does it? I'm not so sure."

However, the bond enabled one thing. His ability to feel the weight of the mantle she carried.

"I've seen so much, Cord. Done even more."

"I guess I don't really care." He tucked her in even closer.

"Then you need to face reality. In order to save everyone, I'll probably die."

All of a sudden, Sam started nudging at Kayla's space, for the only person who filled his heart was his daughter. "Not if I have anything to say about it. Or the rest of this cell or other cells, I imagine."

"And if dying is my choice?"

Cord let go and cupped her face with his palms. "You talk about free will all the time, but you seem to have forgotten."

"Forgotten what?"

"I—we have free will too."

Cord bent his head. Her lips tasted like fine wine, to be sipped at first and savored, and then the sharpness, the first bite, mellowed into sweetness. She started, then her mouth opened. He would have loved to dive in and plunder every crevice, taste the sweet and the nip and the heat until she quivered beneath his touch. But Sam bore the mantle of a queen and a mere human, newly turned vampire, would never measure up. Or would he?

A question to be answered in the future. For now, Cord simply drew back, refusing to take advantage of the situation. He let go but couldn't quite sever their connection completely. He picked up her hand and traced the lines of her fingers.

"A wise decision."

"One I'm already beginning to regret." Cord waited for the fire in his belly to cool. "Now isn't the time, Sam. There will be one, though. I'm sure of it. And when the time is right, I'll make you melt, that I promise."

She started to smile, then her smile faltered. "Your arrogance will be your downfall someday."

"Already has been," he acknowledged. "Will be?" He shrugged. "I guess the future remains to be seen."

With a great deal of reluctance, Cord let Sam go. "I will intrude no more." He bowed, kissed the back of her hand, and left.

WHEN CORD FLOATED IN THE SEA, HE FELT A SENSE OF PEACE. NOW HE sat on a stone bench on the grounds, and the silence grated. Lia's death burned in his chest. He couldn't imagine what Sam felt and had no way to comfort her.

A cold wind kicked up and the night sky swirled as it began to lighten. He could sense the coming of the dawn but felt weary of mind, not of body. A storm approached, and he stood right in the middle of it, well aware of his promise, not as sure of his abilities.

"Dr. Stuart?"

He hadn't really heard her approach, yet now the beating of her heart gave her away. Cord imagined he would always hear them, including his own. There would be the blood and could only ever be the blood. Lia had tried to warn him and so had Sam. "Dr. Roberts?"

Cord rose. Hunger and need welled to form a tight knot in his belly. He swallowed.

"You would be safer if you stayed away."

She stilled, leaving a distance between them, a distance that he could cover before she could even blink. "I'm told it gets easier," Tori said.

"Indeed." He clasped his hands behind his back. "Lia didn't trust me. I'm not so sure Sam does either. In any event, Lia fed me."

Silence. Then a deep whoosh as she sighed. "You were bonded. My sympathies."

"I didn't know," he whispered, answering so many causes and effects. Yet Lia's face filled his vision.

"You couldn't. Any more than Hunter could have known that an enemy existed from two thousand years in the past who was hell-bent on destroying him, or that Sam had a brother in blood hell-bent on destroying anything and everything in his way."

Cord huffed out a bitter laugh. "What we don't know is supposed to make us stronger."

"Details," she agreed.

"Damn little devils."

Tori smiled and then her lips fell. "We have a great deal of work to do. May I call you Cord?"

"As long as you let me call you Victoria."

"Tori, please." She indicated that they should begin moving toward the house. He allowed her to circle him and followed. The blood rushing through her veins roared inside his ears. He longed to cover them with his palms. Instead, he clasped his hands behind his back even tighter.

"I have a surprise to show you, but before we go downstairs, understand that every being on this planet has a stake in what we do. Or don't do."

"No pressure, eh?"

Her heart pounded faster in his ears, and he wondered at the cause. She laughed softly and said, "Choices. You could kill me right here, drain me dry, and no one could get to me fast enough to stop you."

Consequences. "I could also die."

"You know about that rule?"

"Sam said it's forbidden. So is creating new vampires."

Tori continued up the grass next to him. "As a doctor, I don't like being responsible for someone's death. Call it a physician's arrogance if you must, but I don't like being unable to control. My oath is to do no harm and to save lives, not take them simply by existing. Can you imagine the chaos without those rules?"

"I can. I've seen movies where vampires rule the world and humans are bred as food." The weight of his actions crushed his soul even more than the rock tomb Sam had used to imprison her brother.

"Then you also know that one being stands in the way of that scenario becoming a reality."

"Yes." How could he have been so gullible?

She walked up the steps to the patio with strong, even strides. "With a little help from her friends."

He held the door for the doctor and tried very hard to block out the knowledge of the treasure so close to him. They walked through the cafeteria, eerily silent and filled with shadows. Good place for a horror movie. Or perhaps, he already played a part in one. One thought pounded in his brain with each beat of her heart. Blood.

They reached the elevator and Tori pressed a button to open the doors. A cool waft of air floated over him as he stepped inside. His hands ached as he clenched his fingers even tighter. Saliva flooded his mouth, and he fought for control, focusing on the vibration thrumming through his body as the doors closed. Refrigeration units.

When the doors opened, he stepped out quickly, not being polite by letting her go first. He walked into the middle of the room, breathing heavily. It took a few minutes before he circled the room with his gaze.

"Wow." He'd stepped into a fully integrated laboratory complete with incubators, refrigerators, analyzers, a mass spectrophotometer, and was that—? "Is that a molecular microscope?"

Stacy, sporting a ponytail and white lab coat, grinned as she walked toward him. "Welcome to our home away from home."

Cord inhaled her tantalizing scent, far more tempting than Tori's. "You should not be here, Stacy."

Stacy sobered, her steps slowing. "True. But just as I believe you meant no harm with your discovery, I believe you mean me no harm now."

"I'm not sure I'm strong enough yet," he strangled out, trying desperately to find the float. When that didn't work, he focused on the laboratory, making mental notes of additional equipment he would need.

"We don't have the luxury of time," Tori answered. "What you created has caused consequences beyond repair."

Consequences.

"I need to take specimens of your blood," Stacy added, her grin gone and her face tight. "You're newly made by a royal."

He could feel anger emanating from Stacy and a picture came to him of a grinning man with dark brown hair pulled back into a ponytail. "I seem to be the giant elephant in the room." He raked his hand through his hair, focusing on her anger to blunt the hunger. "His name?"

Stacy stared. "Pritchard, Captain Jeremy Pritchard. He died saving my life."

"Your anger with me is justified. But you must understand. I didn't mean to create a weapon. I was trying to save my daughter's life."

Cord's fingers trembled. He unclasped them and curled them into fists. Images of sinking his incisors into Stacy's neck filled his vision.

Both Tori and Stacy seemed to understand. "You could," Tori told him. "And neither of us could stop you. But what would happen to your promise then?"

Yes, his promise. His promise to save them.

Looking around the room, he wondered about Chaz and Hunter.

"They aren't here," Stacy added, her tone gentle. "Sam's holding them back."

Cord began to hyperventilate. He couldn't stop shaking. He slammed his hands down onto the countertop for control and gripped the edge. He swore he could feel the granite bow beneath his grip.

"You need to be able to work with us twenty-four, seven," Tori pounded away at him. "Sink or swim time."

His insides began to piston just as they had the first time he'd fed. All of a sudden, Sam's face filled his mind. She didn't speak, for he had to duke this fight out on his own. But knowing she stood with him, simply focusing on her, helped wipe away the terrible need until he could breathe again. Cord shuddered once and lifted his head.

"I'll be all right now."

I told you I would manage.

Cord straightened and picked up Tori's lab notebook. The work mattered now, nothing else.

In the time it took for the elevator to go up and down, Chaz and Hunter both burst into the room. Hunter looked like he wanted to start barking at Tori, and Chaz looked none too pleased as he gazed at his wife.

"Oh, ye of little faith," Cord joked.

Both of them whipped their heads around. "Do you have any idea how close you came to dying?" Hunter growled. "With pleasure?"

"Yes," Cord answered, understanding the razor's edge he strad-dled. "But I'm not here to kill."

"It's our nature," Chaz replied with sadness. "Antu turned Casper-ian, Hunter's former master, and Casperian tried to kill Hunter. And the first vampire he turned rogue, Mikhail Kirilenko, the leader of the Paladin, was like a father to me. Mick killed Jeremy and almost killed Stacy."

"The Paladin?"

"The vampires sworn to protect other vampires from rogues."

"Consequences," Cord breathed. "What I created was meant to stimulate the mitochondria of humans, not vampires."

"We know," Tori said. "We also know Morgan tried that but couldn't turn off the mitochondria once they'd been turned on."

"Morgan? Dr. Morgan Mackenzie?"

"It's Kent now," Stacy added. "She's our sorority sister."

What a small world. "The same thing happened to me, so I began gene sequencing."

"But mitochondrial cells are all different," Tori answered, "Depending on the cell that they're in."

"Exactly," Cord said. "And I kept failing. So I started with vampire mitochondria."

"Of course. Just the mitochondria and nothing else," Tori exclaimed. "What cells did you put them into?"

"I started with skin, then tissue, and finally muscle."

"Like going to like?"

"Yes." Tori didn't ask where the cells came from. She didn't have to. By her thoughts, he understood her connection to Casperian and his utter lack of caring for both vampires and the human race. "They all died."

"Because human cells can't withstand vampire anything, right?"

Stacy agreed. "They're not strong enough."

"Yes. But I don't understand what happened with the vampire muscle and tissue cells. They have a property to them that ruined my experiments."

"It's the protein that enables you to heal fast and knit human skin," Tori answered. "It's the protein inside the Lethe."

"Protein? Interesting." God, to finally talk about his experiments with people who understood the science. "Anyway, I thought gene relocation would slow the mitochondria down once I turned on their engines. It didn't. But put human mitochondria 'on speed' and put those mitochondria into a vampire cell. It stimulated the entire cell, and the cell went crazy."

"Nirvana."

"I didn't know. You have to believe me. And I never got to my next step."

"Next step?" Stacy asked.

"Take one of those stimulated mitochondria out of the vampire cell and put it back into a human cell. To save my daughter."

Cord didn't need to hear Tori's thoughts to feel her chagrin or be a mind reader to understand Stacy's anger. "I really messed up, didn't I?"

"I nearly lost Hunter."

"I nearly lost my life," Stacy added.

Even though his body ready to scale skyscrapers, Cord's mind wearied. "I'll take some of the blame but not all. Sam and Antu—"

"Blame gets us nowhere," Stacy continued. She seemed more sympathetic while Tori reminded him of Sam in a way, stern but fair.

"Antu's getting smarter. He's figured out that if he makes the vampires and then gives them the Nirvana, they're even stronger than when Casperian was their maker. Even Lia couldn't stand up to these new soldiers."

Lia's face loomed in his mind, this time with her signature sarcastic smirk. His insides hollowed, and a slow burn lit his veins. Antu had to be stopped.

"Wait a minute," Cord said. You said Casperian tried to kill Hunter. He used the Nirvana, didn't he?"

"Yes," Tori said.

"What's keeping him alive?"

"Sam's blood. Royal blood seems to slow the effects of Nirvana."

Cord watched both women share a look. "How?"

"We took dental pulp stem cells and grew them on royal blood agar plates."

Cord's heart began to pound. A rushing sound filled his ears. It took a moment for him to realize the sound was his own blood flowing through his veins. "They slow the mitochondria down, don't they?"

"So far, yes," Tori continued. "But only temporarily. As you know, it doesn't matter whose blood or where it came from, blood cells die, and you need to feed again."

Cord wondered at the sadness in her tone. Then he realized. "The stem cells don't last so they aren't a complete cure."

"No."

"Did Sam make Hunter?"

Tori cocked her head and stared at him. "No. Antu."

Cord began to pace. He went over each step of his logic trying to tamp down the adrenaline running through his veins. So engrossed, he didn't even hear Sam enter, didn't even feel the swirl of air from the elevator or hear the doors open and close.

And when he was sure of his logic, Cord muttered, "Then, Houston, we have a problem."

"What problem?" Sam asked.

He whirled. Tall and straight, pale and ravaged, Sam walked toward him, every inch a human, and every millimeter a queen.

"We can't kill Antu."

"Why?"

"Because his blood may be part of the cure."

Chapter Twelve

CONSEQUENCES.

Lia's death. Turning Cord. Casperian and Nirvana. Antu.

Sam rubbed her temples with her fingertips. The hollow ache of loss wouldn't let go. Was it as simple as fate, as simple as the flow of a stream that goes in one direction no matter how many obstacles blocked its path?

Sam wasn't sure. The same flow of water gouged out a path over time so it could reach the destination it needed to reach. She walked into the laboratory knowing what had to be done.

"The Mother and The Father set us upon this course a long time ago. They may have been prescient, able to see into the future, then again, they may not. They had to realize humans would grow in time. To become what they have become? I don't know."

Sam breathed deeply, releasing the air in a soft whoosh. She lifted her head and straightened her spine, tightening her back and shoulders to be the queen she should be. "But I do believe they saw a time when priests and priestesses would no longer be necessary."

"No!" Tori cried. "We'll always need you."

Sam watched Chaz and Stacy nod in agreement. Hunter simply bowed his head in salute. Their thoughts warmed her heart but none more than Cord. The poor organ had been chilled and dormant since Lia's demise. "Thank you."

She held up her hand, asking to finish. "I have known since the beginning that there would be a moment when the world would continue without me." She laughed lightly. "Arrogant, I know." She let the smile on her lips fade. "Hunter, you see what I see. Miklos. Hiroki. Both desire to be Head of the Council. They respect me as the eldest but only so far. "

"Mercy knows what she must do."

"I'm sure she does. But do they? I wonder." Reality could be bitter sometimes. "Neither leader sees that they are trying to set a course in their own image. As I have done." And reality could be terribly painful. "As The Mother and The Father have done."

"You're different," Stacy protested. "You lead by example."

"With a firm hand and a mother's heart," Chaz added.

"But always in the image I was given, an image I now see is not as pure as I thought." She turned to Cord. "You say I cannot kill Antu, that his blood may be the cure. Perhaps," she shrugged. "But without us, the rogues that have already been created can be destroyed and never be created again."

"Are you sure? I mean, even *I* can see the toll this kind of war will take," Tori said.

"Yes," Sam agreed. "The cost will be very high, I fear."

"Then let me do my job," Cord bit out.

Sam grimaced and swept her arm out to encompass the entire laboratory. "What you, my friends, have done in such a short time is truly a miracle but to deny reality for the heart's sake will lead to destruction. Antu will enslave everyone. He must be stopped."

Sam met each of their gazes in turn. From Hunter, she received a warrior's respect. From Tori, deep friendship, the kind given once in a lifetime. From Chaz, the brotherhood of the Paladin. And from Stacy, simple human warmth. But from Cord, she felt anger and frustration.

Because he cared, because he felt guilty, or both?

"I swear to all of you, I didn't know Antu survived," she insisted. "Once I was certain, I saw this ending. I don't see another."

"Look harder," Tori told her.

Cord marched up to her, and his gaze flashed fire. "Get me some of his blood and I'll get you a cure," he bit out. "Then he can face all of us on our terms, not his."

Sam's heart swelled. Yet the truth remained. "The terms will never be ours. Antu made sure the odds would always be in his favor when he killed everyone in the temple." She turned to pace but walked over and fingered the rim of a beaker instead. "Except for me. Because we were mates? I don't know. Why did he wait so long to show himself? Why didn't he kill Lia sooner? We are filled with emotions, and he deems emotions a weakness. Did killing Lia become a small part of his plan, or does he have a larger, more nefarious strategy waiting for us?" She shrugged. "I do not know."

"Do you believe he is stronger? Hunter asked.

"He is made of The Father. I am made of The Mother. We each have our strengths and weaknesses. No doubt he is clever, but I am steadfast. I guess you could say he is made of the wind, mercurial and fleeting. I am made of the earth, the rock our race is built upon. Is any one element stronger than the other? At times, I suppose."

Sam looked up at Cord knowing her next words might wound. She didn't want them to, but what she wanted wasn't important anymore.

"When we trained in the temple, Antu and I were a matched pair. Every fight, a draw. Perhaps being a matched pair meant we were supposed to be mated. We all know that when Antu sees something he wants, he takes it. But with me he took care, as if he knew he had to woo me. Terrified of being a part of someone else's being, I begged not to be mated. My God, I couldn't imagine, to be completely joined, to know every thought, every wish, every deep dark secret? But Antu became gentle. He gave me sunsets and most of all, time.

"But a man who is the center of his own existence doesn't need to understand the concept of love. At first, I thought his indifference was my fault." Sam blew a short breath out of her nose. "I learned. He doesn't understand goodness and caring and doesn't want to learn them. They are words without meaning. But I believe in them with all my heart. I believe love and goodness and caring make all of us stronger. This is the strength that knits us together.

"I could sacrifice myself also and seduce Antu into believing what we were can be again." She heard Cord draw in a hissed breath and smiled to herself. "Antu's ego will allow it but only for a time. Eventually, he'll see through my performance. However, the time I give you should be enough to manufacture a cure and destroy his minions."

"Not an option!" Tori cried.

For a moment, Sam concentrated on Cord. If she opened her mind, she would hear his thoughts, but Sam always treated people with respect. She watched his scientific mind process, but her heart lightened at the pain in his gaze. He shook his head ever so slightly from side to side. She comprehended he was living through her self-imposed torture and hated hurting him.

"I can't stop you," he said. "I can only beg. None of us want this kind of sacrifice."

Sam smiled, the warmth his words created wrapping around her heart. "And yet, each and every one of you would trade places with me."

Hunter cocked his head, a confused frown on his face. "You would not ask such a forfeit of us."

"No."

"Then why do you ask it of yourself?"

Love comes in different forms, with a mate and lover, or with a comrade who would die by your side. She wondered which carried more powerful. "Of all the insights, of all the thoughts and feelings The Mother and The Father overlooked, they completely misunderstood one—loyalty. They thought loyalty stemmed from command. It doesn't. Loyalty comes from the heart. Antu rules by fear, by command, as his due. I do not rule. And yet all of you would lay down your lives for me and for each other. Every vampire in your cell, Hunter, would take the blade of an axe before allowing the steel to cut another. Antu cannot and will not understand brotherhood, we do. Our bonds will give us an edge."

"How much of an edge? Chaz asked, pulling Stacy into his side as if to meld his mate to his flesh. "Rogues are still rogues. And the ranks of the Paladin are getting thinner and thinner."

"We will fight them as we did in New York, at the estate. In units.

We'll train as units until each unit becomes a single fighting machine," Hunter answered.

"Can we win?" Stacy asked.

"We have no choice. We must."

SAM PREFERRED TO USE ONE OF THE CABINS ON THE ESTATE WHEN SHE visited. The cabin she chose was Spartan in comforts, with just a bed and a few shelves, but huge in solitude. She rested in a place no one knew about, not even Antu. A gift from The Mother? Perhaps, but it was oh so necessary. Sam thought of it as an altered state, perhaps even a different dimension of sorts, but always a place where she could shed the mantle of ruler and just be Samira.

Here, she felt no guilt, no pain. She didn't need to make decisions that affected the lives of others, she could simply float or swim or rest with no thought at all. This place became her sanctuary, one of peace. Every being had one, the place they went to, to rest without blame or remorse or regret. She understood Cord's need to float in the sea all too well.

The place could be whatever Sam chose. Sometimes she surrounded herself with her bedroom and the rock walls of the home she built. Sometimes she walked in a field filled with flowers, and sometimes she raced the wind on the back of a white stallion, immersed in the bunch and release of the horse's strong muscles.

In this moment, Sam simply wanted serenity. Lia came to her as a picture, with the tiniest of nods and a brilliant smile. Sam took comfort in knowing Lia rested in her own place, happy and at peace.

Sam decided to float, and after a time Cord began to invade her thoughts. She pushed him away and tried to sink deeper into her float, but Cord became stubborn. His gaze seemed infinite as if he discerned her every thought, her every emotion. She'd started out having difficulty separating Cord and Nuya. Now she wondered why. Cord's features were lines and edges, Nuya curved and round. Cord had the look of a scientist, curious and intelligent. Nuya radiated feeling and caring. Yet deep in Cord's gaze, Nuya shined. Had Nuya's soul returned in Cord's body? Was this the time they were meant to share or just some tease of fate?

Sam wasn't sure how she would know. Here in this infinity, all felt possible, yet nothing seemed real. When Cord stood before her, a bemused smile on his face, she recognized the impossible had become possible.

"What are you doing here?"

"I don't know," he answered. "I'm aware that I'm sleeping and yet I'm not. Where am I?"

"You seem to have invaded my infinity."

Cord smiled. "You don't sound happy."

He dared her to tell him how she felt with his gaze. Unsure, she declined the invitation. She craved solitude but found herself also craving his contact. "Is Nuya with you?"

His head cocked as if listening. "I sense a presence surrounding me. I feel gentleness and purity. I hear laughter. Ahh, now a voice. He says he is not perfect and asks why you have made him that way."

"Every life needs a perfect memory, a perfect moment, a perfect person."

A vision of Cord looking down on Kayla at her birth filled her mind. "I understand."

Sam realized she didn't know Cord at all, she'd always looked at him and seen Nuya first. But Cord's chin looked longer and straighter, his eyes lighter in color. The truth hit her like a one-hundred-foot wave. Sam would always love Nuya but never as a mate, always as a brother.

A sense of peace surrounded her. Cord nodded but Nuya really asked her to let go of the guilt. "He says what happened was just as much his fault as yours. He could have held you back from the procession that day."

Yes, and she could have been born a boy or not at all—the chances of fate were endless.

"What procession?"

"A high priest came to our village to gather the next chosen for the temple. He saw me, and even though I was only five, he went to my father and told him I'd been selected."

Cord frowned as if listening again. "I feel pain but no blame. Why?"

"Do you remember your first feeding?"

He laughed softly looking down at his wrists. "How could I forget?"

"*I drank from Nuya first.*"

She felt Cord reach out as if to comfort. There could never be any. "*You killed him?*"

"*I drained him to the brink, but I couldn't kill him even though I'd been ordered to end his life. The penalty for refusing a direct order of the temple was death. I waited for the bite of steel that would end my life. Nothing happened.*

Sam immersed herself in that moment again, frozen with shock yet filled with the knowledge she'd done the right thing. The seconds ticked by so slowly, ever so slowly. "*Antu stood next to me. My mate. My twin. In my heart, I rejoiced for surely Antu would end this terrible play, this madness, and defend me, defend my decision. Life was precious. All life.*"

How could she forget the hole that opened in her heart as she looked up at Antu and watched his incisors grow? "*Antu drained Nuya before I could even move, just as he did with you. These were the lessons I had to learn. All beings are flawed. No one can be fully trusted. And love can be broken by a single thought or deed.*"

"*Yet you still care.*"

At last. Someone besides Lia who could truly understand. "*Because Nuya was goodness and light. Because his love for me couldn't be more pure or untainted. Because he didn't even know how to be jealous when I mated with Antu.*"

Cord laughed gently. "*He says that last statement might not exactly be true.*"

Sam quirked her mouth. "*And we both know he'd be teasing.*" *She drew in air and released her breath in a soft whoosh.* "*The Mother showed such cruelty that day. She became so cold a piece of my heart froze.*"

Sam did something she'd never been able to do, something a long time in coming. She let go of the regret. "*She also showed compassion and strength in her cruelty. She let me live so I could protect our race. If I hadn't learned how to hate, I could not have learned how to kill.*"

"*That's some price to pay.*"

Sam straightened, lifting up her shoulders to take up the mantle of responsibility once again. "*But a necessary one.*"

"*By whose standard?*"

If Sam knew anything, she comprehended her next words. "*There has to be balance.*"

She could sense Cord's uncertainty. "*Sometimes it seems as though the scales are tipped in a single direction.*"

"*Then it is our job to tip them back. Help me save our people.*"

"I promised I would before. I promise I will again. But I can't be in two places at once. I must know my daughter is safe. I must get home. It isn't far from here."

Sam frowned, hating the words necessity and expediency. *"She's not there."*

"I don't understand."

"The metaphysical is hard to grasp. Just as we are communicating now. When Antu drained you to the brink, he sensed all of you. He's aware you have a daughter and that she is your weakness. He had no trouble finding her, nor did I. So when I brought you to Sanctuary, I brought Kayla as well. She is being guarded by my soldiers. She is safe."

"Safe? Among a bunch of vampires?"

"Who have sworn an oath to die before touching her? Yes."

"And any of whom can be corrupted."

Sam shook her head. *"Our greatest strength is our brotherhood, our loyalty to one another. She will be safer in Sanctuary than anywhere else."*

"You don't know the future and neither do I!" he roared.

"No, I don't. Nor do I expect you to understand the bond of centuries of service. However, I feel your fear. My plane will be ready to depart immediately. I will go and bring her here."

"Without me?"

A parent's anguish and helplessness. Sam had never understood them before. She did now. *"You have a promise to fulfill."*

He quit her dream-state, and Sam opened her eyes to a well of sickness in her belly, something that hadn't happened in five millennia. Choices killed people, ideas, even feelings. Would he ever forgive her?

Chapter Thirteen

CORD WOKE UP TO THE MEMORY OF A DREAM THAT WASN'T A DREAM. Had Sam left him behind? Could she be that cruel?

He searched the grounds, the cabin she'd slept in, everywhere he could think of in the mansion. Eventually, he found himself at the place where he'd consoled her, the rock ledge on the cliffs of the Hudson River. Finally, the panic gave way to weariness. Once he let go, he Lia nearby. Her presence soothed, but each time he thought of Kay, his heart jerked and began to pound anew. Sam had shut him out. She'd taken charge of a responsibility that belonged to him and him alone. Was she already on her way to her plane? To Sanctuary?

Cord wasn't used to seeing New York City from the other side of the river, but even the glittering lights and starlit night couldn't take his mind off his fear. The tall buildings felt cold and sterile like a test tube without blood in it. The blood carried life within, not the glass. And he'd become as hollow as that empty tube. He listened to the echo of an ambulance siren across the water, and his heart wanted to stop.

Telling himself to breathe, Cord closed his eyes and opened his mind, but he couldn't find Sam. So he tried to find her soldiers. She blocked them too. He wanted to hate her with all the passion of man whose choices had been taken away. Yet, he couldn't. Why?

Cord heard the snap of a twig and the crinkle of a dried leaf. He swung around but didn't see anyone, yet he felt a presence.

"You shouldn't be out here alone."

Charles, Stacy's husband. "Sometimes even a vampire needs to be alone, Charles."

"Call me Chaz." The vampire walked up next to him and sat down. "And you're not."

"All right, Chaz." He would've liked to be alone in his misery. "Not what? Alone? I know."

Chaz laughed softly. "No, I meant a vampire."

Cord wasn't in the mood to play games. "Not a vampire? What are you on, Nirvana?"

"Not funny," Chaz bit out, the smile gone from his face. "No, I meant vampire, a true vampire. You're a Paladin."

"You used that term before, and I've come to understand you're some kind of like vampire cop. You destroy rogue vampires, but I have no desire to join you, so I don't understand the distinction."

"Which is why I figured I should probably explain." Chaz picked up a dead leaf and began crumbling it with his fingers. He let the pieces fall. "This is our race."

Cord got the metaphor. "I'm working on a cure."

Chaz brushed the remnants of the dead leaves off his fingers. "But you'd rather be somewhere else."

"Wouldn't you if it were your daughter?" Cord asked, drawing up his knees and wrapping his arms around them to keep from breaking something. Anything.

"Yes, but not every vampire would say the same."

He let his chin rest on top of his knees. "Now you're simply being cold."

"Am I?" Chaz quirked his mouth. "You've dealt with some of the vampires here. They are very…singular."

"Yes. I wondered why."

Chaz answered with a question. "You wanted to die when Sam created you, didn't you?"

Cord nodded. But he didn't see the point of the inquiry. "At the very least, as a scientist, I know it is impossible to fight the laws of nature."

"But you didn't die." Chaz had been playing with a twig, digging in the dirt. Now he stopped and looked over at Cord. "Not exactly."

"Oh c'mon. You're joking."

"Not in the slightest." Chaz threw the twig away and adopted Cord's position, his arms linked around folded knees. "I believe there's still an essence inside you that makes you more human because of your decision to die. You rejected the gift; therefore, you were able to keep some of yourself. It's why you're fighting so hard with yourself to go save your daughter."

Cord thought back to the moment when Sam gave him her blood. He thought he'd died.

"My real name is Charles, third guard of the Tower of London, circa the 12th century. We arrested a vampire. Obviously at the time, we didn't know he was a vampire. The jailer had been given a pendant as payment to release the vampire. The jailer reneged on his bargain. The day the accused was to be executed, I was part of the guard to accompany him to the gallows. As soon as the door opened, an angry and hungry vampire jumped out of his cell. We never knew what hit us. All the guards, the jailer, we were dead in a matter of minutes. Except me."

"But Sam gave me her blood."

"To seal the bond, every vampire must drink from its maker. I didn't. I ended up wandering the countryside, watching my wife die of the fever because I nearly drained her, not knowing who or what I'd become until Mick found me. He fed me and he became my mentor, my father, my friend." Chaz sighed. "As the leader of the Paladin, Mick showed me my true purpose, to defend and protect. Nirvana killed him." Pain and grief etched Chaz's features. "And I took his head."

"I'm sorry." Cord felt terrible. "I don't know what to say." After Chaz shuddered and turned to stare out at the skyline of New York again, Cord asked, "Why are you telling me all this? To make me feel guiltier?"

"Because you needed to know. Because none of us can fight what we are. Because those same feelings allowing you to feel guilty, the ones making you besides yourself about your daughter, are the same feelings that make you care about our race."

"And yet I sense from your tone, you've received ostracism and hate from the ones you are sworn to protect."

"Yes." Chaz picked up a rock and threw it.

A soft plunk made Cord realize he'd been able to reach the river with a single throw.

"I have no choice," Chaz said. "I'm a Paladin. And so are you."

"I can say no."

"Ummm, yeah. Sorry, you can't. Like I've been trying to tell you. You don't have a choice. And the sooner you accept and let Sam do her thing, the sooner you'll be able to do your thing."

Cord wasn't convinced. Chaz didn't say anything more, he simply left, leaving Cord to stare at the Hudson and the lights for a long time. Several times, he thought of jumping into the river, swimming across, and finding his way into New York and onto a plane. He'd arrive too late to make a difference, but at least he'd be doing something. Anything.

Why he didn't, Cord wasn't sure. He rose and ran back to the compound. He found himself in the lab staring at the one place that made sense to him. He hated the sight of tubes and beakers and machines that would end up being the instruments of Kay's death. But they were also the instruments able to give her life.

Tori came down first. He sensed the tension in her without having to hear her thoughts. Obviously, she knew Sam left. From Hunter? "She did what she thought was right."

Tori, ever the doctor, set several blood bags on the counter. He stared at them, not wanting their succor. If Kay didn't live, how could he?

Hunter walked into the lab next. Hunter stationed himself next to the elevator and sent a clear message. To leave this place meant going through the vampire leader and all his soldiers.

Cord watched Tori walk over to Hunter and marveled at Hunter's restraint as their heads leaned in and touched. He could hear the tantalizing rush of her blood through her veins and thought better of his first decision. He drained the bags quickly.

"Sam will get to her, and you'll see. Kay will be fine."

Cord didn't feel as certain as Tori sounded. He looked down at the empty plastic containers, hating what he'd become. But then he lifted his gaze to the couple who'd done nothing but show him respect and care. Tori and Hunter looked at each other again, then Tori's eyes filled with tears. He felt a terrible sadness emanate from her. "I had a daughter. Kelly. Thieves killed my entire family in a home invasion."

Horror hollowed his stomach, souring the blood he'd ingested. He wanted to reach out to offer comfort but didn't think he had the right. "I'm so very sorry."

She squeezed Hunter's hand and let go to wipe her fingers under her eyes. "The men were criminals, and at least one was a drug addict. They followed my parents home from the mall. What should have been a simple robbery turned into a melee when my father decided he'd had enough. They threw my daughter up against a wall, breaking her neck. Within a month, I'd lost all of them."

Cord felt sick. "There aren't any words…"

Tori nodded. Cord watched Hunter pull her into his arms and simply hold her. After a few moments, he let go except for one hand. "I haven't been able to come up with any, that's for sure," she replied with a shaky laugh. "But Hunter has shown me I don't have to, either." They clasped their hands tighter. "I believe humanity comes from within. We all choose how human we want to be, or not at all. I wake up every morning with a question—did the man who threw my daughter up against a wall so hard he snapped her neck really want to kill her, or had he simply become so frightened and desperate for drugs he didn't know what he was doing? I always tell myself it's the latter because if it wasn't, I'd want revenge."

Tori looked up at Hunter with the kind of love few get to experience. After a long moment, she added, "If there's anyone on this planet who had the right to revenge, it would be Hunter against his former master Casperian."

Hunter continued. "I didn't want revenge. I wanted the home and the family taken from me. I suffered the same as Tori. I lost a child as well. Casperian murdered it before it could be born."

Consequences. "I had no idea. I'm really sorry. I didn't know."

"You couldn't." Hunter inclined his head and Tori leaned on his shoulder. "But I have both now, a home and a family."

"I can't take back what has happened," Cord whispered.

"The point is, none of us can," Hunter replied.

The dream that wasn't a dream came back to him and his stomach hollowed. "Even so, she had no right to take the decision out of my hands." He assumed she'd use a private jet, modern and fast. Fast enough? "How could she just up and leave without me?"

"Antu already knows where Kay is. You don't stand a chance." *You don't know how to fight.*

Don't tell me what I can and can't do, Hunter. She's my daughter. I need to save her.

No, Sam will.

Cord looked over at Hunter feeling a bit perplexed, which seemed superfluous considering the fear swimming inside his guts. "There's a connection between us I don't understand," he said trying not to focus on his fear. "Almost like the one between Lia and me."

"Because Sam made you, and Sam and Antu are connected. I share a small part of that connection as well," Hunter told him. "Antu is my maker, and Sam's blood continues to save my life."

Continues? In spite of his fear, Cord's brain kicked in. Hunter needed Sam's blood to keep his cells from going into overdrive. "Technically, then, you should be my lab rat."

Hunter looked, well, offended. Tori bit her lip to keep from laughing. "I'm getting the feeling that the effects of her blood don't last, do they?"

They both shook their heads in unison. "Then I still need him." Cord sighed. "I'm guessing you haven't even scratched the surface with vampire genetics."

Tori grimaced. "Hard to do when blood cells don't last very long. And the right samples are hard to come by."

Meaning Antu and his ability to show up or not show up at will.

"He's mercurial. And terribly unpredictable. But he does have a singular purpose."

"Making you think plans and strategies will work. They won't," Tori answered. Hunter simply nodded.

"So much for logic then."

"The 'pile it higher and deeper,'" Tori replied, "Doesn't always win."

"Does heart?"

Respect grew in her gaze. The same respect filling Hunter's face. "We'll find out," he said.

Cord looked at Hunter, but the vampire turned neutral as if he was waiting. But for what? Tori caught Cord's gaze for a moment, then looked up at Hunter, as if trusting her mate implicitly. She didn't say anything. They simply seemed to wait.

Sam invaded his mind. *"He wants me buried alive, Cord," she said before he could even think of forming a word. "Is your daughter worth that sacrifice?"*

Ready to scream out at the top of his lungs 'YES,' Cord choked. Sacrifice? The light bulb went on way too quickly and even more brightly. Sam wasn't simply talking about her own life but the lives of every vampire walking the earth. And what about the humans who had no idea vampires existed?

"I can't fight him buried under tons and tons of rock," she continued, her tone weary. "For this is what his ultimate goal is. To do to me what I did to him. And while I work to get free, what do you think will happen? Who will stop him? Who will stop his rogues?" Her sigh shuddered through his mind. "Can you hear him? His laughter? He set this whole thing up perfectly."

"Yes," Cord answered, not ashamed of his selfishness, for what parent wouldn't do anything to save their child? But he did feel guilty that he never thought of anyone else. 'And if I can't find the cure for the rogues, he wins that one too."

"I can fight." Hunter? Able to exist simply because Sam's blood kept him alive?

"We both can. We decided." Tori? He'd been so engrossed he hadn't realized they were both part of the conversation.

"We?" Sam asked, sounding none too pleased by their answers.

Hunter didn't sound one bit abashed. "He won't suspect us."

"I'm certainly not a threat," Tori added.

"Nor am I." Wait a minute, a vampire with Hunter's skill not a threat? *"But one plus one equals a whole."*

Confused, Cord didn't understand. Then Hunter said, "If I drink from him, I might regain my full strength."

"And in his arrogance," Tori added. *"Antu will dismiss me as human."*

Cord waited for Sam to answer. When she didn't say more, he realized she'd bowed out of the conversation, and Cord found himself back in the lab with Hunter and Tori.

"Excuse me, but would someone like to explain please?"

Tori began. "As you know, when Casperian tried to kill Hunter, we were able to reverse the effects of the rogue blood by creating new vampire cells on royal agar plates. I believe an infusion of Antu's blood will give Hunter back his full strength."

"And?"

"I became injured during Hunter's fight with Casperian. I kind of got in the way of Hunter's sword." Hunter and Tori exchanged a glance. Hunter didn't look happy. Tori kind of shrugged in answer.

"Some of the pure vampire stem cells were used to save my life, keep me from bleeding to death," Tori continued. "We used them to knit my skin together. I'm stronger than a human, but I'm not a vampire. I eat human food, and I don't want to drink blood. We already know how to save your daughter."

"We couldn't tell you," Hunter added.

The whole world and everything around him seemed to cave into this kind of gray hole as if he was surrounded by an invisible fence. If he stayed in this one place, things made sense. If he approached the barrier, his mind tried to tear itself to pieces.

He found himself holding his head in his hands and it took a long time for him to let go. "You didn't trust me."

"We didn't know you," Tori shot right back. "How could we? You created a drug that could destroy us all."

Trust. Such a small word. Consequences. So much larger.

"And just so you know it all, Sam asked us to keep the information from you. Until we could take your measure," Hunter added. "We know you now. Apologies."

Blazing hot anger filled his veins. *Apologies? Apologies?*

Damn Sam, damn them all for playing with his daughter's life. How dare they make those kinds of decisions. His fists clenched, and he wanted to slam them into something. But as his blood cooled, Cord made an effort to see their side. After all, he built his life on logic.

Cord uncurled his fingers one at a time. He was still damned angry, he had that right, didn't he? "If you'd known her before she got sick, you'd understand."

Hunter clasped his shoulder. "We do. Now."

Did they? Feeling incredibly betrayed, Cord wondered. He shrugged off the hand and walked toward the interior of the lab. "Well, if you want the monster to work, you'd better get over here."

Tori walked toward him, her gaze part sadness, part necessity, all tinged with guilt. "Cord, I—"

He shook his head. "Don't. I think we've all done enough damage to each other, no?"

She nodded and shrugged into her lab coat. Cord did, too, thinking of his daughter and the way Kay used to be, whole and strong and the light of his life. Determination filled his mind and then everything clicked. Sick and diseased mitochondria. Kay's blood? The cure? "Son of a bitch."

Tori stared at him, but Hunter who answered. "He knows Cord. Antu figured it out. He'll never make a trade. He'll taunt us with her, play cat and mouse, and let as many people who are willing to die, try to free her. Then he'll tire of the game."

As much as Cord hated to admit the truth, Hunter had the bastard pegged to a tee. "And then?"

"He'll end it."

"Then we're all screwed."

Tori gasped, realizing the path his thoughts were following. She'd been coming from the place of strength, the place of fighting fire with fire. But what if the right way to go about a cure was the exact opposite? What if the disease could become the cure?

The strength ran out of his bones. Cord wanted to sink into the float. The problem with the float was that it became a substitute for oblivion. A moment later, Cord decide that a rock wall simply wouldn't suffice. "And Sam, not Antu, has screwed us most of all."

Chapter Fourteen

SAM HATED LEAVING CORD, HATING HIM HAVING TO FIND OUT A TRUTH she created from someone else. Sam always accepted the consequences of her actions. And now she had to accept the gravest consequence of all. There would be no trade. But the rest?

With Hunter left to assume guard duty, Charles became the logical companion for this burden. The Paladin would be necessary to help destroy any rogues they found.

"Before we left, I tried to explain to Cord about being a Paladin," Charles told her.

Sam nodded. "He will be what he chooses. The Mother gave us free will."

Terrible and beautiful in a cold way, Vanessa Demineure accompanied them. Not Sam's favorite vampire, for Vanessa unwittingly created the trap Casperian used to poison Hunter, but a welcome fighter. The redheaded Paladin was as fierce as they came.

"I could get used to this life," Vanessa remarked, her fingertips caressing the leather of her seat.

"You have enough money to afford a private plane ten times over," Charles said. "Who are you trying to kid?"

Vanessa rolled her shoulders and waved her hand at him. "I try never to spend my own money."

He snorted. "Which is why you have so much."

Sam shook her head and rose, sliding into the aisle to go up to the cockpit. She had no desire to listen to childish squabble.

"Of course, darling."

Hours later, they landed in a small, private airport and several big, sleek, blacked out SUVs were there to pick them up. Sam had remained in the cockpit with the pilot and felt glad to be able to stretch her legs as she climbed down onto the tarmac.

Charles seemed concerned as they stood next to one of the vehicles. Her soldiers stood next to the others awaiting orders.

She would be remiss if she didn't at least thank them all, so she said, "You've accepted my command and you know what awaits us. You are brave and loyal, and I count myself lucky to fight by your sides. You all know the plan."

No one answered, not even Vanessa. Just nods of respect and the quick clasp of long slender fingers around her wrist from a woman who was never short on words.

The SUVs took them to boats that flew across the water. Once they reached Sanctuary, Sam watched the Paladin and her soldiers scale the rock wall with ease. She felt a sear of guilt that she hadn't let Cord accompany them. Shaking her head, she began climbing.

When she finally reached the top, she smelled blood, too much of it, and raced through an opening into Sanctuary.

The bland ice tone of the next words spoken, chilled her bones. "She is safe within these walls."

A voice she hadn't heard in many millennia. Sam rose to her full height as she slowed, then walked inside the room. She stared down at the vampire who'd spoken with disdain. "Bahir. You seem to show up in places where you're not wanted."

"You do not sound pleased, my lady."

He smiled, reminded her of something two-faced, like a Janus cat. He sat on a bench made of stone, refusing to rise at her entry, a clear measure of disrespect.

Sam thinned her lips, and a small tick began vibrating at the base of her temple. "Press me and lives will be lost this day. Yours will be first."

Bahir smiled again. This time, though, he rose and bowed. "I am always at your service, my lady."

"Mealy mouthed pig." Sam swallowed hard. She clenched her fists. She looked over at Charles, who stood ready to make an end of this farce.

Pain filled her, and the truth blossomed inside her belly. "I should have known. Only you could have defeated Lia."

The vampire waved his hand. "My master is kind and generous, and oh-so-wise, do you not think?"

"What I think has no bearing here," Sam shot back. "What I know is that this may be the time when the honey on your tongue will not allow your neck to slide out of the noose."

"You cannot prove anything," the vampire said, his arms crossed and his chin stuck in the air.

Sam answered with disdain. "I need no proof."

"Where is Cordell Stuart's daughter?" Vanessa roared. Obviously, she had no patience and decided enough with the games.

Bahir looked down his nose. "Piss-ant. Flea. So unworthy."

Stop reacting. He's baiting you. And lying. Kay isn't here. But she is alive. Sam looked up to make sure both Charles and Vanessa heard her.

Sam began to circle Bahir, rubbing her chin as she considered his fate. "Where is she, *iwiw?*"

Bahir drew back in outrage and whirled to face her. "I am not a dog."

Sam's entire being filled with fury. "I am The Mother! On your knees to me. NOW!"

"Never!"

Both Charles and Vanessa stepped forward. One of Sam's soldiers drew out a slightly curved, wicked looking blade.

Sam held up her hand and shook her head. "Take him to the shackles. Let the sea take him."

"Oh, goodie. I like this idea," Vanessa said, clapping her hands with glee.

"Sam," Charles protested. "We're not like them. You can't."

She looked over at Bahir.

He smirked. "He's right. Touch me and many will die."

There could be only one way to end the stalemate. She leaped and jumped on Bahir's back. With a roar, she sank her incisors into the vampire's neck. Bahir tried to shake her off, but Sam had to find out exactly what Antu planned.

Blood, sweet and powerful, filled her mouth but this blood tasted different. It carried images and memories of a time long gone, a time she'd tried hard to remember and not to remember. Sam learned a great deal before Bahir was able to throw her off.

She wiped her lips and spat out the remnants of the blood in her mouth. Her turn to smirk. "I could have drained you, pig. No one would have stopped me. However, I didn't."

Sam looked over at Charles, letting him see the picture in her mind.

"It looks like a tomb," he said.

"It is. Antu wants *me*, he wants his last revenge to bury me alive as I buried him."

She turned to Bahir. "Your master chose well. Tell him I will come alone."

Bahir cackled. "My master is great in all things. He bests even you."

Vanessa leaped forward. Before Sam could react, she had a wicked looking dagger with its point under Bahir's chin. Vanessa pressed the blade, and Bahir rose onto his toes. "I say we kill him now."

"Hold!" Sam commanded.

Vanessa looked like she wanted to argue but withdrew the dagger slowly. Vanessa grinned as a small well of blood blossomed, staying on the blade of the dagger. The vampiress stuck her tongue out to lap up the drop. Sam couldn't blame her for the nick in Bahir's neck or the taste.

Sam turned to Charles. "Is everyone in place?"

Charles nodded. "They are."

Sam turned to the fallen vampire. She should have rejoiced. Instead, she only felt sadness. Why, she asked? What purpose did all these games serve? "Your master has abandoned you."

"Has he?" the vampire asked, jutting his chin but with the slightest tremble in his tone.

"You already know the answer. You've always been expendable. Caring is the difference between your master and me. Caring will always be the difference between your master and me. So I ask you, why should I care?"

Sam watched fear fill Bahir's gaze. He tried to brazen his way out. "You will not kill me."

"I won't?" Sam asked, lifting a brow. "Why are you so sure?" She motioned to her soldiers. "Take him. Let the sea decide."

Vanessa laughed and clapped. Sam held up her hand and threw the Paladin a look. This was not and could never be a joyous occasion. "Miklos and his men scaled the walls as we spoke and have surrounded your master's soldiers. Your soldiers. They will be given a choice, join us or die."

Bahir didn't answer, but his gaze flitted around the room as if seeking escape.

"I wonder how his betrayal sits with you now?" Sam wondered out loud.

Bahir didn't quite hide his fear this time as his Adams apple bobbed. "I live to serve, my lady."

"You've known the blackness in his heart and yet you stayed with him all these years?" she asked, the question haunting her. "Why?"

Bahir didn't answer. He simply countered with a question of his own. "Was Lia any different?"

Sam sighed. "No."

"Sam, please. You can't do this," Charles protested. "Even though we are Paladin, and Antu has made Cord a vampire and tried to use his daughter as bait. The Mother—"

"Would offer this piece of offal a choice," she interrupted. "And so I shall. Clean and quick or slowly as the water rises with the tide?"

I offer a trade. Bahir for the child.

Sam refused to acknowledge the voice that had reached her. "Take him away. Place him in the shackles in the sea."

Charles looked like he couldn't believe his ears. "Sam? What are you doing? He offered an exchange. Even I heard it."

Vanessa's gaze narrowed, catching Sam's. Seems she had heard the offer as well. "I vote thumbs down."

"No," Charles countered. "That's not our way."

"This pig killed Lia," Sam cried. Her lips compressed and she hardened her features. "He must pay."

"You can't mean that," Chaz whispered, clearly horrified.

Sam decided not to reply.

"If you kill him, you're as bad as Antu," Charles bit out.

Sam widened her eyes as each word found its mark. She motioned with a flick of her wrist to take Bahir away.

"Charles," she began only to have him stare at her with distaste. "Chaz. You've always trusted me. Don't lose faith now."

"My lady?" One of her soldiers appeared at the doorway. "Miklos requests an audience."

Sam walked back inside and turned to enter another chamber. This room sat empty but for a plain stone platform and bench. She climbed up onto the platform and sat down on the bench to wait. Vanessa followed but Charles made leave to go.

Sam shook her head. "Stay. Please."

He nodded, and the look on his face told her he wasn't quite sure what she wanted of him. "Send Miklos in," Sam asked.

One of Miklos's soldiers brought a chair into the room, bowed, and left. Then Miklos limped his way into the room. "My lady," he said, bowing with respect.

Sam bowed her head in return, and Miklos fell heavily into the chair. Lines creased his face, etched as she knew from the pain he constantly carried. But she saw an ease in his gaze that made her suspicions fall into place. "Thank you for your aid."

The vampire leader waved his hand. "It was nothing. My duty is to protect my people."

"Your duty," she repeated not liking the words as they rolled off her tongue. "Your act, you mean?" He stared at her. "Almost enjoyable to watch."

"Act?" he asked, not at all surprised by her knowledge.

"Come now, old friend. Did you think I wouldn't find out?" The old vampire didn't answer but his fingers tightened around the head of his cane. "He promised you everything and you fell for it."

"He promised me what is mine by right!" Miklos thundered back. "Do you really think that insignificant piece of horse dung Hiroki could possibly be more worthy?"

Sam stiffened, and she nodded imperceptibly to Charles, but she never took her eyes off the crafty old lion. "The Council makes all decisions. There cannot be a single leader."

"There must be," Miklos insisted. "They are all idiots. We have the right to exist."

Charles drew himself to his full height, hand on the hilt of his sword. He seemed to understand her request now. "So do humans."

She could feel Charles' anger and held up her hand before he could continue. "Your prejudice has become your downfall," she told the elder vampire. "Your error in judgment will be your death. You believe his soldiers will turn against me. You believe Antu will win."

Miklos stuck out his chin and cocked his head, arrogant to the bitter end. "I chose life for my people."

"You chose glory for yourself."

"A win-win," he smirked.

She shook her head, simply sad now. "He'll kill you when he no longer needs you, you pathetic fool." The vampire elder still dared her to prove he was wrong. "If you don't believe me, go talk to Bahir."

Miklos looked confused for a moment. He didn't know Bahir.

"Bahir has been by Antu's side since the beginning, since our making. He now resides in shackles in this domain." She gave Charles a quick look and watched the vampire's mouth quirk. "It is my will that the sea takes him. You are more than welcome to join him."

Miklos didn't answer. He lifted his chin and cocked his head. God help the sin of pride. "You think you can fight Antu, don't you?"

"My fighters are the best in the world. They've been trained to withstand every hardship. They'll fight forever. And once his soldiers see we are better, stronger, they will fight with us."

What a fool. Antu would let them fight each other until they were all dead. Why couldn't Miklos see the truth?

"What happens when they're all gone?"

The picture in her mind made all the sense in the world, her suspicions confirmed. "He gave you his blood."

Miklos lifted the leg of his pants. Vanessa gasped. Chaz started then snared her gaze. The calf muscle had healed completely.

"Now you understand," Sam said to her compatriots.

Chaz nodded. And to be honest, part of her commiserated in a way. It couldn't be easy living an eternity in constant pain. However, wrong can never be anything but wrong. She brought her attention back to Miklos. "Poor fool. You're already dead."

"Maybe, maybe not."

She rose from the bench. "Where did he take the girl?"

"To the place where the hatred began."

The place where it would end too. *Fitting.* But for some reason, she didn't quite believe Miklos. He was as much a snake as Antu was a serpent.

"Rise," she commanded. Miklos stood. "Your cell and your soldiers belong to The Council now. As do Bahir's."

"Do they?" Miklos scoffed. "My soldiers are loyal. To me. They'll take three of yours for every one of mine. His are nearly our match. They will fight under my command. Are you willing to risk such a cost?"

Again, Antu planned well. "If even one of my soldiers dies, your life will be forfeit."

Miklos didn't look frightened. Because he knew she wouldn't start a war, or because he knew Antu's plans? "You don't have the balls," Miklos taunted.

Really?

No, Antu wouldn't confide in someone so beneath him. Miklos was just another pawn. "I don't? Are you so sure? I am The Mother!"

The room thundered with her last word. Miklos blanched. But he rose and threw back his shoulders. He clenched his fists and scoffed, "Your chains won't hold me forever. And my men are—mine."

"The chains will keep you out of trouble for now." Sam motioned for his soldiers to take Miklos away. "And your men? Are you so very, very sure?" The old man went, but Sam watched as he frowned. Obviously, Miklos didn't trust Antu entirely.

"Have the plane refueled and ready to leave," she told one of her soldiers.

Vanessa stared at her, as if trying to figure her out. The vampiress would never succeed. "We're not going to fight? What about Miklos' soldiers? What about Antu's?"

"We'll take Miklos with us back to New Jersey. I don't think his soldiers will attack without him. For now, I will leave Antu's soldiers here in the care of my guard. Should Antu decide to mobilize, and if they manage to take the day, it will take what is left of them time to reach Hunter's cell."

"You knew Miklos wanted to revolt, didn't you?" Charles asked, a slight smile playing about his lips.

"I suspected. Antu cannot always hide all of his thoughts from me, and I caught a glimpse of Miklos walking without pain."

"What about Kayla?"

"I've made a mess of things, I'm afraid. I sensed Bahir and thought he wouldn't trust such an important confrontation to anyone else. Instead, Antu sacrificed a bishop for my knight. Finding Bahir here without Kay means Antu wants to continue the game, and the stakes will go higher."

"Damned right," Vanessa replied. "Do you have any idea where he's taken her?"

"Soldiers are expendable for Antu. With his plot thwarted, my guess is he wants me to go back to New Jersey, so he can bring the fight to me. Miklos won't wait long before he sends word to his fighters to attack. Rogues, soldiers, it doesn't matter to Antu. Just as long as I suffer."

Sam's guilt didn't sit well in her gut. "Plus, he's dangling Kay like a carrot. He wants to see if Cord can will come up with a cure, or if he'll break and try to find his daughter."

"My kind of guy," Vanessa remarked, her tone dripping disdain.

"Antu thinks Cord will fail. On both ends."

She watched Charles swallow his distaste. "What about Bahir?" Charles asked, caution riding his tone. "Will you kill him?"

"He killed Lia. I should. But again, this is where we differ. I cannot simply kill out of revenge although I was tempted for a moment." Sam blew out a deep breath. "Very tempted."

"I'm glad you didn't," Charles said.

"I'm not," Vanessa added.

She knew. Each vampire became a foil for the other. The leader of the Paladin had chosen well. "Bahir wouldn't have drowned. He would have put himself into stasis, a deep vampiric sleep, that only ones with royal blood can achieve. Ultimately, this sleep is what saved Antu after I buried him, and why I had no knowledge of him after I found out he was Hunter's maker."

"When all of this is over," Vanessa said. "I would be honored if you'd give me leave to take Bahir's head."

Honored. The word so entwined with the other—death. Sam had begun to despise them both. "We have to win first."

Chapter Fifteen

CORD STOOD ON THE PATIO OF HIS HOME AND QUIVERED. EVERY FIBER of his being ached to chase after Kay now that Sam had returned, but who could he trust? He wasn't even sure he could trust himself.

As a human, in his angst and worry about his business and then Casperian, Cord had let the grounds of his home go to seed. The railings of the paddocks were chipped and dirty, the fences and barn not as pristine white and green as they were in his mind. He felt as dismal as his home looked.

"There is the blood and can only ever be the blood."

Cord didn't turn. "Can the blood lie?"

Hunter drew level with him and clasped a hand on his shoulder. "A year ago, I would have said no. Now? Now I'm not so sure. I believe Antu can corrupt anything."

Cord stared at a tall weed growing in between two shrubs at the edge of the patio. The weed didn't belong there. Then again, the poor thing was simply trying to live. "I'm not so sure I like this world I've stepped into."

He looked over at Hunter to see the vampire's mouth quirk. "No different than the human world. Smaller, perhaps, and a bit starker."

"Did you tell Mercy to be careful with the specimens?"

The vampire leader didn't often smile. "You did. At least twenty times."

He had. "I've got all my notes and notebooks. Although I wonder if Tori isn't way ahead of my work." Cord felt his body relax for the first time since they left the estate. "You look stronger."

"I feel better." Hunter let go and clasped his hands behind his back. "The more I drink from Sam, the stronger I get. Especially after an infusion of new cells."

"She's becoming your maker."

He watched Hunter lift a brow. "You may be right."

Cord couldn't suppress the agonizing question tearing his guts apart. "Sam doesn't believe he will, but do you believe Antu will kill Kay?" Just asking the question pierced his heart, but he believed Hunter wouldn't lie, and in order to keep going, he needed an honest opinion.

"No, actually I don't."

"Why not?"

"You heard Sam. Antu loves to play games. Kayla is still a very important piece in all of this."

"Until she isn't." Cord sighed. He tried to banish the emptiness in his soul by picturing Kay taking her horse over the fences as they once were, shiny and white in the sun. He placed the memory close to his heart. "I need your help, Hunter. I'm about ready to jump out of my skin and go off half-cocked, and I don't even care where. So tell me. Help me understand him. What is Antu like, what's he capable of?"

"Just about anything," Hunter snorted. "He's colder than a polar ice cap and just about as unfeeling. There isn't an ounce of remorse left inside the man."

Not what Cord wanted to hear. "Great. Just great."

Ever enigmatic, Hunter shrugged. "You asked for the truth."

"And you don't pull punches."

Hunter's head moved slowly, side to side. "Antu believes every living thing on this planet is meant to serve him."

Cord wondered. "I understand arrogance, I have my own, but not to the exclusion of all else. Is it possible he's searching for something?"

Hunter drew his brows together and thinned his lips before asking, "What do you mean?"

"Like kindness or compassion."

Hunter stilled, and Cord figured he continued to process.

"You're not making any sense," Hunter said.

"I guess not. But maybe he's buried his real self so deep he can't find himself anymore."

"Perhaps." Hunter nodded slowly, looking like he was still thinking things through. "But he has been this way for millennia."

"My point exactly," Cord replied. "He's forgotten what emotions feel like, and he's frustrated. He keeps using substitutes because he can't find the real thing anymore. He searches, he fails, until it all becomes a vicious cycle."

Comprehension filled Hunter's gaze. "One, I'm afraid, which may become never-ending."

Cord shuddered thinking of the devastation. "Unless we can stop him." He tried to draw in a deep breath, but the knife piercing his heart would allow no more than a small draught. "Can we save Kay?"

"We?"

"I won't be able to work or even concentrate until I know she's safe."

"You made a promise."

"Which I intend to keep!" Cord clenched his fists until he could get his lungs to stop heaving. "As soon as she's not in that monster's hands anymore."

"I do understand, you know." Cord kind of shrugged as Hunter continued. "Look, we have the element of surprise. I'm not quite a vampire. But I'm nearly healed. And Tori is much stronger than she looks. We've been sparring, and she can hold her own, even against me. But Antu believes she's human and will scoff that we sent such an emissary."

"And not question the Trojan horse?"

Hunter snorted. "Arrogance breeds the fool. Antu thinks both of us are insignificant. He doesn't know the truth because he can't read my mind and reading Tori's is beneath him. But he can read yours through Sam. Do you sense him?"

"Not right now."

"He will come. And soon, I'm afraid."

"Then all he'll get is this." Cord showed Hunter the picture of Kay jumping a course of fences.

"Good. Very good." Hunter almost smiled. "Antu actually wants me to challenge him. I'm the only vampire he's never defeated. At the time, I think he gave me my life as a reward for my ingenuity. Now? Now, I'm simply dangerous and need to be eliminated." Hunter's face turned deadly serious. "Beware the serpent, Cord. Especially the one with honey coating its tongue. When he is ready, Antu will speak."

Cord stilled and watched Hunter do the same. "I think he already has."

"Miklos."

CORD LOVED HIS HOME. HE REMEMBERED HOW HAPPY HIS FAMILY HAD been before his father died and wanted his daughter to know that same warmth and security. He'd tried to create an atmosphere for Kay after her mother left where his daughter would always feel safe, secure, and most of all, loved.

Where the hell was Sam?

Cord walked down to the barn, needing to take his mind off everything. Even though he could see in the dark, he didn't want to take the chance with *Perfect Gentleman*. He threw on the flood lights around the main ring before going to the stall. His horse, affectionately called 'G', looked fit and ready to run, so Cord hooked a lunge line to the horse's halter and led him out to the ring. With a slight nip in the air and not having regular work, G was feeling full of himself, dancing and high-stepping, shaking his head as they walked.

Cord started the horse in a smallish circle, letting him have his head and play a bit before asking the horse to work. He clucked and swung the end of the line as incentive to get G to move, then he reversed direction.

"You shouldn't be out here by yourself."

Cord whirled. Sam. Silent as a cat and just as dangerous, aloof and then warm, sometimes in the same breath. She could drive a man crazy—if he let her.

Surprise gave way to a slow burn deep inside his guts. *You bitch.*

Yes. She didn't even defend her actions, and she certainly didn't seem like she wanted to try.

Cord's blood nearly boiled in his veins. "Where the hell is my daughter?"

She didn't answer. One minute she stood outside the ring, then next, she simply stood before him, waiting. Cord turned his back on her to find his horse standing and waiting as well. He asked the horse to pick up where they left off. At least someone cared about his wants and needs.

"You haven't answered me," he bit out. The soft footfalls of the horse and the jingle of the lead-line broke the terrible silence. He clenched his jaw, a thousand words begging to get past the lock in his throat.

"I could counter with a question of my own," she finally said.

"Oh really? And what might your question be?"

"Where the hell is my cure?"

Both of his brows shot to the top of his forehead. "Wow," he choked. "You really are cold, aren't you?"

He dared not turn around. "Choices aren't always easy to make," she said with a sigh.

Cord curled his fingers around the line, tightening them until his knuckles turned white. He'd never thought he could hate her. Still wasn't sure he did now, making his blood boil even hotter. He thought about throwing every knife in the drawer at her and ask her why she didn't tell him about the cells. Then he wondered why he should bother. She didn't care. She couldn't.

"How do you live with yourself?"

Somehow, his question reached beneath her armor. "Damn you, I'm not prescient. I don't have access to the future. My *choice* has always been to protect."

Really. And what protection was there in keeping the truth from me? "At what cost?"

"What do you want me to say? That the needs of the many

outweigh the needs of the few? Or the one? Sometimes there is no lesser of two evils."

He whipped his head around to stare at her, not believing a word. "Kay's *my* daughter. *My* daughter. *My* choice."

"Yes." Yet, she couldn't quite let go. "And no."

"So you just thought, screw him, I'm going to do what I want to do."

"What I had to do!" she fired back. "Antu wants you dead. You're the threat. Not Kayla."

Cord's fingers trembled. He swallowed several times and then answered in the coldest tone he possessed. "Do you see the horse?" He turned his attention back to 'G.' "Can you see his gait? Nearly perfect, each hind hoof stepping into the imprint made by the front hoof."

He could feel her walk toward the outer track of the ring. "He's magnificent."

"We're bonded. G trusts me. I've spent years working with him. He knows I would never put him in a position of compromise. And if I make an error in judgment coming up to a jump, he knows I'll do everything I can to rectify that mistake and get him over the fence."

The next thing Cord knew, Sam stood next to G. She stopped the horse with a light tug, unhooked the lunge-line, and sprang up onto Gs' back with the grace of a woman used to riding. A push forward, a request to walk backwards, a couple of pivots, with no reins, simply the pressure of her weight and legs.

In his mind, he saw her flying like the wind on the back of a white stallion across a stretch of hardpacked sand.

He came back to the present to watch her tap G with her heels. His horse lifted onto his hindquarters, then start cantering around the ring. Soon they were galloping on the straightaways but slowing just enough so G wouldn't lose his footing around the corners. On one pass, she kept riding him straight. She gathered a bit of mane in her hands, and she simply leaned forward onto her knees. She cleared the outside fence, which had to be over four-and-a-half feet, with ease.

She rode him around the outside of the ring to get him to slow down and came back to the gate. She sat back with a satisfied smile. "Guess he trusts me too."

G started blowing and stamping, wanting to run more, but Cord grabbed his halter. The horse had enjoyed enough excitement for one night. Cord attached the line and watched Sam slide down off his back with practiced ease.

She walked over and G nudged her as she ran her hand down his nose. "I'm sure," he replied, biting out each word. "If you betrayed him the way you betrayed me, he'd have behaved differently."

The joy in her gaze faded. Cord should have felt satisfied, not hollow. "Betrayal is a harsh word. I did what had to be done."

Cord began walking so he wouldn't have to examine the cause of his internal emptiness. "Expediency isn't an excuse." She wore her neutrality like a cloak and Cord wanted to dig. No, he wanted to excavate so she'd feel something, anything. "You had no right to take the decision out of my hands."

"Events were unfolding. I had a rebellion to quell."

"I *have*—" He drew in a deep breath and let the air out slowly. "A daughter I need to save."

"And you wear a set of steel blinders. When will you understand that I am all things to all people?"

"When you realize that the great Queen Samira wears the biggest blinders of all," he shot back. "You see the forest but walk right past the tiny bush, the lowliest weed."

He watched the tension leave her shoulders as she bit her lip to keep from smiling. "You are not a weed."

Incensed, Cord reared back, making G jerk his head. Cord barked at the horse to calm down. When he could speak properly and with an even tone, he said, "I didn't call myself a weed."

She cocked her head. "You didn't?"

Cord refused to reply. He snapped his jaw shut and walked the horse into the barn. Once the animal was on cross-ties, he brushed G out then put him in his stall with a handful of grain as a treat. The horse deserved it. She didn't. And yet she had no idea what a perfect picture she made sitting, her back straight as an arrow on a haybale, knees crossed, and hands folded in her lap.

"Let me go, Sam."

She rose, her tone just as weary as his. "I'm not holding you here."

Same tree, different route, all leading to the same place. "I promised."

"Exactly. So your decency and your conscience are making you stay."

"I keep seeing flashes of some kind of farm. The place is in disrepair. Red-tiled roof and white stucco. I don't know where. But I'll find it."

She flashed him a look of pure pity. "What you seem to be describing is an estate in New York where Casperian and Hunter last battled. She's not there. My men have checked already. No one was there except Antu's soldiers waiting to ambush you."

"Damn it!" he exploded. "The bastard is always one step ahead."

"Yes," she cried. "And now you understand. I've been trying to keep you safe until you have a fighting chance to win."

"Win?" Cord stormed out of the barn and started walking up the hill to his house. He stopped midway and rounded on her. "The longer I stay, the more chance you get for your cure. So don't tell me about winning."

"Then go!" she shouted. "Run off half-cocked without a clue. I don't care anymore."

"Fine, I will." She marched past him, and Cord wanted to break something. No, he wanted to break her.

He caught up with her just as she reached the house. He grabbed her shoulder, whirling her around to face him. He needed her to understand the rage and frustration roiling in his belly, the helpless fear of a parent whose daughter was in danger. He opened his mouth to yell and yanked her into his body instead. He kissed her, staking his claim, helpless no more.

Their tongues fenced and twined, each touch a spark igniting a fire in his blood. He broke away for a moment but couldn't draw in enough air. Seemed she couldn't either. He reached the edge of a precipice. One more step and they'd both fall into the irrevocable.

Her face filled with desire, but her gaze remained guarded. His arm wrapped around her waist, giving her a taste of what she could have if they both let go. Then he pushed her away and felt the tiny sear of hurt she couldn't quite hide.

"Don't come near me again until you find my daughter and a way for me to rescue her."

She didn't say anything. She simply brushed past him and left. He listened to a car engine roar to life and then fade away. He'd wanted to punish her the way he thought she'd been punishing him. Not his best idea.

Chapter Sixteen

SAM REACHED THE MANSION WITH HER STOMACH SWIMMING AND DOUBT attacking every choice. She touched her lips, remembering the kiss. She'd shared hundreds but couldn't get the taste of him out of her mind. And now she had to tell him the truth, she had the ability to cure his daughter. If he hated her now, what was he going to do after he found out?

Sam walked out onto the patio of the house overlooking the grounds. Each blade of grass became part of an emerald expanse that could stretch on to infinity if winter didn't force the grass to die and renew itself each spring. Could she really be responsible for each blade, even at the expense of her own wants and needs? Hadn't the needs of the many always outweighed the needs of her one? When would her responsibilities end?

"You seem upset."

Sam heard her strong heartbeat and recognized Tori approached. She also needed—a friend. "Kayla wasn't at Sanctuary as I surmised."

Tori opened her arms and hugged Sam. Multitudes of words could be found in one gesture. She squeezed hard and let go. "She isn't at the estate in New York either. I don't know where she is, and I put myself at great risk by drinking Bahir's blood. Which revealed nothing as to her whereabouts."

Tori rubbed Sam's upper arm before stepping back. "You miss Lia, don't you?"

Amazing. Simply amazing. How had Tori known her innermost anguish? "She always gave me the right words when I needed council. You share her intuition."

Tori seemed taken aback. "I wouldn't presume to step into her shoes. But you do have friends here."

Sam walked around the outermost area of the patio before turning to smile at her friend. "I know." She felt the sickness fill her gut again. "I was wrong to take the choice out of Cord's hands. And now?"

"Yeah. We heard. The news about Miklos and his treachery reached us faster than you did."

"Email." Sam shook her head. She didn't want to talk of war at the moment, so she changed the subject. "I'm sorry I haven't had time to take you up on your offer for a girls' night out."

Tori snorted. "You've been a little busy."

"Still, I would have liked to share some good with you and Stacy. You've both worked so hard."

"Everyone has. We're a family." Tori reached out and squeezed Sam's hand, once hard, before letting go. "What's wrong, Sam?"

She didn't know if she should confide in Tori and yet, wasn't that why she stayed and allowed Tori to approach? "Cord is already angry with me for making him keep his promise to find the cure. I can't imagine what he'll do when he finds out about the cells and what they can do."

Tori's face fell. "Houston? We have a problem. He already knows, I'm afraid. Damn those little white lies, eh?"

So much made sense now. No wonder he'd gotten so angry at his home. Why hadn't he said anything? Why had he decided to keep the truth from Sam? "Not so little anymore." She sighed, folding her arms over her chest. She walked over to a planter filled with flowers. So beautiful and fragrant. "Sometimes I would simply like to be Samira."

Tori crinkled her nose and answered, "Not your fault. You made a decision you thought best at the time."

"At the time," Sam repeated. "You know how frustrated he must feel."

"He'll forgive you." Tori paused. "Eventually."

The words ran past her lips before she could stop them. "He kissed me." Taken aback, Tori simply stared at her. "He didn't seem to care that I was, well, a queen."

Her friend grinned. "Queen? Didn't you just say you wanted to be Samira?" After Sam nodded, Tori said, "You have feelings for him. There's nothing wrong with trying to be human."

"Feelings? I'm his maker. I feel everything he does."

"Oh Sam, really? You wouldn't be this upset if it were anyone else, and you know why."

Sam shook her head. "I suppose not. But there's a connection between us. Something made up of past, present, and future."

"There's no law saying you can't open yourself up to more than the blood bond," Tori insisted, her gaze warm but full of concern.

Sam wasn't used to allowing anyone inside but Lia. She let Tori see her fear by opening her mind. "Whenever I do, people end up dead."

"A good reason not to open your heart, but it seems like you can't help yourself. Be honest with him. Let him get really mad, then he can cool down and listen to reason."

Sam couldn't help flashing Tori a grin. "Sounds like you've engaged in this type of scenario before."

Tori threw her a look. "I think that's a boundary you don't want to cross. Hunter wouldn't be pleased."

"He is a very private person." Sam decided to banter back, not something she'd normally do. "And I'm five thousand years old. I haven't exactly been…celibate."

Tori laughed. "Point taken. And now I have to ask. Doesn't it get old after a while?"

"So does life." Sam shook her head trying to throw off what she recognized now as her reaction to her guilt. "Purpose has a way of guiding and renewing. So do people. Thank you. For being my friend."

"Not necessary."

Sam faced another reality she didn't want to touch. "You'll need to postpone your wedding. I'm sorry."

Tori's shoulders slumped and then straightened. "I understand. Not a good idea until we're not under siege anymore."

"Yes." Sam decided to ask Tori the question uppermost in her mind. "Do you ever regret becoming involved, becoming part of our world?"

Without a millisecond's hesitation Tori replied, "Never."

Sam climbed into the elevator, rehashing the mistake she'd made. God, she hated these tiny boxes. But even worse? Having to face the consequences of her actions and look Cord straight in the eye as she stepped out of the elevator and into the lab.

She drew in a deep breath and said, "You already knew about Kay and the cells. Why didn't you tell me?" She didn't even know how to get out her next thought. "Why did you kiss me?"

His gaze held all of the hurt of a man who has been used. "How can you even say her name?" he exploded. He advanced on her, getting right into her face. "Let's reverse the question. Why didn't *you* tell me?"

Sam couldn't answer. Expediency was the easiest word, trust the harder one.

"I mean, my God. Were you ever going to tell me? You had the cure all along to save my daughter and not turn her into a vampire."

Sam straightened, unused to being questioned. Or blamed. Or— she'd been about to say hated. No, she knew all about being hated. "Eventually."

"Awesome." He kept clenching and unclenching his fingers until he finally threw up his hands. "Absolutely awesome."

Expediency. The easier word sat like a bitter herb in her mouth. "I didn't make Nirvana, did I?" she asked, angrier with herself than with him.

He winced. "Low blow even for you. So beautiful and yet so cold." He whirled away from her and marched into the center of the lab. Sam followed but kept a good deal of space between them.

"And not infallible. I'm sorry." As the anger ebbed, Sam began to pace. She wanted to take a beaker and hurl it against the wall. There would be satisfaction in the sound of breaking glass. But in the end, she'd only be obligated to pick up the pieces.

"I made the omission so you would agree to work with Tori and Stacy." She stopped and locked onto his gaze. "And now I've placed Kayla in grave danger, put her in the middle of a war that isn't hers. You see, we all make mistakes."

"Not good enough," Cord shot back.

Sam didn't answer. How could she? What else could she say at this point? She simply opened her stance and accepted every dagger his gaze threw at her.

"Damn you!" He stared to advance on her then after a step, whirled away, then turned back. "Will Antu keep his promise not to hurt her? Will he keep her safe?"

The question strangled out of his throat, and the knives tore at her insides. "As long as I continue to play puppet, then yes. I think so."

"And his soldiers?"

"First, her blood has to be far from appetizing. Second, they are as loyal to him as mine are to me. Perhaps, even more, but I think not. He rules with fear."

She watched Cord's jaw clench. He stormed past her and slammed his fist into one of the rock walls surrounding the lab. The entire room shook. "For the record, Tori doesn't even know what she is yet. How could I possibly do that to a child I don't even know?"

He leaned his forehead against the rock with his palms against the wall. "It doesn't matter. Those cells mean she can live."

"What kind of life?" Sam argued, rounding on him. He had the right to be angry with her for the omission, but he wasn't thinking straight. "Never human, never vampire. A specter in her own world? Would that be fair?"

"Yes!" he yelled as he turned to her.

"My God, Cord. Listen to yourself. You would die to save her, but you would also kill her so she can live? Condemn her to an existence she may never understand? And for how long? Who's being selfish now?"

He didn't answer, just stared at her, breathing hard, as if trying to deny the truth.

"Cord?"

Neither of them had heard the elevator go up or come down. Tori stood in the elevator doorway with Hunter right behind. They stepped out. Cord's shoulders slumped as he walked away from the wall. He seemed to cave in on himself, and Sam hurt for him. "Am I being selfish?" Cord asked. "Isn't it a parent's duty to protect at all cost?"

"Yes," Tori answered. "I would have given my life for Kelly in a heartbeat if I'd been there. But the choice to use the cells was mine. And though she's a child, I think the choice belongs to Kayla, don't you?"

Sam watched Cord nod slowly. *I am truly sorry.*

He didn't answer, and she didn't really expect one. Perhaps, one day, he would. Until then, she owed Cord a debt she needed to fulfill.

"Just so you know, Antu sacrificed his oldest and most loyal servant to put us right where he wanted us. Bahir killed Lia."

Never had she heard such surrender in a voice as when Cord said, "Let Bahir go."

She whipped her head up to stare. "He is Antu's instrument. He placed your daughter in grave danger."

"No." He shuddered. "I did that."

And then she understood. Creating Nirvana had become the stone Antu had cast, and all Cord could do now was try to stop the ripples in the pond. "She could already be dead."

"Very true. But I think, no I'm positive, I'd know. And right now, my heart is telling me she's alive." Cord turned to stare at her. "You know better than anyone. Miklos, this Bahir, they're just toys for Antu to play with."

Shaking her head, Sam stepped down from the 'dais' feeling the entire weight of the world. "So am I."

"I can feel Lia here with me," Cord added, strength returning to his voice. "I won't ask how this is possible or how I know, I just do. She's not happy with your answer."

Oh, my friend, I miss you. "Lia was there at the beginning. Being chosen as my, I guess the word you would use is handmaiden, meant she came as close as anyone to The Mother and The Father. She had extensive knowledge of their faults."

"And their miracles."

Sam quirked her mouth. "Those too."

"How did we get here?" Cord asked again.

To answer, Sam had to share the memories of her past. Were they ready for them? "I must share the beginnings with all of you. But we must wait for Chaz and Stacy. They are on their way."

About fifteen minutes later, the Paladin and his wife walked in. "You have the right to hear the beginning. I'm glad you came."

Chaz lifted the corner of his mouth. "Did you think you could keep us away?"

Stacy and Tori hugged. A tiny sting of jealousy reminded her even a queen can be human. "Your choice as always. I fear for Stacy's life, Chaz. No other reason. You should take her away and hide."

Chaz interrupted. "Where? No place is safe now." He grimaced and went to stand by his wife. "Miklos is an arrogant old fool."

"So am I." Sam sensed her friends were about to protest, and she held up her hand. "We can debate later. Right now, you all need to understand Antu. So you must understand the beginning." Sam opened her mind to let them in.

Chapter Seventeen

"*SAMIRA. SAMIRA ANAI-SEBAT.*"

Sam froze. Her heartbeat filled her ears. Thud! Thud!

"*Samira. Samira Anai Se-Bat.*"

She turned in a slow circle. She saw no one there. She circled once again. Still no one. She shook her head to clear her mind. How could there be a voice inside her head when no one spoke? What devilry was this?

Samira crouched as if to hide. But how could she hide? Where? Where could the body go when the mind sat naked and completely exposed?

"*Do not be afraid, little flower.*"

A voice she knew. And yet she did not. One she loved, but now she could not trust. Nuya had promised to save her when the time came, not let her be taken by the Temple. He promised he would protect her, love her. Always.

She had no place to hide, the same as this moment.

Her heart pounded even faster, and her fingers trembled. She wanted to curl inside herself, but Samira was now a child of the very temple she feared. So she practiced breathing as Mensah had taught her and searched for the place of peace within.

Once the dread left her, Samira regained her innate curiosity. She straightened from her crouch and arched her back, lifting her chin in defiance. Still, her body remained tense and ready to run should the need arise. *"Who are you? How do you speak inside my head?"*

"Do you not know, child?"

The Mother!

Her first instinct urged her to fall on her knees and prostrate her body in submission, but an invisible hand held her upright. *"You should never do a thing if your heart, mind, and body do not agree. Are you not too proud to debase yourself in this manner?"*

"I fear that I am, my lady. Mensah has told me so many times."

The Mother did not reply, and Samira worried she had caused insult for having the temerity to speak. And yet she could not quench that innate part of her, the need to know.

A light tinkling, like a small stream running over stones or the gentle sway of palm fronds in the breeze filled her head. Samira realized she could hear The Mother laughing.

"So curious. So proud. Just as your teacher described."

A picture painted her vision, that of a scorpion. Not a normal scorpion, a larger and more fearsome creature, the size of a small dog. Then there were two and where the knowledge came from, Samira couldn't say, but she knew this was the true form of The Mother and The Father.

Samira swallowed her disappointment. Surely—after all the legends—they were at least, well, more than this.

The Father shined black as night, a stripe of red down his back from head to tail. The Mother glowed red beneath her black scales. The colors of the temple had been born from the colors of the Mother and the Father.

"We can take many forms. But for you, child of the truth, we give you the truth, we show ourselves in our natural form. But think not that we are less than all you have ever been taught. We do not do so with you, why do you do so with us?

The Mother was right. Sam had allowed her arrogance to cloud her opinion. She bowed her head. *"Forgive me, my lady."*

"Is this better?"

A statuesque, perfectly coiffed, completely unblemished woman sat upon a golden throne beneath a golden headdress, her pure black hair glinting blue in the rays of the sun, her golden eyes without depth but seeing all.

Samira couldn't help but laugh. *"Yes, my lady."*

"You see, the truth is…"

"Simply the truth," Samira cut her off. *"I had no right to judge."*

The Mother stared at her with a strange look. Perhaps strange was the wrong word, for what god would admire a mere human? *"And yet, if you did not judge and acknowledge your failure, you would not have passed the test."*

Samira drew her brows together tight. *"Forgive me, my lady. I do not understand."*

The Mother rose and began to pace, not as much out of anger at her ignorance but as a teacher trying to get a student to grasp the point of the lesson. *"To be a leader you must know the truth and make your judgements accordingly. You think of the scorpion as a tiny creature, but also fearsome and deadly. You think of the scorpion as loathsome by sight yet mighty in ability. It can wait for days until its prey approaches and kill with a single sting of its tail."*

She watched The Mother still and turn. *"But did you also think of the scorpion's need to survive, how deep and strong that need must be to be such a patient hunter?"*

The question blurted out of her mouth before Samira could even think of holding it back. *"Do you speak of the scorpion, my lady? Or do you speak of us?"*

The vision inside her head clapped her hands and laughed in obvious delight. *"Mensah said you were quick. Well done."*

She couldn't help but ask, *"What else did Mensah say?"*

"If I told you, your head would swell."

"We should not have that happen now, should we?" Samira sassed back.

The Mother shook her head and bit her lip. To keep from laughing again? Possibly. She continued to pace, five or six steps, then turn and cover the same ground. *"We have visited thousands of worlds on our journey,"* she said, sobering. *"Never have we stayed in one place so long."*

Images of purple skies and flaming treetops filled her mind. Strange looking flowers and bushes lined a path, their leaves already glowing with a strange light that made her able to see in the dark. The warmth of the air filled her, and her steps were as light as the mist rising from the ground.

Samira's jaw slackened at the next vision in her mind, of never-ending water as far as the eye could see, whose great waves crashed against huge rocks. What manner of place was this? She wanted to stay with The Mother and immerse herself in these wonders more than she wanted to draw breath but shirking her duty would be wrong. Samira closed her mind and asked, *"Why do you show me these places?"*

"To make you understand you are infinitesimal in the infinite."

"Then why do you stay?" Samira already discerned the answer. The blood. *"And the temple? The priests and priestesses?"*

"Our gift. To thank you for the gift of life you give to us."

"Gift?"

The Mother turned and sat back upon the throne, regal and proud. She stared hard at Samira, her features turning as stark as the empty dessert. "How dare you!"

Samira fought the urge to prostrate herself and beg forgiveness. The words screaming inside her head needed to be said. "Is your gift not a burden as well? Does there not need to be balance in all things, all ways?"

She watched The Mother's face clear, and her gaze soften. "Yes. Therefore, you must use our gift wisely."

Sam didn't think they had. So she spoke to the vision in her mind, the vision as clear now as it had been then.

"Great Mother, we face our true test, the one you tried to warn me about. But the test, I fear, was of your making. You passed onto us the gifts but also the faults. As a woman, a female, you imparted the nurturing, the curiosity, and the innocence of life. As a man, The Father is stern and strong to defend, but he is not just. He never was. You always kept him in check. I don't know how to keep Antu in check. And I fear, if we both leave this world, chaos will reign. If we do not leave this world? I fear that even more."

Sam pulled the vision into her mind. Two thrones, both as great as the other. Golden spired headdresses, each with two scepters in their arms denoting strength and purity. The Mother robed in scarlet and gold, The Father robed in black and gold. Both tall, near seven cubits, with the whitest skin she'd ever seen but dark rich blue-black hair gleaming in the many torches lighting the room.

"Great Mother. Great Father. Hear me as I call to you."

Sam paused and drew in a deep breath. *"We have reached the cross-roads you predicted. The faults have always lain with the gifts for there can be no such thing as perfection. You saw this, understood this, and trained us so we could continue.*

"But I fear deception lay deep in one of your hearts. Or perhaps both. The Father can be mean and petty like a spoiled child. The Mother can be secretive and deceptive like the young girl who lies while she smiles."

Sam finally asked the questions that haunted her. *"Was this simply another test? Could you not see that you doomed us from the start? Did The Father not pick Antu because of his flaws? Did The Mother not pick me to counteract those flaws? Could you not see the outcome?"*

Sam's heart hollowed. Then her fists clenched. Not without a fight. *"Great Mother. Great Father. We have grown. We are a race of beings, no better and no worse than any other beings on this planet. Such was the gift you gave us. Surely you cannot mean to take these gifts away?"*

Determination filled her. She waited, steel growing in her spine and strengthening her fingers. And then the voice she'd been waiting for.

"No. You have finally learned the lesson we tried to teach. No race, no species, no beings are perfect. You have grown much, and we are pleased."

"Then how do I defeat Antu? How do I stop him?"

The vision shifted, blending the two thrones into one and then none. Sam felt a terrible need to shield her eyes to the blinding light. *By The Mother and The Father!* Of course. So simple. There for her to see if she'd just looked.

The blending of the thrones. Had Cord seen the vision also? She opened her eyes to watch his widen. Their race had the best chance of survival without both her and Antu. The blending of the thrones canceled out their power, leaving those who remained to continue. Would chaos reign? Would the Miklos's of this world try to take all of the power? Or would the Hunters of this world be able to stop him?

"Have faith."

Such a small word. Faith.

The rest of the people she cared about most in the world stared at her, waiting. They wanted to know what she'd seen but would never force her to tell. Another piece of the brotherhood Antu would never understand.

About to explain, Sam stopped. Nuya stood before her, a slight smile on his lips, not Cord. Was this a message, The Mother coming to her in a form she needed to see? Could this be another trick from

Antu, the master of trickery? Or perhaps her own need projected a thousand-fold to fill her gaze.

She shook her head. She could hear the thrum of refrigerators and scrape of a rotating platform, and she could see it wobble under the number of samples on top. The vampires in this cell still trusted, were still willing to fight. Her friends continued to try to find a cure.

Sam looked at all of them, and they stared back either curious or patient. When her gaze finally rested on Cord, he angled his head slightly to ask what her next steps were going to be. He'd seen the vision, but did he know the answer? Perhaps the vision was an answer for her alone. Maybe another test? A clue? She wasn't sure yet.

"The Mother and The Father have given me a vision but in doing so, now make our paths diverge. It is time for there to be no thrones at all." She paused. Not one of her friends spoke. They must have accepted she would do what was best.

"By The Mother and The Father!" she continued. The saying has always been this way. Now I know why. It is as I feared. Antu and I must neutralize each other. The vision was of the thrones blending together until they were no more."

"No!" In spite of what she'd done to him, Cord became the first to shout the word. Well, at least he didn't want her dead. The others followed swiftly after. Sam's heart warmed.

She spoke to Hunter first. "You must protect our people. You must now accept the role of protector for all life, human and vampire."

She turned to Cord. "To save the people, you must find a cure for the rogues Antu is creating."

His face lit up with comprehension. *Kay's blood.*

Yes. I'm sorry.

"If we know, then he knows." Sam watched their gazes focus on Cord. "I didn't put two and two together. The very same reason for creating Nirvana may be the cure. Kay's blood. It may be crucial for curing the rouges he's created."

Comprehension lit Tori's gaze. "The diseased mitochondria."

"Yes," Cord answered.

"Or is she just another game he's playing?" Hunter asked.

"I don't know. With Antu, anything is possible," she replied.

"Damn it!" Anger made Cord's entire body shake. And he had a right to be angry. Again, they'd all thought of their race first. "Right now, I don't give a crap. I want my daughter back in my arms."

Of all the people to try to console him, it wasn't Tori but Hunter who clasped Cord's shoulder. "We also need a cure."

"Don't you understand?" Cord asked. "I won't know if she's 'the cure' until I can test her blood. I certainly won't know until I take the diseased mitochondria and introduce them into the pure vampire cells."

"And then see if the new cells can overtake the old," Tori added.

"At least, we can try," Stacy added.

Sam could feel the thousand thoughts flying through Cord's mind. As his maker, they were connected, and he kept tearing himself apart inside. "Would all of you mind leaving and allow me to speak to Cord in private? We need to talk. Some of you need food, some to feed, and all of you need rest."

Hunter's mouth quirked. Did he understand the task before her? He bowed and clasped Tori's hand, gently pulling her away. Chaz turned to follow with a nod, but Stacy broke away and came over to her, throwing her arms around Sam's neck. "Whatever you decide, whatever you do, we are with you," she whispered. She let go, turned, and walked out of the room.

Cord looked terribly pale, his skin stretched tight across his cheekbones. His shoulders slumped and he bit out, "Alone at last."

God, the words were bitter. "You know what must be done. You also know I'm going to ask you to stay away."

He stared at her hard.

"What I ask of you is impossible. I'm going to put you in the position of having to choose between your daughter and a race of people you don't know, a race of people you joined unwillingly and share no loyalty with."

Sam sighed when he didn't answer. "I can't force you to listen just as I couldn't force Chaz and Stacy to stay away. I knew what Miklos planned. He's wanted supreme power ever since he became a vampire. All I could think of was what would happen if Stacy got caught in the middle of a vampire coup."

"Her choice, their choice."

"Yes, and now yours. You see, The Mother and The Father asked for unquestioning obedience, but they never took away free will."

"Where is my free will in all of this, huh?" He fought with himself, rubbing his face with his hands until he got himself under control.

"I'm sorry. You're right." She watched his shoulders lift and his jaw clench. "But everyone is not simply one person. You are the scientist, but you are also the man. I am the queen, but I am also Samira. You seem to believe the queen doesn't care. She cares more than you will ever know."

"But the needs of the many still outweigh the needs of the few, or the one."

Sam's heart turned over in her chest. "Yes. You may not want to hear me, but I understand. By The Mother and The Father, I understand."

"You were right," he told her, turning to face her. "Once I stopped thinking of trying to keep Kay alive, I started thinking of her stuck at the same age, a grown woman in a child's body for age upon age. Almost made me want to kill her myself." His gaze became utter chaos, just what Antu wanted, pain and rage and fear and love. "Is he spiteful enough to turn her?"

Her heart sank. "I won't lie. He is. But we both still live with the teachings of the temple, which were engraved upon us as children. It is forbidden."

"How forbidden?"

"A very good question."

Sam didn't know if he'd accept her offer, but she held open her arms. He stepped into her embrace. She simply wanted to give him someone to hold onto.

He bent his head so that his breath brushed her neck, sending tiny shivers through her body. She closed her eyes. Together they used the other's strength, and when at last they became strong together, he lifted his head.

But not before his cheek brushed hers.

Her blood rose, and her belly hollowed. She banished the feeling immediately. Now was not the time. Yet he shared her feeling, for a slow smile grew upon his face as he lifted up. Then worry and anguish filled his gaze and he let go.

"Bahir said that the end would take place where it all began," Sam said. "But I think he was lying when he said Kay had been hidden in that place."

"Antu's had ages to perfect his lies," Cord answered.

Sam agreed wholeheartedly. "Bahir has spent those ages with him learning every technique."

Cord rubbed his chin and frowned. "There is a truth within the blood," he answered slowly. "A truth we both know and understand to a certain extent. You drank from Bahir, didn't you?" She nodded. "Bahir dismisses it as insignificant, doesn't he?" She nodded again. He reached out and clasped her shoulders with his hands. "Will you share with me exactly what you saw when you joined with Bahir? Allow me to sink inside the blood?"

She closed her eyes. She began to project. All of a sudden Cord's grip tightened. "There's a curtain of darkness."

"Antu has created the curtain," she said. "He fights my entry."

"Whatever's behind that curtain," he whispered. "I'm not sure we want to know."

"All right," Sam soothed. "We'll get there soon enough. Sink into the past. Let the ages fill you."

He began to speak. "Ancient Greece. Beautiful, pristine, not aged by the millennia. I see Bahir speaking to people, simple people. They are getting angrier and angrier. Now I'm in Constantinople at the end of the Roman Empire. There are riots between the Orthodox and the Catholic people. The city has fallen to the Turks. So many dead."

She watched Cord shudder. "Keep going."

"Famine. Plague. Surely Antu couldn't have created these as well."

"No. But he can place fear inside already frightened men. He can pit them against one another to create war."

Cord reared back and shook his head and Sam recognized what he was seeing. The terrible devastation of not one but two world wars. "I think I'm seeing only what Antu wants me to see."

"Then fight the blood. Go beyond both of them."

"I see a red tiled roof. Dead trees. Blackened ground." Cord doubled over. "I feel pain."

She wrapped her arms around him and drew the pain into her body. "Such a waste to feed one ego."

Cord straightened slowly. "Bahir trained them. He's gloating. He thinks he's got you in checkmate."

"Does he?"

Sam cupped Cord's cheek with her palm, bringing Cord back to the present. He leaned into her touch. "He showed me the choice you gave me."

"I made you a promise to end your life." She smiled softly. "Are you saying you don't want to die anymore?"

"Yes."

"Then you must close your thoughts to both of them with all the will you possess."

Deep inside Sam understood he wouldn't be able to, so she played his weakness into a strength. "Antu will set the stage with exquisite care. He will exact his revenge with delicate precision."

Sam watched his gaze harden, felt his muscles tense beneath her fingertips. "I believe Antu is going to force me to make a choice between killing him and saving your life. He loves creating impossible choices."

Cord clenched his cheek muscle, and it vibrated beneath the skin. "He already knows what I believe The Mother and The Father want to happen," she added. "He also knows your life is necessary to our race. He has and will continue to use your daughter as bait. What he doesn't know, what he will never know, is the deepest part of my heart. Do you know what I will do?"

She watched him smile. "I think I do."

Chapter Eighteen

PICTURES FILLED HIS MIND, NOT FROM ANTU BUT FROM SAM, AND Cord barely noticed the sounds of the refrigerators or the rotators. They faded away as did the modern world and he realized he reached back into Sam's consciousness and the beginning.

The desert spread out before Cord, barren and beautiful and so immense he felt as significant as a grain of sand. But what was a desert? Grain upon grain of sand, no?

In the distance, the oasis seemed the mirage, green life in a brown and beige sea. Behind the oasis rose a cluster of rocks that hid a group of vampires and humans. Sam sat upon a white steed, magnificent and strong, her back straight, shoulders square, and her armor glinting in the light of a full moon.

Though her blood rode high in her chest, Cord recognized Sam wanted no part of what was about to take place. "This is a slaughter, Antu."

"You grow weak," he spat out. "Are they not traitors to the thrones?"

Cord could feel her heart constrict as it had so many millennia ago. "They are. And they should be punished. But why does your answer have to be so unyielding? Has anyone taken the time to ask why they rebel? If they were happy, why would they risk their lives this way? Surely, they know only death awaits them."

Cord watched Antu tuck his chin and widen his eyes. "Ask them? Why would we ask them anything?"

Cord watched her frown, not understanding why Antu's set his stance in stone. "Because there is no reason in this madness. Perhaps their grievances are just."

"Grievances? Just? Enough! They are traitors!"

He watched Sam grow just as angry. "By whose judgement?"

Antu lifted his chin as if his existence gave him the right. "Mine."

Cord watched the vision unfold, a very one-sided battle, and he could feel the reticence in Sam's heart. She drew her sword but to protect herself, nothing more. She killed no one, actually even tried to defend some of the rebels from imminent death.

She met Antu in the center of the battle. He stood over an injured man ready to deal a deadly blow.

"Hold!"

Antu held still, but he lifted his head with brows running in a straight line. Sam dismissed Antu and asked the dying rebel, "Why? Why do you rebel? Why do you bring this slaughter upon yourselves?"

The man choked and coughed up blood. Cord, so deeply connected, could feel his mouth water from the scent of it. "We have the right to be free."

Sam seemed confused. "But The Mother and The Father gave us all the gift. They gave us all a choice. They allow us free will."

"Allow?" The man coughed again, and Cord could almost taste the blood on his lips. "How can a body allow free will?"

In that instant, Cord understood Sam's motives. Allow and free created an oxymoron. Free was free—or else it wasn't.

Cord came back to the present with a jolt. From a shift in time or the sear of her shame?

"My life became a lie. Everything I believed, everything I sacrificed for—a lie."

Cord felt sorry for Sam but couldn't quite bring himself to forgive.

"I cast Antu out. I denied our bond. I broke the unbreakable."

Cord could feel the wind on his cheeks as he rode with her, drying unshed tears. "I flew back to the Temple."

"Let me guess. The Mother wouldn't see you."

Sam blew out a deep breath. "Wouldn't even acknowledge my existence."

Once again, Sam opened her mind. Cord found himself drowning in her distress, anguish, and anger. But most of all, the emotion he shared with her was the hollow emptiness of betrayal.

"I refused to drink. Days turned into weeks. I took back control of the one thing I thought I *could* control. Mensah refused to let me starve. He brought the one person he was certain would save me.

"Nuya," Cord whispered. "But I thought Antu killed him at your first feeding."

"So did I." Sam leaned her palms on a countertop and hung her head between them. "Icing on the cake."

God! Cord wasn't exactly fond of Sam in this moment, but boy this Mother of hers had turned out to be a real sweetheart. And so, he guessed, was her mentor.

"Little bird?"

Cord felt his heart pound with hers. "Nuya?"

"Do not die. Please Samira. Do not die."

"But I wish to join you in the afterlife."

A hand touched hers and with it, his. His skin rippled in sensation. "But I am not dead, little bird. See? I am flesh and blood." Cord's skin rippled again. "I am here."

"I do not understand."

"You spared my life"

"But Antu drained you. I watched him. I heard your heartbeat fade."

"Mensah brought me back from the brink of death. He saved me."

Another lesson learned. Cord felt a piece of her heart freeze and shivered for her. "No, dear one. Mensah saved you for just such a moment. You are dead and yet you are not. He has not let you slip into the afterlife yet."

"Why would someone, anyone be so cruel?

"Because Mensah was positive the truth would break me. He knew you were the only one who would make me want to fight, make me want to live."

Cord watched everything unfold through Sam's eyes. The elder man, the one she trusted the most, the father figure who raised her, complicit in all the lies. He saw the anguish in her teacher's gaze, but the emotion left his visage way too quickly.

"Now you know," Mensah told her. "You are made of her—The Mother. You are all things to all people. The illusions were necessary to make you into the queen you must become. The world is a balance of good and evil. You

needed to know the depths of both so you could rejoice in the one and fight the other."

Sam lifted up from her position of submission. She let Cord see The Mother in her mind as if the past didn't exist. "The foundation has been dug deep within. The stones have been set upon the foundation. Break the house and chaos will reign."

Cord could feel the one word struggling to break free of her throat. His throat as well. He shouted the word with all the pain they both felt. "Why?"

The Mother answered. "Because of your strength, child. Your courage. Your ability to go beyond the obvious. You are my chosen. And now you must drink."

With The Mother holding her immobile, Mensah opened Nuya's wrist and poured the last of his blood into her mouth. She drank because she had to, she drank because she had no choice. There was the blood and could only ever be the blood.

Samira lived because she had no choice. But how she lived became her choice.

Cord came back to the present with a jolt. Sam spread her arms wide and dropped them to her sides. "Now you know."

She turned on her heel and left. Cord didn't pay attention to the sound of the elevator. He walked over to his makeshift desk and sat down, picking up a pen and twirling the plastic in his fingers. He wanted to feel sorry for her. He wanted to feel sorry for himself. Instead, he felt nothing at all. No, he felt everything.

When he returned to the present, an email from Morgan Kent sat staring at him from his laptop. She'd sent her notes on the gene sequencing that enabled her to speed the mitochondria up. But replacing the correct amino acids back in the chain didn't reverse the process and removing the string simply killed the cell.

Killed the cell.

Cord threw the pen down on the desk and snapped the laptop closed. She understood what it was like to be betrayed. So what? She thought being kindred spirits made everything all right. Right?

Bullshit. She screwed him over and would do it again to save…everyone.

Damn you, Sam! Cord wanted to hate her, he wanted to make her bleed the way he bled, but he couldn't. Because, in spite of her past she still felt compassion, she carried Nuya's gift with her.

A man's face, his own face, stared back at him in his mind, with a slight smile. What was it with these people? They were all aware of things he didn't know, and he became the last to find out. He slammed his fist down on the desk, making everything on top rattle. Past, present, and future didn't seem to matter anymore.

Nuya stuck his tongue out of his mouth at Cord. About to get insulted by a figment of his imagination, Cord froze. A stillness invaded, the same stillness he'd felt when The Mother spoke. Nuya made a lapping motion with his tongue. At first, Cord didn't know what to make of the gesture.

What the hell?

All of a sudden, the light bulb went on. *The Lethe!*

The picture faded and the hold on him let go. Of course! The mystery protein. The 'alien' protein. Removing the string killed the cell. But what if he had a way to protect the cell once he removed the string? The mitochondria would slow down because the chain had been altered. The cells would be changed, but the ramification of the change could be investigated. Tori was both human and vampire.

Cord jumped up out of the chair and began to pace the lab. The logic. So simple. Yes Sam, and of course Antu, would be the cure. They were the carriers of the alien genetics. Their blood would introduce the protein to help the cells stay alive. But the effects faded after a time because red cells died and the protein with them. But the Lethe closed the wounds on human skin almost immediately, so the protein must be concentrated in the saliva.

Cord nearly screamed at the top of his lungs. He stopped himself just in time. There were humans in the building from the donation center. Hunter came down first.

Cord didn't even greet the vampire. "I need a tube of your blood. Now."

"I was just about to visit Sam."

"Sam's blood is and always will be a patch, a band-aid. And I think I know why."

Hunter simply lifted a brow. "Why?"

The elevator went up and came down and Tori stepped out yawning. "What's going on?"

"The Lethe. The protein you can't quite pin down. I think it's alien, from The Mother."

Tori looked like she woke up in a hurry. "And your point is?"

Cord ran to the laptop. "Read the email from Morgan Kent." Hunter kind of just stared at Cord while Tori read. "When Morgan removed the string of amino acids causing the mitochondria to speed up, she killed the cells. She had no way to protect them. But what if we did?"

Tori grinned. "The protein. But what about the missing string?"

"We would have to see what the effects are by removing it. If they're severe or the cells continue to die, we'll have to reinsert the entire chain again using the 'virgin' vampire cells you grew and see if we can rebuild the damaged cells. This time, using the protein as protection."

Tori began to nod. "Sounds like a plan. But we still have one thing to figure out. Right now, transfusions are the only way to get the protein into the body, and the effects don't last. What do you propose?"

Cord rubbed the back of his neck. "I don't know yet. We're going to need a vehicle of some kind. But at least we can start with the rest."

"You bet." He watched Tori rub her hands together, her excitement palpable.

"And Hunter?" He paused, watching the vampire leader lift the corner of his mouth. "You can't feed from Sam. We need you to get weak so we can make your cells strong again."

Hunter threw him a look. "I had a feeling you would say that."

Chapter Nineteen

SAM WALKED INTO THE CONFERENCE ROOM. SHE FACED THE COMPUTER screen at the other end of the table. The heads of the European and Asian cells filled the boxes on the screen. A piece of her marveled at the technology able to bring faces from around the globe to this one place and

time. Jason had flown in from California, and she nodded her thanks for making the trip.

To her friends, the depth of Antu's intentions were clear, but The Council didn't have this knowledge. Time to tell them. "As all of you are aware, my brother Antu is not only alive and well, but he has decided he wants to rule us all. To this end, he has sacrificed Bahir, his most loyal follower, as you would in a chess game, and turned Miklos, one of our most loyal Council leaders, against us. He will go after each one of you with what you want most and offer it on a silver platter as he did with Miklos. His price will be your freedom and the freedom of the vampires you protect."

Sam leaned forward, placing her hands on the back of the chair at the end of the conference table. "The lies, the deceptions, and the strategies will grow more complicated until he has what he wants—total domination."

How many, she wondered, had already been offered their gilded cage?

No one spoke so Sam continued. "The good news is, we have found every drop of Nirvana Dr. Stuart made and destroyed all but what he needs to use to find a cure. Also, I don't believe Antu has had the time to find someone to continue making Nirvana, so I'm fairly certain Antu's supply of Nirvana is now limited. Hopefully, very limited. My brother has never been rash, but caution is not his forte. He may use it all, he may not. No matter what, we need to deal with what is in front of us. So I'll ask him to begin. Dr. Stuart?"

Without going into too much detail, Cord explained his theory. There was only one question from Danika. She asked how fast he could come up with the cure. When he couldn't answer, Sam watched several expressions grow from disappointed to guarded.

Charles and Vanessa went next to give an update on the number of rogues the Paladin had found and destroyed. Too many, as several of the cell leaders added to the Paladin totals.

What a terrible price they were all paying!

Then each of the cell leaders gave an accounting of resources and soldiers willing to fight. Not enough. Never enough.

Finally, the discussion ended, and Sam was able to continue. "Antu has left two of his best generals in enemy hands. We must be wary. My brother is certain to use them and soon, so time is of the essence. Antu will attack, make no mistake. Dr. Stuart is working on the cure, but if he isn't able to do so before the attack, I'm going to need full cooperation from all of you. Are we agreed?"

Each cell leader nodded. "The first and perhaps most important battle will be here in New Jersey." Sam looked over at Mercy to see her expression grow grim. "The New York cell is one of our largest and most important for supplying blood to our people. Disrupting our pipeline here would be huge blow to all of us, not to mention the loss of Mercy's soldiers."

They discussed tactics and numbers, after which there wasn't much else to be said. "We've made our plans as best as they can be made. Thank you all."

She shut off the computer and watched everyone leave the room.

She wanted to reach out to Cord, but he left the room before she could try. The cut wounded.

Sam motioned for Hunter to remain. He nodded, knowing where they needed to go. Tori glanced at them but left with Stacy to continue working in the lab. Chaz followed as a guard for his wife, while Mercy and Jason left discussing their perimeter defense. As patient and steadfast as ever, Hunter followed her as they went down into the bowels of the cell.

Every vampire cell kept a prison handy in case they found one of their members going rogue. Hunter's prison had been built with titanium bars engineered into the bedrock of the Palisades. Meant to keep rogues from destroying vampires. Meant to keep enemies?

Bahir grimaced as he rose from his seat on the solid rock floor. Sam merely smiled. "The accommodations aren't to your liking?"

Belligerent to the end, Bahir answered with acid dripping in his tone. "I've endured worse."

Sam turned to Miklos. "And you, old friend. What good is being whole when you cannot move?"

Miklos didn't rise and Sam could've forced the issue, but now wasn't the time. Instead, she projected a scene to each of them where they were given a syringe full of the unknown. Nirvana? Or something else?

"You wouldn't dare," Miklos scoffed.

Bahir knew better. At least he had the intelligence to be afraid. He'd glimpsed the steel The Mother forced into her spine through his blood bond with Antu and had watched firsthand as her blade bit without remorse. "Our deaths serve no purpose, my lady. But our lives? Our lives are bargaining chips to be used at your discretion."

"Poor fool. Your master will not bargain, and you know it, Bahir. I would have expected a better reply."

"What about the child?" Bahir asked, his voice turning sly.

Sam nodded. "Now you're coming closer. But I tasted your blood." Sam grimaced as she remembered the taste and Bahir lifted a brow as if he were insulted. "Your master is indeed wise. He didn't tell you where the girl is being held. You have no leverage."

Bahir swallowed several times, then turned on his compatriot. "He does," Bahir pointed. "Miklos knows. My master gave the girl to him to guard."

He's lying.

Hunter was right. Although Bahir had learned the art, he hadn't quite mastered the craft. He didn't have the balls or the flair to carry off a lie, so he wrapped his lies around the truth. Using Miklos to guard the girl made sense, but the depths of her bones told her Miklos didn't know where anymore. Antu would move Kay frequently to keep her hidden.

"Perhaps we should give them the Nirvana," Sam said. "Then leave them locked together?"

"A tempting idea," Hunter replied.

She made sure they each saw her vision of their future. Fear filled Bahir's gaze. Miklos tried to remain nonchalant but couldn't quite help the tensing of his muscles.

"Miklos seems to believe his soldiers will rescue him. What do you think?" Sam replied.

Hunter still had his reputation, and she watched Miklos lift up from his slouch, interested in Hunter's answer. "An error in judgment," Hunter said. "To go up against one cell is to go up against The Council and *all* its resources."

"Are you willing to sacrifice so many?" Miklos retorted. "Hunter, you have been known to protect your people at all costs. Are we then so different?"

"I would never sell my soul," Hunter spat out. "And don't pull the pity card with me. Not all scars are physical, though I bore my share of those too in my human life."

"My leg should have healed as soon as I became a vampire." Miklos shrugged. "I found out too late that although vampires can heal themselves using the Lethe, vampires can't grow missing flesh. Only royal blood can."

"Buyer beware," Hunter muttered as he wrapped his fingers around one of the prison bars. "Every member of every cell makes his or her own decision about how he or she will live. Or die. Their choice. As Sam has told us time and time again, our gift is free will." He flexed his hands to show the bars wouldn't budge. "But I can answer your question personally with another question. If I choose to fight, is my choice a sacrifice?"

"Ultimately," Miklos replied.

Sam noted Bahir didn't say anything, his gaze flying back and forth to watch each of them speak. The priest turned manservant always tried to find the better position by listening and waiting. Sam had to give the little bastard his due, once a serpent, always a serpent.

Sam thought of Lia for a moment. A part of her wanted revenge so badly she could taste it. She made sure Bahir saw the vision of her separating his head from his body with her sword. He blanched. But now she'd bound herself to promises, and her first promise was to save Cord's daughter.

"Especially if you lose," Miklos added.

Sam watched Hunter incline his head and smile. He lifted back from the prison bars, dragging a single fingertip down the steel. The scraping sound shivered down her back. He moved his gaze to Bahir. "Tell your master I know he is close. Tell him anytime he wishes to conclude our fight, let me know where and when. I am at his service. Tell him, this time, the fear of a newly made vampire won't save him."

They left the prison. Hunter kept his next question private. *Was goading Antu a wise move?*

I don't know. Was it? When Hunter didn't answer, Sam continued. *He would expect such a response.*

Hunter smiled. They walked back up the path hewn out of solid stone in single file. But once they were able to face each other, Sam frowned. "Don't underestimate him, Hunter. Antu is not the general who sits and watches the battle unfold. I have seen him ride into a hundred spears at the head of his men."

"Not this time, Sam. He's waiting."

She nodded. "For me to make a mistake."

"Perhaps."

"Both Miklos and Bahir were too composed to believe they would do anything but be rescued. The attack will be sooner than we thought."

"What about Kayla?"

"Antu is nearby." Hunter nodded in agreement. "We both feel him."

"So if you were him and wanted to be close to this battle, where would you go?"

Hunter replied without hesitation. "The city. New York."

"And you'd hide Kay in the city too, wouldn't you?"

He nodded again. "An easy place to get lost in."

Hunter rubbed the back of his neck, and Sam felt his frustration. "If Miklos's men are guarding her, they could be anywhere."

Sam frowned as she considered. "I'm not so sure. Antu would pick a place that would serve more than one purpose."

"Then he would choose a place where he would not be interfered with but could set a trap." She watched Hunter grimace. "Cord has asked that I not feed from you, which will leave me weak. I won't be able to help you."

Sam reached out and patted Hunter's shoulder. "I'll manage."

"You always do. But this time," Hunter replied. "Be careful."

Sam followed Hunter into the mansion. She thought about the perfect place for an ambush. She swallowed, her stomach hollowing as a picture came into her mind. "I think I know where she is."

Chapter Twenty

CORD BEGAN TO HATE THE BLACK ROCK WALLS OF HIS LAB WITH A passion. The huge refrigerators holding the blood that held his life, all their lives, thrummed, setting his teeth on edge. The slow swish and roll of the rotator didn't soothe anymore. But his own ignorance had become what bothered him most about not being able to get out of this lab. Every idea he came up with kept coming up short.

What kind of vehicle could he find that would introduce the protein?

Cord had been struggling for hours, racking his brain for any kind of mechanism he could think of. His problem? They were just mechanisms.

Why? Why would a vampire blood cell already containing the protein be able to keep Hunter alive? Was the answer simply Sam or Antu's blood as the carrier? Because Sam and Antu's blood contained more protein than ordinary vampires?

If he carried his hypothesis to the correct conclusion, then Hunter should be completely cured. He wasn't. So the answer? Obviously, the direction The Mother wanted him to go in from his vision of Nuya. Every vampire could close small puncture wounds with a swipe of the tongue. The protein at work. And yet the protein seemed completely inert when introduced to either type of cell.

Cord needed to come up with a different idea.

He set Tori and Stacy on the task of extracting out enough of the protein from vampire saliva samples to use for testing. Most proteins could be separated out of saliva samples using centrifugation and filtration. It seemed the alien protein was no exception.

Once he had enough concentrated protein, Cord tried injecting a minute amount into the cell. The alien protein didn't seem to do anything, albeit a vampire blood cell or a human blood cell. Next, he tried introducing an even smaller amount of the protein concentrate into the mitochondria. The protein, being alien, simply sat there. It didn't become part of the mitochondria, and it didn't become part of the nucleus of the cell. The cells simply didn't recognize it as a protein.

What had the ability to invade a cell and pass on genetic material, or in this case a protein? A virus or a bacterium. He decided not to use a virus. Viruses could be too unpredictable. But a bacterium? He remembered reading in a magazine not too long ago about using bacteria to introduce proteins into the brain to help reduce the effects of autism. Could he do the same? But what bacterium would work? Why not one that was everywhere like *E.coli*?

He injected the protein into an *E.coli* cell. It simply sat there. Okay. Step number two. Take the altered *E.coli* cell and grow lots of them on agar plates. And wait. And wait. Hours later, Cord introduced the proteinated bacteria nuclei into one of the 'clean' neutral vampire cells Tori had created. Then he took this cell and introduced the proteinated mitochondria into a diseased cell to see if it could take over for the diseased mitochondria. The mitochondria worked because the diseased vampire cell didn't die.

"Tori, look at this!"

Tori ran over to him. He sat back and watched as a grin became a huge smile on her face. "Oh My God, that's it! We can remove the DNA string, causing the cell to speed up, and use the protein to protect the cell from dying."

"Might not even need to. We'll have to see," Cord replied.

"I'll bet we can put the protected cells into some plasma, and we can make an infusion. Damn, Cord. It works."

Promise fulfilled.

Cord figured Tori couldn't help herself. In her mind, she called for Sam. Cord heard and hurried out, already on his way. He'd had all he could take. He'd fulfilled his promise. Ripping off his lab coat, Cord grabbed his jacket. Now he was going to go save his daughter.

The elevator door opened, and Sam walked in. "Going somewhere?"

A wall had sprung up between them made of choices neither wanted to make. Cord wasn't even sure how to talk to her anymore. But he was certain of one thing—he needed to find Kay. Now. He stopped and stared as Sam barred his way, white hot anger sending him to a place he warned people not to go. "I don't know, and I don't care. I need to get out of here and start searching for my daughter."

She planted her feet and steeled her body. "Brilliant idea. How do you propose to find her?"

Another spurt of anger shot through his guts. Cord didn't care. "Move." She didn't, which angered him ever more. "You heard what I said. Don't make me move you."

She rolled her eyes. *Really?* "You don't know where she is."

"So what?" he exploded. "Antu has her, and I have a direct line."

Sam snorted. "A direct line? Are you serious? Antu is worse than every trickster known to walk through the hallowed halls of a comic book. Combined. Don't you understand? You're a toy, a plaything, the cat at the end of a string. He'll play with you until he's tired of you and then brush you aside as insignificant."

"And you, oh, Goddess Queen, know where she is?" he yelled. Cord curled his fingers into fists. To keep from throwing something, he held his arms tight at his sides until the fury in his gut cooled. "As in, you never get led down the wrong path. You're too smart and all-seeing, all-knowing to succumb to his nonsense?"

"Not always," she admitted.

Good. At least she had the balls to be honest.

"But I'm not the point," Sam added. "Kay is. And I think I know where Antu has her."

"Where?"

Sam crossed her arms over her chest. "Promise to obey my orders so you don't get yourself killed and I'll tell you."

"Why do you care? I've done my duty," he spat out. "I've done everything I promised. I'm finished." He got in her face. "Tell me!"

She started to pace, the way she often did when she worried, but stopped. Something unexpected filled her gaze as her voice rang with the truth. "I don't want you to die."

"I won't."

She snorted. "Says the lamb going to slaughter. It's a trap."

A spark lit deep inside his belly. He pushed what he thought he saw away. "I don't care."

"By The Mother! You are one stubborn-assed man. Don't you understand? I don't want you to get hurt."

"I won't."

Because of the circumstances surrounding his making, Cord had never really felt like a vampire. Sure, Sam had forced him to acknowledge the truth, but he'd always felt deep inside that he'd become a human with some really neat enhancements. Now he had to embrace his true nature. If he didn't, he would surely die.

"Yes, you will."

All right, he had no fighting skills. But he did have his brains. They'd been enough in the past. Were they enough now?

"He'll kill you," she continued, something growing stronger in her gaze. "If for no other reason than to get back at me." Back at her? She hesitated and twin dots of pink lit her cheeks. "He knows I care for you."

"You care for me? Wow. I mean, double wow." He opened his mouth to continue, but not a word came out. He had to swallow a few times before he could say, "You have a strange way of showing it."

She shook her head. Cord realized she didn't want to continue their discussion in front of an audience.

"Cord. Please. He's created a trap. We need you."

He quirked his mouth. "We?"

Cord couldn't see behind him, but he was certain Tori and Stacy were staring at both of them, wondering who would win.

Sam drew in a deep breath and stared straight into his gaze. "I need you."

"And I'm not the one you lost." He paused to let that one sink in, then decided he'd like some privacy. "Let's go." Cord grabbed her arm and pulled her into the elevator. Once the elevator doors shut, he demanded, "Where is she?"

Her gaze filled with worry. "Do you promise not to do anything exceptionally stupid?"

He nodded. Her face fell.

She had no choice but to tell him. "Your offices in New York. It's close enough for coordinating his attack on the mansion, but completely private. The police have cordoned off the area as a crime scene making the place off limits to humans."

"Crime scene?" he asked, his stomach hollowing.

"The man in the office next to yours. Your Vice President. Derek Allwood. Bahir drained him. He didn't recover."

Comprehension dawned. "Ah, God, no."

"I'm sorry. So very sorry."

"You've said so before." Derek, no nonsense but quick to joke when the necessity arose. No family but his numbers. He'd invited the man over on a few holidays, but Derek always declined. A loner, Cord supposed. Still. *Killing Derek served no purpose.*

None. Antu doesn't care who he hurts or how. Or what deviltry his minions create.

He shuddered, his anger a raging storm inside. There would have to be justice. Somehow, someway. Cord released a huge breath. "It's a perfect setup. I should've thought of it. Why didn't I?"

"Because you were busy trying to save our race. Thank you."

"For what?"

"For tearing yourself into pieces. I know how much this news hurts you."

"You don't know the half of it."

She sighed. "Perhaps. I know you would have joined him in death if I'd let you. I know you wanted to be anywhere but in your lab, trying to find a cure. Your efforts on both counts, though, would have been futile. Antu would never have let you find her."

Futile? For Derek? Absolutely. For Kay? Cord tucked his rage into a place where he could bring it out later and sighed, raking his hand through his hair. Time to focus on what he *could* fix. "I guess so. I would have run around like a chicken following clues like kernels of corn. Until the game began to bore Antu. Then he would have cut my head off. My time was better served here."

Seemed Sam didn't like being right. "Yes."

"I keep coming back to one small problem though." The elevator stopped and put them into the main area of the house and the cafeteria. "How do you know you're right?"

"I don't. But Hunter agrees."

Hunter came walking toward them. "I agree to what?"

"You need to go downstairs to the lab," Cord told him. "You don't need to feed off Sam anymore. Tori and Stacy are working on the cure."

In his typical stoic fashion, the news didn't seem to affect the vampire leader one way or the other. Instead, Cord watched Hunter focus on Sam. "You can't go alone."

Chaz approached from the hallway leading toward the living quarters. "He's right. I'll get my gear."

"No," Sam said. "Not this time. I need you here, Charles. Both of you. Hunter, I need you to work on a defense for the mansion."

"The cell belongs to Mercy."

"And you know best how to defend the place you built," Sam answered. "Charles? I need you to guard Tori and your wife while they finish figuring out how to get the cure into all of the rogues Antu has created."

Ever the scientist, Cord put up his hand for quiet. "Wait a minute." They all looked at him. "We believe we have the cure. We think it will work. But what we've created hasn't tested yet. We really need a person, a test subject, a rogue to try it out on."

Sam frowned. "We don't have the luxury of time. We'll simply have to trust you."

Cord shrugged "Great."

"Are you sure you don't want me to go?" Chaz asked.

Sam kind of grinned. "I have someone else in mind."

"You rang?"

Cord whirled toward the voice. He couldn't miss the shock of bright red hair.

"I'll meet you at the car," Vanessa told them. "I have a few accessories I need." She threw Sam a leather coat, which Sam caught with ease.

Cord watched Sam shrug into the sleeves, noting the slits up the sides for easier maneuverability, and saw the gleam of gold from the handle of her sword.

He may not know how to fight, but Cord figured he could use a little help in the self-defense area. "I need a weapon."

Vanessa guffawed. Sam sighed. She nodded to Chaz who ran back down the hallway and emerged moments later with a wicked looking blade, which he slid into a leather shoulder holster. He threw both to Cord. "This belonged to a good friend. Captain Jeremy Pritchard, a Paladin."

"Stacy told me about him."

Chaz nodded. "Use it well."

Wrapping his fingers around the hilt, the long dagger fit his hand well. "I intend to."

They met Vanessa by a sleek black car. She climbed into the driver's seat. "Hang onto your hats, kiddies."

Sam immediately slid into the back seat, leaving the passenger's side for him. "Try to at least slow down if you sense the police," Sam pleaded.

"No promises."

Luckily, they only encountered one patrol car, which didn't stop them because Vanessa acquiesced to Sam's request. The city streets were nearly deserted, and Vanessa screeched the car to a halt in the underground parking garage Cord used next to his building.

"He knows we're coming," Sam said. "Cord, listen to me. He wants me dead, but he wants you dead as well."

As if he hadn't figured this out already. He clenched his jaw, letting go slowly. "He has a great deal to answer for."

"Vanessa? He has soldiers placed on the stairs. I can hear their heartbeats. Can you take them out?"

Vanessa barked out a laugh. "Consider it done.

Sam opened her door to get out of the car, and they followed. "I cannot open my mind to find Kay. You have to. Do you feel her?"

Cord opened his mind a fraction. He saw Kay sitting in her motorized chair, staring out a window at the sky. Her bewilderment and fear washed over him. "She's here. Thank God, she's here."

"You have one job," Sam told him. "Get her out and get her back to the mansion. Do you understand?"

Cord nodded. He turned to find Vanessa already gone not even realizing she'd left. He and Sam ran up the ramp of the parking garage and out onto the street. He pulled open the door to his building and followed Sam through. "No security guard," he told her, ducking behind the large circular desk to look.

"Still alive, I hope," she answered. "There's no telling how corrupted his soldiers have become."

Awesome.

Cord followed Sam to a bank of elevators. A set of doors opened, and he ran inside. "C'mon. Let's go." All he could think of was Kay. *So close. So close.*

Sam stepped inside, hesitant, one foot at a time, caution filling her every move. All of a sudden, his insides turned hollow with horror. Just as the doors started to close, she cried, "He's inviting us into the elevator. I don't trust him."

Sam grabbed his arm and threw him out of the elevator. She scrunched her eyes, her gaze filled with sorrow, and her brows drew together. And though he couldn't hear the words in his head, her intentions were clear. She had to go alone.

Hail and well met sister!

Chapter Twenty-One

SAM WOULD NEVER HONOR HIM AGAIN WITH A SALUTATION. *BROTHER.*

Sam hit the up button. She tried to keep her fingers from trembling. "Take the next one, Cord. He wants to play with me first."

"I see you still hate small places. A fitting end, no? To die in a tiny box the way you wanted me to die."

Sam grimaced. "I won't and we both know it."

"Yes, well, I guess I can't have everything."

Sam could see him in her mind, still incredibly handsome but in a cold way, like the beauty of a statue. She could appreciate his abilities, but what was a man without heart? Simply a tin man. Could Antu simply be looking for all he'd lost, caring and compassion and feeling?

"You were right to suspect the first elevator. But what about the second? Or all of them?"

Sam looked up. The lights on the numbers told her they'd reached the tenth floor. Another game. Another perfect storm?

"Your friends. They will both die before they reach the child."

"I don't think so."

"But I am curious," Antu continued. "On several counts. Is he your lover?"

"You have no right to ask the question, so why do you?

"No particular reason. Why is this sickly young thing so important?"

"You already know. She's innocent of any and all crimes except one. Her existence."

The elevator reached the fifteenth floor. Nineteen to go.

"Yes, well, fate often dictates action."

"Fate? Have you really lost all of your humanity, brother? Don't you remember anything about love? He's her father. She's a child."

"My Father gives me all I need."

"I wonder. Let the girl go."

"She is free. She simply doesn't have the strength to leave. Which makes her unworthy."

"But also makes her the prize."

Antu laughed. *"You understand me too well, sister."*

The twenty-second floor came and went, and Sam wasn't so sure. She focused deep within herself to create a wall, then reached out to Cord.

"I don't know if my elevator is rigged or not. I don't know if yours is either. Get out now. Stop the elevator at the next possible floor. He wants to play with both of us."

Sam watched the light for 25 come on so she hit the button for the twenty-seventh floor. As soon as she hit the button, the elevator lurched, shuddered, and screeched to a halt. Sam's stomach heaved as the steel box rolled up and down, and she slammed a palm against a wall to steady herself. The doors didn't open. Had the elevator moved enough to reach a floor? No. Surely, Antu stopped this mechanical monster between floors. If so, how close was she to an exit?

"You are trapped, dear sister. Just like you trapped me. How do you like the feeling? Is your heart racing? I can hear it, feel it. Do you feel fear? Is there a hole in your belly? Is your throat dry as the desert sand? I know your hands tremble. I'm not ashamed to admit I felt the same."

"Why would you feel shame? Courage is admitting your fear and overcoming it."

"Yes, well, to overcome a thing, one must understand that thing. I find humans to be clever souls. Don't you? They have defined my emotions into what they call stages. The first stage they term shock and numbness. Oh yes, my sister. At first, I didn't know what to feel. I couldn't believe you would betray me so."

"We can debate betrayal another time. Or do you consider Mensah simply collateral damage?"

He ignored her outburst. Instead, he continued saying, "The second stage they call yearning and searching. My hands roamed over the rock walls for months seeking any crack. You could not count the number of times I simply pounded my fists so that the wall would crumble only to find more rock behind my imprint."

Sam climbed to her feet. She'd known the moment of reckoning would come. She hadn't imagined playing out their pain in a steel cage, but he'd set the terms and this was his game now. *"You created an escape tunnel. You knew my plans. In your complete and utter arrogance, you thought you could escape before I trapped you inside."*

"You're right, I did. A slight miscalculation on my part."

"Slight miscalculation? Is there no end to your hubris, your egotism? Your conceit led you to believe killing the other priests and priestesses was necessary. How did you reconcile all that death, all that waste, as you sat alone with nothing but your thoughts?"

"My thoughts, dear sister? Oh, they did not fill with guilt. They filled with vengeance. And then I realized I would consume myself if I kept it up. So I reached the third stage, acceptance and recovery. I decided to wait and to sleep. And I dreamed. I would take everyone you ever cared for away from you. Lia became the first. This man, the one who is Nuya but is not. He will be next. Along with his daughter."

Sam looked up. She spied an emergency escape panel in the ceiling of the elevator. She bent her knees and sprang upwards. She hit into the panel with sufficient force to break it open. The panel didn't budge. Then Antu placed the picture of a chain and clamps with plates and multiple bolts inside her mind. She tried again, this time with more force. The panel broke open at the hinge, but the chain didn't budge.

Sam fell to the floor. She landed awkwardly and toppled onto her hip, pain shooting down her leg. She bit her lip, and she got up. She was not going to die in a steel box.

Looking up, Sam saw a space where the hinge broke between the plate and the top of the elevator. She jumped up again and wedged her fingers in the space. The elevator rolled up and down, and she dismissed the roiling in her gut. Hanging by one hand, she began pounding away at the cover beneath the chain. The links stretched but didn't break.

Vanessa. Where are you?

Not sure. Little maggots are everywhere.

I could use some help.

Gotcha.

Sam dropped to the floor again. In her mind, she saw Antu smile. She pulled the picture back and saw him standing and leaning in from a floor above her. One of his soldiers held a cable cutter. The elevator lurched and listed to one side as the soldier cut one of the cables.

"If you cut the other cable, the safety brakes will engage."

"And you know I've already disengaged them."

"So? I will not die."

"No, but I will bury you as you buried me. I'm sure it will only take days to free you, but you will know the pain, and you will drown in the helplessness I felt. A small satisfaction but worthy nonetheless."

Sam watched the soldier cut the other cable part of the way through. The elevator tipped even farther.

"You don't have much time, dear sister. But allow me to wish you Bon Voyage. Enjoy your trip."

Antu's laughter sent a chill up her spine because of the delay escaping her confinement would cause. He'd taken her freedom, her freedom of choice and her freedom of action. Pissed, she surveyed her situation. Antu had taken away her ability to pound away at the chain.

He thought she'd simply give up. *Not a chance.*

Sam jumped up as gently as she could, hooking her fingers in the space as she had before. Her stomach hollowed as the car swung back and forth. She heard a 'twang' and wondered how many cable threads were left.

Using her right arm and shoulder and every ounce of strength she possessed, Sam pushed at the cover and chain. Her best bet was to snap the brackets holding the chain. Would she be able to break them before the pressure on the cable became too much to bear? Sam sent up a silent prayer to The Mother. The Mother appeared before her, touching her shoulder. A surge of power ran through her body and the clamps tore away with a terrible shriek of metal on metal.

Sam pushed off the cover and slid her arm through the opening. Just as she pushed herself through, someone grabbed her arm and pulled. As she hung by the grip holding her, Sam caught a familiar scent. Cord?

"What the hell are you doing here?" Sam asked.

The elevator swayed as he pulled her all the way out and set her on her feet on top. "Love to chat but no time to talk. Grab the ladder."

He let go of her and jumped to the maintenance ladder built into the elevator shaft. He rocked back and for but held on then shifted to one side. Sam jumped but slipped and lost her balance. He reached out to steady her as she grabbed the ladder, drawing her close. He bent his head and lowered his lips to hers.

For the first time in her life, Sam closed out all feeling except where their skin touched. He locked his arm around her waist, and he pressed harder. A piece of her opened.

He let go with a shaky laugh. "To be examined later."

She nodded. "Thank you for saving me."

He lifted his brows and kind of rolled them as if surprised by her words. "No thanks necessary. Let's go save Kay. I couldn't get to her on my own. Too many soldiers."

"Vanessa?"

He started climbing the ladder. "Not sure." He came level with the open doors Antu had used. He jumped through the opening and into the hallway. "Hurry."

Sam climbed up the ladder after him. Just as she reached the opening, there was a splitting sound and then a whiplash of air across her cheek as the last cable broke. As Sam leapt through the opening, she counted inside her head. Just as she reached nine, the entire building shook, and a cloud of dust flew through the elevator shaft.

Cord wrapped his arms around her and wouldn't let go. His heart beat almost as fast as hers, and she decided not to examine why. Not yet. Instead, she wedged her palm between them and pushed gently. He kissed the top of her head and let go. "The stairs?"

"This way."

He ran and she followed on his heels. Once they reached the

thirty-fourth floor, Sam nodded for Cord to turn the handle and open the lock gently. She peered out.

"Something's wrong," he bit out.

Sam agreed. She'd expected a guard around Cord's daughter.

Sam pulled her sword out of her coat. Cord pulled the dagger out of his holster. She lifted the corner of her mouth. "Try not to get hurt."

He grinned and started half-running down the hallway. "Which office?" she asked.

"This way."

They continued and both stopped to stare at one another as they heard the faint beat of a human heart.

No locks, no guards. Sam's heart clawed its way up her throat. They burst into the room. A girl was slumped in a motorized chair and faced a huge glass window. Cord reached Kay first. His cry was one she wouldn't forget.

"Kay? Sweetheart?" He swung the chair around. Two puncture wounds dripped watery blood. "Please darling. You can't die. I have a cure. You have to live."

Cord began crying and speaking and begging all at the same time. Sam recognized the exact moment he decided to undo his sleeve so he could tear at his wrist.

"No."

"I have to! She's dying!"

"You can't. It's forbidden."

Sam heard Antu's laughter and shivered. Cord pushed her away so he could bend down in front of the chair. Sam flashed over to him, but rather than restrain him, she simply knelt next to him and placed her palms on his cheeks.

"Cord. Listen to me. Please." She waited until some of the panic left his gaze. "The Mother doesn't want your daughter's death. She gave me the strength to free myself from the elevator. She has given me the ability to hold Kay immobile long enough to get her back to the mansion. She is very weak, but I think I can help her hold on until we can transfuse her. She will know about vampires now, but that cannot be helped. Besides, you're her father. I think she'd find out soon enough."

"Can you save her? Please. I'm begging."

"I can impart a tiny spark of The Mother's power. The tiniest of sparks. To keep her heart beating."

"Will she become a vampire?"

"I don't know. I don't know what she will be. I fear her heart will outlive the rest of her body, but this is something she will have to deal with when the time comes. All I know is The Mother is pushing me down this path. Before you consent, understand that your daughter will never be completely human again."

Cord nodded and Sam let go. He rose. "Tori was right. Give me a moment."

Cord closed his eyes. She could hear him reaching into Kay's mind and repeating the questions Sam had asked him. When he opened his eyes, he said, "She wants to live."

Sam channeled The Mother's power into her fingertip and touched Kay's chest right where her heart rested. She withdrew after a fraction of a second. The girl's heart started beating stronger and stronger. "Her heart will keep beating now without my help. But we must still hurry. She's lost a lot of blood."

Vanessa ran up to them, gulping air. "I…was just…starting to have…fun and they retreated." Sam watched Vanessa wipe the perspiration off her brow. "She doesn't look too good. She gonna make it?"

Sam nodded. "Get the car and bring it around front. You'll need to use the stairs."

"Yeah. I heard the elevator crash and felt the building shake. Glad you weren't inside."

Cord lifted Kay and Sam picked up the chair. "Let's go."

They ran down the stairs as fast as they could and found Vanessa waiting for them. Sam called Tori once they were on their way. "Tori? We have Cord's daughter."

"Thank God."

"She needs a transfusion."

"A positive," Cord called out.

Obviously, Tori heard him as she replied. "Got it."

The city streets were quiet. They encountered one police car, but Vanessa slowed down in time, and Sam held the officer immobile long enough for him not to realize they'd passed.

Then Vanessa floored it down route 9W, and even Sam became a bit nervous as they rode up and down and around some tight corners. Finally, the gates of the mansion opened, and they screeched to a halt. Cord lifted Kay out of the car and sprinted up the steps. Tori and Stacy were waiting with a gurney. "I only have two units, but we've put out a call for more."

Sam watched Tori place a stethoscope on Kay's chest. The doctor's eyes widened. *She needed a little help.* Tori nodded and started the infusion right on the front steps. Cord held the blood bag as Tori and Stacy took the girl into the mansion. Sam heaved a huge sigh.

"Kid wasn't doing too good to begin with," Vanessa said. "Why'd he want to drain her?"

"To vex me. Just like he wanted to bury me in the elevator. The same way I buried him."

"Some family, huh?" Sam simply stared. "Mine wasn't better." Vanessa shrugged. "Nothing like brotherly love, eh?"

Sam started walking up the steps to join everyone inside. "Nothing brotherly or loverly at all."

Chapter Twenty-Two

"You need to feed," Tori said.

Cord looked up, wondering how he'd gotten into the lab. Looking over at his daughter, a lump formed in his throat. "I'm fine."

Tori gave him a stern 'doctor' look. "No, you're not. You're dead on your feet."

He frowned. "Was that, was that a joke?"

She laughed softly. "Maybe. But not the order. The more you test your willpower, the harder it'll be to hold out."

Cord looked back down at Kay. "I used to watch her. Just like this. For hours."

He watched Tori's gaze darken, and her eyes fill with tears. He reached out. "I'm sorry. I didn't mean to hurt you."

Tori shook her head. "You didn't. Grieving isn't wrong and I can't live without feeling anymore." She wiped at her eyes and Cord hurt with her. "I'll be fine."

He cocked his head and caught her gaze to make sure. She turned brusque as if to cover the pain. "I'll get you some bags and then set up a bed right here. Okay?"

"Thank you."

When Tori returned with the blood, Cord said, "It's funny, but I still crave coffee. And the taste of cinnamon donuts."

"Not at all. Chaz buys a bag of beans just to grind them for the smell. He was carrying one when we met. And he's never tasted coffee before. I think if he did, he'd be disappointed."

Having had many a bad cup in his human life, Cord agreed. "Big difference."

Tori checked Kay's vitals. "I think part of our humanity remains with us no matter what form we take. Even it is no more than memories."

Cord nodded and hopped onto the gurney she'd brought. He slipped into this kind of twilight, neither awake nor asleep. They were both scientists. The first time he met his wife Allie, Cord stumbled over his words like a seventeen-year-old. How could he not as he stared at the model in the lab coat? Dirty-blonde hair and warm brown eyes, Kay looked just like her. And when he married Allie, Cord thought he'd found a compatriot in life and in work. Turned out, Allie liked money more. She stole his heart, then his secrets and sold them to Avery Duncan.

She sued him for divorce so she could marry Duncan; Cord counter sued for his daughter and his pride. They settled out of court. He lost his patents but kept custody of his daughter and enough money to keep their home and start CoRRStar. Who'd have thought he'd end up here?

Cord jerked awake, his mistakes bitter on his tongue. He sat up to find Sam standing not too far away. The lab was deserted and judging by his inner time clock, too early for Tori or Stacy to get up yet.

He glanced over at his daughter. She'd taken the two units of blood, and her color looked better. Her chest rose and fell slowly. His first instinct? Get back to work. He had a cure to finish.

"I'm sorry about everything, Cord."

The queen who never apologized, just apologized. "Perhaps you're not so cold after all."

"We seem to have misjudged one another," Sam answered. "Thank you for saving me. Surviving that elevator crash wouldn't have been pleasant."

"Choices. Turned out I was right.' He paused. "You saved Kay. I'm grateful."

She didn't answer.

"What?" He pasted an amazed look on his face. "Where's the bad-assed queen I always have to deal with?"

She snorted. "Same place as the arrogant-assed scientist." She picked up a test tube, rolling the glass between her fingers before replacing it in the rack on the counter. She had incredibly long fingers, slender and strong, and Cord imagined for a split-second they were wrapped around his cock instead.

She must have sensed his intent because a thin streak of pink suffused her cheeks right above her cheekbones. He stepped forward, and she stepped back. "Love's hurt us both, hasn't it?" she asked. He nodded. "I couldn't help but see the pictures in your mind."

She shifted from foot to foot as her head turned to scan the room seeking escape. She could easily push him away, and he braced himself. When she didn't, he looked down to watch the rapid rise and fall of her breasts, and what he remembered from their size and their outline as pear-shaped globes beneath her blouse.

The power of the predator surged through his veins. He could take her, right here, right now on the top of the workbench. Nothing had ever stopped him before, so he wondered why he couldn't move. Then he realized. Deep inside her gaze rested the innocent shyness of a fawn, wanting to trust, while every instinct said don't.

After Allie, Cord had learned all sorts of secrets about women. They could be warm and wonderful or cold and vindictive. They were complex creatures like chains of amino acids, with the same basic sequencing. But change a link here and there? No wonder men could never understand women. DNA always had the ability to mutate.

But with Sam? She was a whole different story. Fascinated, Cord stepped forward and cupped her cheeks with his palms. Surprise, surprise. She didn't pull away.

"Samira. Samira. I can't get enough of saying your name."

He feathered his fingertips up and down the sides of her face. Tiny beads raised in her skin. Seemed the queen wasn't quite as immune as she thought.

He bent his head ever so slowly. Anticipation fluttered in his belly. She had decided to block her thoughts. Out of self-preservation? Cord wondered for she'd become unsettled. Her weight kept shifting as if trying to escape, twisting her hips while he held her head immobile.

The route didn't exist anymore.

Their breaths mingled, hers short gasps of wonder, his a complete need of oxygen. The dam broke with a torrent as she stilled, reached up with her hands, and pulled his mouth down onto hers. She swept the inside of his mouth with her tongue like a rapier, swift strokes looking for the sweetest spot to land. In doing so, she teased his incisors. Sparks of feeling, electricity, he had no idea what to call them, shot through his body and went straight to his groin.

Oh, how he wanted to give in and jump into the rising river.

The queen held him back. Playing with this kind of fire merely ended up burning holes in a man's soul, and he'd been there and done that already. Cord still remembered Allie depositing Kay in his arms like a she was some kind of a pizza or something, turning her back, and walking out of the lawyer's office without so much as a goodbye.

Cord retreated, breaking the kiss. He lifted up and opened his eyes to find hers still closed. She seemed to be experiencing every nuance of the last few moments. She raised her eyelids with a shaky laugh, opening her mouth to say something, then deciding not to. She moved away too quickly and backed up into a cart with racks of tubes on it. They clicked and jangled, and she reached out to stop the cart from flying. Cord bit back a smile, pleased he'd affected her so.

"Stop standing there grinning at me like a peacock," she said.

"You're adorable."

"I'm what?"

"Underneath all the queen layers and the Sam layers, there's a young girl waiting to come out."

She huffed out a short breath. "The child remains in all of us." She looked down at his crotch and grinned, a dimple of delight creasing her cheek. "I'd wear a lab coat for a few if I were you."

He laughed. "You have a point." He walked over to his and put it on. "Until next time."

"If there is one."

SEVERAL HOURS LATER, JUST AS HIS VISION BEGAN TO BLUR FROM TOO many hours looking at a microscope, Cord heard the word he thought he'd never hear again. "Dad?"

He almost forgot to move slowly. "Kay?"

"Can I have some water, please?"

"Sure, sweetheart."

A jug sat on the table next to the hospital bed. He poured her a glass and held her head up so she could drink. She still smelled sick, but he was certain she'd be all right. Sam's touch would always remain. The rest? The choice to use the Tori's cells had become Kay's and Kay's alone.

God help all those parents who had watched their baby birds spread their wings for their first flight, praying they make the right decisions, hoping beyond hope they'll be safe. From first steps to driver's licenses to old age, the fear never went away.

He sat on the edge of the hospital bed and brushed the hair back from her forehead. "How do you feel?"

He could hear her heartbeat, fast and strong, and he swallowed the need welling in his mind. There could be the blood everywhere else but not with his daughter. End of discussion.

"Very strange. Jazzed up and tired all at the same time." She lifted up enough to put her hand under her head and looked at him. "Dad, what's going on? Where are we?"

"My new laboratory. We're in a private mansion in Alpine."

"Alpine?" She appeared to digest this information, then asked, "I remember sitting in your office building in the city. I was looking out the window. Then this man came in. He had black hair hanging down to his shoulders. I thought he looked kinda cool, then I felt a pinch in my neck. It hurt and I wanted it to stop. I don't remember much after that except this really bright light. Did I die?"

Cord grimaced. "No. But someone tried to hurt you to hurt me. I'm terribly sorry."

She brushed off his apology. "Why does my heart feel like it wants to pound right out of my chest? I feel like I should be running a marathon right now."

"Sweetheart, I have to confess something to you, and I don't think you're going to understand. Try to keep an open mind, though. Okay?" She nodded, her gaze accepting and trusting. "I was in trouble. Financially. I needed cash. So I teamed up with someone I thought owned a diagnostics company."

"They weren't mobsters or something like that, were they?"

"No. Worse, I'm afraid. And when I tell you, you're going to think I'm crazy."

"Would it make you feel better if I told you I already thought you were crazy?"

He stilled. "No games, Kay. I'm not playing." Her smile faded. "I know you know all the movies and stuff, but some of the legends are true. I'm a vampire."

"A vampire? Really?" She started laughing. "I'd have thought you'd come up with something a bit more original, you know?"

"I'm not playing, Kay."

"C'mon, Dad." A thought must have occurred to her because she frowned. "You haven't gotten into smoking stuff you shouldn't smoke, have you?"

"No, darling," he sighed. "Wouldn't affect me, even if I did. I think. Something I'll have to check."

"Check? You're joking right?"

"No joke. I'm being serious, very serious. In trying to find a cure for you, I made a formula that would turn vampires into rogue vampires, vampires with an uncontrollable thirst."

She laughed again, but this time a bit shaky. But a laugh, nonetheless. "Now I know you've gone bonkers. You sound like a bad movie."

"I said the same. No movie I promise."

He smiled, and she could see his incisors were slightly longer than the rest of his teeth. "Okay, Dad. Fun-time's over with. Stop with the games and the fake teeth."

"I'm not the one who likes playing them. The man with the black hair loves them. Which puts you in a great deal of danger. I'm sorry."

He watched Kay shake her head. "Please tell me you're kidding." He shook his head. "Dad, stop. Please."

"I wish I could. For the record, I had a hard time accepting the truth too."

She stared. "Who says I'm accepting anything?"

Cord reached out. Kay flinched. His heart broke. He started bleeding, hating himself with no one else to blame. "You don't have to. Not now, not ever. Just know I'm still me—your father—inside, even if the outside's changed a little."

She'd hurt him and hurting others would never be his daughter's style. She reached out and grabbed his hand. Her eyes widened. "You're cold."

"Yes." She didn't shrink back, but her next thought was like a stiletto in an already damaged heart. "No, I won't drink your blood. How could I?"

"Wait a minute. What? How did you know what I was thinking?"

"The look on your face. Pretty obvious." He tried to smile, wondering if he'd be able to pull off the feat. "Besides, we've watched way too many movies together." He squeezed her fingers. "Kay, listen to me. This mansion is a vampire home. Nearly a hundred vampires live on this property and in the surrounding area. You're human."

"Human? You want to…oh, my God…I'm a meal now?"

"Damn it, Kayla! Stop!" She did because he only used her full name if he really got angry. Which he wasn't but it got her attention. "You're my daughter. I'm your father. Nothing inside of me has changed."

"Easy for you to say," she muttered.

"A lot of people went to a great deal of trouble to save your ass. Behave."

"Me? What about you? They wouldn't have had to if you hadn't gone and done something stupid."

Cord yanked his hand away and rose. "Trying to save your life is a crime now?"

He heard someone approach and looked up. Stacy? What was she doing here so early?

"Excuse me." She turned to his daughter. "Hi. I'm Stacy." She turned back to him. "Would you mind if we talked a minute?"

"Of course." He retreated to a far corner of the lab knowing full well he could hear everything they said. Stacy knew too.

"Hey."

"Hey."

"I'm human." He glanced over to see Stacy hold out her hand and have Kay grasp it. "Very."

"Thank goodness."

"But my husband, Chaz, isn't."

"No shit."

Cord had to have a talk with his daughter about her language.

"Yes." A silence fell between them, and he looked over again. Stacy stood next to the bed rail. "Your father's trying to tell you that physically he and my husband are vampires. And yes, they drink blood to survive. But only just enough. There are rules about how much they can take."

"So they don't hurt anyone?"

"Exactly. Do you know what this place is?"

"A home for vampires?"

He heard Stacy laugh softly. "No, a blood donation center. So no, you're not a meal."

Kay huffed. "Easy for you to say."

"Not really. I struggled with the concept too." He heard Stacy sigh. "There isn't a man on this earth more human than my husband. I'm beginning to believe the same about your father. And, so we're very clear on rules, everyone here takes an oath. If they drink from you, they can die."

"Really? I mean really die?"

"Yes. No joke."

"But doesn't your husband want to? Like all the time?"

"Yes." Stacy laughed louder this time. "You seem to have forgotten a very important word. I trust him not to hurt me just as you've trusted your father all your life not to hurt you. Why would a simple change make you stop believing in him?"

Kay didn't answer. Although he wanted to open up to her thoughts, Cord decided to respect his daughter's right to privacy.

"He loves you, Kay. The same way Chaz loves me. Well, not exactly but you get my point. My husband never lost his humanity, the essence inside which makes us all human. Your father didn't either."

He heard Kay rustle in the bed, then settle down. "Does your husband drink from you? Is he allowed?"

"On occasion. He sips."

"Oh. Oh, yeah. Gotcha."

Stacy laughed again, and he watched her reach down and hug Kay. *Stacy, thank you.*

You're welcome.

"Tori, sorry, Dr. Roberts, will be down soon to check on you. She's a real doctor and human too. Her fiancée is also a vampire. I woke up and came down first to find out how you're feeling."

"A little tired. A little jazzed. Hungry."

"Good. I'm going to remove the I.V. but you still need to rest. And I'll see what I can get from the kitchen. I think they've got vegetable beef soup on the menu for today."

"Menu?"

"Yes, menu. We make sure to feed everyone who donates. We've got drawing stations all over the city. Many are homeless. They can use a good hearty meal after they donate. We pay them too."

"Wow." Kay paused. "You're right. This is a lot to take in."

"Try not to absorb it all at once. I've always found the easiest way to digest something is human bites."

They both guffawed.

After Kay had something to eat, and he'd messed up three experiments because his heart lay next to her in her bed, Cord finally walked back over to his daughter.

"I love you."

She nodded. "I know." And then he saw what he'd been searching for in her gaze. "I love you too, Dad."

Chapter Twenty-Three

SAM STAYED OUT OF THE WAY, LETTING CORD HAVE TIME WITH HIS daughter. He also seemed to be nearing completion with his 'cure.' Good news. She'd been in contact with the Council several times. They were all preparing to fight.

Miklos remained enigmatic as ever, Bahir just as slimy, and Sam had to wonder how long they would remain in their prison. She placed them in Mercy's care as Hunter had now become Cord's guinea pig.

All of which left her sitting in the eye of the hurricane. Or pacing in her small cottage. She yearned to visit with Cord's horses again, but the respectful thing to do would be to ask permission, and she didn't want to bother him. So when he came to her cottage, Sam was quite surprised.

"Hello."

"I get the feeling you've been trying to avoid my company," he said.

"Not exactly. Tori tells me you're making progress. I didn't want to interrupt."

He nodded with a tiny smile. "I need to go back to my home. I have a small cryo unit there and some specimens to retrieve."

"Cryo?"

"Cryogenic freezer. The samples have been frozen in liquid nitrogen."

Sam shook her head. Liquid nitrogen. To think they'd advanced so far. "Do you need my help?"

His smile widened. "No. But I keep seeing G in my head."

"I've been trying to figure out a way to ask your permission to ride him again. It may be the last chance I get."

He frowned, not liking her last sentence. So he focused on the other one. "Permission? The great queen asking permission from the lowly scientist?"

"I don't find your teasing to be funny."

"I'm not teasing, I'm being more serious than I care to admit." He leaned on the doorjamb with one hand. "We both know what's going to happen, and I'm not happy with your choice. You don't need to sacrifice yourself."

"I've tested fate in the past, but I believe every choice has only redirected the flow of the inevitable. The vision was clear. The thrones become one and then they are no more. I have custody of his generals. Antu will attack soon. I will fight him. We will die." Sam sighed as her belly hollowed. "You will cure Hunter and all of the others, and Hunter will rule with The Council. Our race will survive."

"Just like that, eh? So let it be written, so let it be done."

"Not funny," she muttered, getting the reference to the movie. "I'm not a Pharaoh. I've never tried to hold sway over the lives of others. Antu does this and quite well, I'm afraid."

Sam ducked under his arm and started walking toward the mansion. She smiled as she looked over her shoulder to find him scrambling to follow her. "Are you coming?"

He shook his head in what looked like defeat. "Yes."

Sam threw him the car keys and let Cord take the wheel, giving herself a chance to study him. His movements were precise and efficient, underscoring the scientist, and yet he was so warm and caring with his daughter. "How is Kayla?"

"Still feeling strange. Her heart is on speed, but the rest of her tires easily. She seems to have formed a bond with Tori. Must be the 'geek' in her. And she likes Stacy a lot." He glanced over. "You should stop by and say hello."

Sam huffed out a nervous laugh. "I'm not very good with, I was going to say people, but definitely teenagers."

"Better with vampires?"

"Some. Like Lia. My soldiers. Others, perhaps not so much."

She looked over to see him grin. "I think Hunter and Chaz would disagree. Mercy too."

For some reason, a picture of her favorite redhead popped into her mind. "Not Vanessa."

"She's not all that bad," he said with a laugh. "But you have two very good friends."

Tori and Stacy. "Yes, I do. Perhaps there's hope for me after all."

"You never know," he teased.

They pulled up to Cord's home, and Sam found the mix of modern and country pleasing to the eye. The house looked to be a colonial but had a porch and rocking chairs next to the front door that would be called country in a home decorating magazine. She found the combination warm and pleasing to the eye.

They got out of the car, and Sam stilled. The sun sat low in the sky behind some hills in the distance, creating an orange glow. The panorama from the paddocks to the barn to the vista in the distance looked like a painting. "I remember so many nights like this one, the wind cool and, well, perhaps not so fresh as I would like. I definitely remember the air being cleaner back then. The Mother and The Father appreciated the beauty of our world."

"They have a strange way of showing it."

"When we teach children, when you taught Kay, you taught her caring and goodness, you didn't teach her pettiness and jealousy. You taught her respect and trust, you taught her the right way to be, not the wrong. There has to be balance."

"For every action, there is an equal and opposite reaction," he replied. "In order for a chemical change to occur, both sides of the equation have to be equal. I get it."

Sam followed Cord to the stables where he let her take G out. Then he got another horse out of its stall. "This is Charismatic, Kay's hunter. Kay was getting ready to join the junior circuit when she got sick." He paused, and she could tell he watched his daughter ride in his mind. "You should have seen her."

"I imagine she was magnificent."

He nodded. "I have a stable hand. Charley comes over Silver Springs to take care of the horses. She rides them when she can." Charismatic tossed his head and wouldn't stay still while being groomed. "Not quite enough, I'm afraid."

"A hard run will do them both good. You won't need a bridle or saddle. Believe me, he'll know who's on his back soon enough," she said.

Cord looked skeptical but nodded and vaulted on Charismatic' back with ease. She watched him sink into his seat and use his weight and his legs, along with a sharp bark, to settle the horse down.

"You see? All you have to do now is be careful not to grip too tightly or you'll hurt him."

They entered a ring containing fences to jump over. Sam worked with G for a short time and then let him run free around the ring outside the fences. Then she slowed him down to watch Cord work his horse at the trot and the canter, back and forth, and side to side. Once she slowed to a walk, he let Charismatic have his head, and the horse burst forward. She enjoyed watching, she hadn't seen excellent horsemanship in a long time.

They met in the center of the ring. Cord's smile widened, and the light of challenge lit his gaze. "Are you up for jumping them?" She nodded. "Twice around the ring in a figure eight, long side, then both diagonals and the long side again."

He swung his arm in the air to indicate the correct direction. "Done. You go first."

He cleared each fence with ease, but as he rode, Sam imagined him in gleaming armor, flying across the dessert, at one with the bunch and gather of his steed.

She rode well but wasn't as sure about the jumps. Twice G helped her as she misjudged a take-off point. Still, she got around without issue and felt glad.

"You ride beautifully," she commented as they walked the horses out side by side.

"So do you."

"You're being kind."

"Am I?" His gaze darkened. Her breath caught. Every movement of the horse made her extremely aware of her body. She got down and walked 'G' into the barn. Cord seemed to know what she was feeling so she hid behind the work of grooming 'G,' brushing him until he shined and giving him fresh water and some grain.

He reached out as they walked back toward the house, clasping her hand in his. Once they reached the patio, Sam needed to warn him. "Cord, listen. We're connected in a way that transcends normal emotions. Please don't mistake feelings for connection. They—"

He placed a gentle finger on her lips. "You talk a lot when you're nervous."

"I'm not nervous."

He stepped closer and she swallowed. He grinned. "You're not?"

"Damn it, Cord! Haven't I hurt you enough already? Made you into a vampire? Changed your daughter in a way none of us will ever truly comprehend? Dragged you into a war you shouldn't be a part of?" He didn't answer, just stood there with that sexy half-smile on his face. "Don't you think you should be angry with me?"

"Sure." He nodded. "But you saved my life after desperation forced me to do something really stupid. Or do you think I don't realize Casperian would have made me his next meal and his next victim?"

"Antu was better?"

He shook his head. "You put your life on the line not once but twice to save my daughter, along with your principles, your ethics, and your—essence—to keep her alive. About time we called it even, no?"

"I don't want to hurt you. I've done enough already."

"My choice."

Sam lifted her hand to caress his cheek. "Yes." Her blood, already warmed, heated inside her veins. "You'll find coupling as a vampire very enjoyable, far more enjoyable than when you were human."

"Coupling?" He stiffened, and Sam realized she'd hurt him. "Are you so frightened that you can't even call it making love?"

Caught, feeling guilty, yearning with an intensity she hadn't known in millennia, Sam didn't know what to do. "I told you. I don't want to hurt you. It's better to leave things this way. Engage your emotions now and what will you do when I'm gone? Or did you forget the blending of the thrones?"

"Don't worry about me. What about you? Or were you lying when you said you cared for me?"

Everyone built walls for protection, shut out truths for the sake of their own sanity. Sam was no exception. But Cord had already punched a hole through several. "I don't lie."

"You think making love is a mistake."

She nodded, her breath catching in her throat, making her words come out in a whisper. "A grand mistake."

"I don't care."

"Neither do I."

The hole opened, and Sam couldn't believe the torrent of yearning flooding her belly. She wanted. Oh, how she wanted. Pulling his head down, Sam tried to inhale him whole.

He broke away, breathing hard, and Sam said, "Sorry."

"Sorry? I'm not. I've been trying to figure out what's beneath the ice for a while now. Guess I have."

He bent his head and covered her mouth, parting her lips with his tongue and tasting every crevice inside. Sam growled, sweeping her tongue over his and licking at his incisors, enjoying each and every shiver she created.

Sam wanted more. She let go and tugged on his hand, pulling him toward the back door. He fumbled for a key. She leaned in to lick his neck. "Don't make me break the lock," Sam whispered against his skin.

He managed to get the door open and she smiled. They stumbled inside, hands everywhere, mouth's slanting this way and that. Until he finally lifted his head. "Sam. Slow down."

She giggled. "It's been a while."

He lifted the side of his mouth with the crazy, sexy, knowing smirk he'd used before. "For me too."

In gentling her fervor, Cord made her realize the importance of their joining. They knew so much about each other and yet, so little. She wanted to know every spot on his body where her touch would make his skin bead. She wanted to inhale the musky scent of his manhood, lick the salt of his sweat as their bodies became one.

"Easy, sweet. A man, even a vampire, can only take so much. The pictures you're sending are—hot."

"Now you understand."

He didn't answer. He nuzzled her neck and unbuttoned her blouse. Her fingers trembled as she did the same to his shirt. He tangled his hand in her hair and pulled back, scraping his incisors along the slant of her neck. Her core opened, and she fought against the urge to simply rip his clothes off.

Both her shirt and her bra were gone before she could gather her wits. She pushed his shirt off his shoulders, trailing her fingers down and around his firm chest muscles. She continued lower, and he sucked in his stomach, inviting her hand to slip inside the waistband of his jeans.

Tempting as the thought became, Sam decided getting naked was more important. She unsnapped them instead and pushed them down to his feet, her one purpose to free his cock from its manmade prison.

He put his hand on hers. "Do that and I'll become seventeen years old again."

"Your first time?" she teased.

"A gentleman never tells."

She shucked her own jeans and watched as he stepped away from his. He wrapped his arms around her waist. "With you, I'm afraid, I'll always feel as though I don't measure up. You've got millennia on me."

"Boring millennia, truth be told. My encounters were rather perfunctory."

"Encounters? In all that time you never met anyone who made your heart race? Just a little?"

"A woman never tells," she said then grinned. However, teasing him didn't seem right so she decided to be honest. "No, not really." She placed his palm above her breast. Her heart beat madly beneath his touch. "Does this answer your question?"

She turned to liquid at the half-smirk he gave her. He picked up her hand and kissed her palm. The walls inside crumbled. Sam had been afraid of this moment for over five thousand years, the moment when need and feeling urged her to throw caution to the wind.

"Samira."

He didn't need to say more. She jumped up on him, throwing her legs around his waist, wanting him so badly she lost all reason. They fell to the floor with nothing more than an area rug to cushion the impact. Sam could've cared less about the pain.

They rolled over and over, tongues mating, bodies trying to become one until she finally stopped their movement. She sat astride his hips, a slow smile growing on her face. "This was what you wanted, wasn't it? That I should ride you into oblivion?"

He nodded, all laughter gone from his face. She centered his cock and slipped down until she sheathed the tip. He hissed in a breath and Sam closed her eyes, savoring every sensation. She opened them and watched his jaw clench as she lowered herself bit by bit. His hands wrapped around her hips, urging her to finish what she'd started.

She leaned back and with one swift move, impaled herself on his cock until he was imbedded deep inside her body. His hands slid up her sides to play with her breasts, and Sam threw her head back. How long had it been since she felt this way? Had she ever felt this way? No, never.

He tweaked her nipples, rolling them between his fingers, and she gave him a gaze that asked are-you-sure-you-want-to-play-this-game? He drove his hips upwards. She released her breath in a whoosh and clenched her inner muscles around his cock. He groaned, and she started riding him, speeding up, slowing down, drawing out the inevitable in both of them.

At the last moment, Cord sat up. She felt the pinch, felt the draw, then all thought ceased as they erupted together. She screamed out her pleasure. He cried out. Shock after shock rumbled through her body until she finally collapsed on his chest.

Neither of them could draw in enough air. And as she listened to his heart jump inside his chest, nothing could ever make her regret what had just happened between them.

Chapter Twenty-Four

CORD WANTED AN IMMEDIATE REPEAT. NO, A THREEPEAT. HIS COCK still pulsed with tiny aftershocks inside her warm nest. Wouldn't take much to get him going again, for sure.

Sam moved slightly, snuggling closer. Her hair smelled like orange and spice, the rest of the room like sex. He started to grow again, and she lifted up, surprise in her gaze like she wasn't quite sure what to make of him.

"I see you weren't kidding when you said perfunctory." He rolled her on her side and began nibbling on her earlobe. Using a combination of nips and swirls, he worked his way down to her collarbone. "And you were right. Absolutely amazing."

He nibbled along the full length to her shoulder, then lifted back to start on the curve of her chin. "Cord. Please."

"No, Sam. Don't think. Just feel."

Cord belonged inside of her and next to her and surrounding her and being a part of her. She opened her mouth to protest, then simply lifted up to kiss him. In literature, kisses have been described as the sweetest nectar, the most fragrant wine, indescribably delicious. He'd never realized before how right the description was.

He shifted his hips a touch, and she gasped. He wanted more of the wanton woman who couldn't get enough of his body, but his engine began to fire, and he had no way to stop the rising in his blood.

He'd hoped for long and slow but perhaps slower would be more achievable. He pressed light kisses all over her face, her nose, her eyelids. He didn't know how but he knew no one had ever taken the care to love Sam the way she deserved. So he took his time, memorizing every inch of her skin, enjoying the feel of her pert tight breast in his hand, drowning in the way her gaze liquified as he pinched and rolled her nipple in his fingers.

Of course, each time he did, she would close around him and squeeze, and he would have to hold his breath until the urge to move passed. Cord decided to cherish her with each kiss. At first, he could tell she was leery of the feelings inside each trail of his fingertips, but she grew stronger and surer of herself until she let him feel her emotions as well.

Cord rolled her on her back and sank his cock deep inside her core. Her legs banded about his waist, and he lifted up on his elbows even though his weight caused no discomfort. She'd ridden him, now he returned the favor, twisting in and out so he could wring out every ounce of pleasure.

"Cord," she whispered. "You're killing me."

He leaned forward and kissed her, his tongue sliding in and out in the same rhythm as his cock. She urged him on as she had his horse, pressing with her knees and pushing up with her hips.

With long and slow completely forgotten, Cord surged upwards. He met her thrusts, climbing the mountain with her. He could sense she'd reached the brink and slowed one last time to let her gather herself before plunging in.

He wanted to draw out the moment, he wanted to drown in every sensation, but even a vampire has his limits. And when she lifted her head to drink? Oh, the sensation, the ravaging of the dam, the complete rightness between them. Cord had no words; indeed, his mind went blank. He exploded inside of her just as she screamed and convulsed around his cock, which added to the wonder. He kept trying to gulp air and keep it in his lungs, only to need more. Her short sharp breaths in the crook of his neck told him she'd joined him at the top of more than a mountain.

"Is it always like this?" she whispered.

"It can be." He pulled her up so her face could be even with his. "You mean to tell me you've never enjoyed yourself?"

"Antu wasn't kind."

A picture entered his head of Antu and Casperian. "Well, I'll be damned. So that's why Antu kept Casperian around."

"Perhaps," she replied. "In the beginning of the world, pleasure was simply pleasure, no more, no less. The connotations and inhibitions came later."

"Couldn't have been very nice for you."

"Now that you've shown me what could be, I suppose you're right. You don't know what you're missing when you don't know."

Cord actually had to process her statement before it made sense. "I get it."

He let go of her and helped her stand. He took a quick shower and listened to the water run for hers, clenching his fists to keep from joining her.

He gathered his specimens and put the cryo tank in the trunk. As they were about to get in the car, she turned to him. "Cord. For your own sanity. This was a daydream, nothing more."

Cord ran the back of his fingers down her cheek before opening the car door. She got in, and he rolled his eyes, knowing in his heart what he wouldn't let his mind reveal. *Fat chance.*

HOW IMPOSSIBLE TO CAGE THE BIRD WHO HAS KNOWN NOTHING BUT freedom. But Cord wanted nothing more than to keep Sam by his side, protect her, and hold onto her for the rest of eternity.

Closing the car door and watching her walk away once they reached the mansion, the folly of his desires punched him right in the gut.

He lifted the cryo tank out of the trunk and brought it down to the lab. After he finished setting it up, he checked on Kay. She slept, not quite used to vampire time. He sat down next to her, feeling her warmth, listening to her heart beat solid in his ears.

Tori came up to him. "I wondered if Sam's power would be a permanent fix or not. I'm still not sure. I'm not a cardiologist, and I don't have the right equipment. But Kay's heart is slowing. How much so, remains to be seen. The heart muscles are solid and strong, you can hear so I don't need to tell you. At least now she won't be so out of sorts with herself."

"Good. Thank you."

Cord looked down at his daughter, but a picture of Sam flying through the wind kept filling his vision.

Tori tapped him on the shoulder. "You seem a bit distracted. Are you all right?"

"Sam." He let the concern swimming in his stomach fill his face. "She's going to go off half-cocked and get herself killed."

"She'll do what she thinks is best." Tori rubbed her hand across his shoulders. "She believes the vision was clear. She's always done what she thought she must, she'll do no less now."

"I know," he sighed. "I—I think I'm falling in love with her."

"Gotcha." She smiled. "Anyone ever tell you it's a bad idea to fall in love with a queen? Especially a vampire queen on a mission?"

"Hundreds of times," he deadpanned.

"I can tell." Tori walked over and sat on the gurney that had become his bed. "Stick with her Cord. She needs you."

"And simply watch her go get herself killed? How?"

Tori cocked her head at him. "You've never really been in love before, have you?"

"I thought I was." He glanced over at Kay then up at Tori. "Once."

"Right. Well, you'll figure it out. We all do."

Tori walked back over to her workstation, and Cord rose. He bent down and kissed his daughter on the forehead, then lifted the side bedrail. He walked over to his own workbench thinking about Kay and Sam and being able to let go. No cages, just choices. For what else was the most supreme act of love? Everyone had the right to make his/her own choice. He had to abide by Sam's.

He stared down at his lab notebook. If he couldn't control other people's choices, he could control his. Tori and Stacy had managed to synthesize enough protein to introduce to the bacteria. Then they grew a lot of bacteria on plates and then he added the pure vampire cells. And he waited. The time had come to introduce the new vampire cells to Hunter's damaged blood. The mitochondria with the protection of the protein remained in the cells while the diseased mitochondria burned themselves out. The vampire blood cells lived.

Still, the entire experiment was *in vitro*, not *in vivo*, so they still had a last hurdle to overcome. A couple of hours later while Cord finished his notes, Hunter came down to collect Tori.

"You look like shit," he told the vampire leader.

Hunter shrugged. "Are you almost ready?"

"No guarantees." Hunter nodded and clasped Tori's hand. "But I think this is going to work. Tonight?"

"Tonight."

For a moment, Tori dropped her guard, and Cord read absolute terror in her gaze. Then she turned away and tugged on Hunter's arm to go upstairs. "We'll see you later."

Tired and hungry, Cord went upstairs and showered and drank a few units he pulled from the refrigerator. He wondered if he'd ever taste the real thing again, remembering every nuance of the blood he'd tasted from Sam as they made love.

As he walked through the main area and cafeteria of the mansion, people said hello to him or nodded as if he were part of the donation center. He missed the camaraderie of his staff and worried about them. He would have to speak to Hunter about a way to send instructions as to the welfare of his company without arousing suspicion. Right now, Derek was dead and Cord was missing. Better for him to remain that way.

When Cord got back to the lab, he found Kay still sleeping. So he lay down on the gurney and fell into a sort of twilight, neither awake or asleep, which seemed to be the way he rested now. He could feel Sam nearby and wondered if she missed him. He certainly missed her.

Pictures of their lovemaking invaded his mind, and he realized she put them there. *Stop. My daughter is in the next bed.*

She grinned. I seem to be all alone in this one.

An invitation I can't refuse.

Without knowing how but that he would be able, Cord woke up. *What about Kay?*

Stacy will be up soon.

With his daughter's welfare off his mind, Cord hurried out of the mansion and through the grounds to the small cottage Sam stayed in. He lifted his hand to knock on the door. "What the hell am I doing?"

She laughed and opened the damned thing. "I would have thought the answer quite obvious." They stared at one another for what felt like a century before she stepped back to let him in. Once the door closed, Cord pulled her into his arms. Once inside his embrace, he realized just how right she felt in his arms.

"When I'm with you like this, I can't think straight."

He kissed the skin of her neck, finding the sweet spot just inside her collarbone. She jumped, and he did it again. "So beautiful." He worked his way across her shoulder, drowning in the scent of oranges and the tang of spice.

"I don't want you to think straight. I want your blood to boil with mine. I want your insides to fire. I want to drink from you."

Cord let go. She had on a robe but nothing underneath. He parted the robe and dove into the valley between her breasts while unsnapping his pants and pushing them down. There'd be time later for the bed.

He lifted her in his arms and pushed his cock inside. He kissed her and gave her a piece of his soul. He slanted his mouth to drink in more of her, and his insides cooled to molten lava. Thrusting upwards with his hips, she moaned, and he spread her legs wider so he could drive deeper.

Using the wall for balance, Cord gripped the bottom of each of her thighs, and thrust faster and faster. He kissed her, but she tore her mouth away. He felt a pinch and the draw of blood from his neck. Each sip created a live wire to his cock. When she finished, he could smell his blood on her lips, a heady aphrodisiac, but not more than drinking her blood in return. Hadn't she called her blood nectar once? Sweet and filled with power, Cord felt a connection stronger than any he'd felt before.

Physically, he could feel the warm velvet of her core surrounding his cock. But through the connection, he sank inside Sam. He felt with her and through her, if that were possible. He understood which movement would create the most pleasure and which would create more.

Cord withdrew almost all the way out and thrust inside her body faster and faster. He let go of her neck and kissed her again, then broke away to draw air into lungs that wouldn't fill. She spread her legs, and he pushed even deeper, and they fell off the precipice together. He cried out, she yelled in a language he'd never heard before but understood. How could this be possible?

With Sam, anything was possible.

He withdrew, and Sam slid down the wall. Neither of them could catch their breath. He stepped out of his pants and lifted her up into his arms, laying her down on the bed as if she were priceless.

She was.

"What just happened?" he asked, divesting his shoes and socks and sliding next to her.

"Besides amazing? I don't know."

"We—we were connected when I drank from you. For a moment, I became you."

She blushed. What? Sam blushing? "And I you. Very strange but very wonderful. A gift from The Mother, I think."

"Did you just say strange?"

"Yes. I've never connected with anyone before. Ever. Not even Antu."

He rolled over and nestled between her legs. "Maybe we should see if it happens again."

It didn't. But Cord decided he wouldn't give up trying.

Chapter Twenty-Five

SAM STEPPED OFF THE ELEVATOR INTO THE LAB. THEY'D RUN OUT OF time. Cord looked like a bundle of nervous energy. She'd never seen him pace before. Hunter looked weak and tired and more than ready to become a guinea pig. Tori sat by his side, their bond made of steel. Tori believed the cure would work. Cord believed. How could she doubt?

And yet she did. She trusted in the things she understood, and she didn't know science. But The Mother kept moving them toward this purpose, so Sam stayed the course. "This is your fight now, my friend," she told Hunter. "Go for it."

He smiled. "Knowing you stand by my side is enough. Thank you."

Not one to show too many emotions, Sam opened her arms, and Tori stepped inside. "Trust in The Mother."

Sam let go, and Tori nodded. "No worries."

Never a patient being, Sam found the wait the hardest. She would have faced a hundred soldiers rather than one more glance from her friends. She wanted to pace, decided not to, and walked over to where Cord talked quietly with Kay.

He nodded and left as she approached. No help there.

"You're not frightened," Sam commented, sitting down in about the same spot Cord sat. "Good."

With her long darker blonde hair and huge eyes, Sam thought the girl very beautiful. And her irises. Brown and warm. Nuya's eyes. Sam chided herself for being fanciful, blinked, and the feeling vanished.

As Sam stared, Kay drew her eyebrows together. "I know you, don't I?"

The child had a right to know the truth. "Yes. Through The Mother's touch."

"My heart?" Sam nodded. "Dad says you're all vampires."

Sam smiled. "We are. Does this bother you?"

The girl drew in a long breath and let the air out slowly. "It's taking a bit to get used to. I'm used to watching television shows and movies, not being part of them."

Sam huffed out a breath. "When I was your age and still human, the thought of liquid nitrogen freezing specimens would have counted the same."

"Gotcha." Kay cocked her head so much like Cord, Sam found it hard to draw in more air. "Dad says he really screwed up, and Hunter is sick because he was trying to find a cure for my disease."

"He did. But if Hunter and all the others affected can be cured, then your father will have fixed the problem he created."

"And you?" Sam found Kay's stare curious and judgmental and a touch uncomfortable. "Can you fix the problem you created?"

Sam smiled. Intelligent and quick. She liked Kay. "I don't know. Sometimes I follow the direction of my creator without asking about consequences."

"Your creator?"

"Our beginnings stem from over five thousand years in the past. An alien race visited our planet. They gave us many wonderful things but there was a price. There's always a price."

"Like me?"

So very bright. Impressive. "Yes. There is a protein we create that can heal open wounds. We use this protein to close the puncture wounds we create by drinking." Kay stilled. Yes, Sam decided.

Vampires were hard to take in. "We are also to be able to give humans a chemical to make them forget we've sipped."

Kay made a face. "Sipped. Jeez, you make it sound like you're sharing a glass of wine or something."

Sam's first instinct was to become insulted, but ignorance was the decision not to know. Kay wanted to understand. "To us, blood is sweeter than wine."

Kay frowned. Perhaps she didn't need to have all the facts all at once, Sam decided. Time was the greatest accelerator of acceptance. Thus, it would be prudent to end vampire lessons for today.

"Anyway," she continued. "Your father has figured out how to use this protein to fix Hunter from the inside. Tori thinks a tiny amount of these cells will make you whole again. But it will change you, not that you're the same now, but you will never be truly human again."

"I was dying. Dad was desperate."

"Very," Sam agreed.

"Don't get me wrong. I'm grateful. But I think Dad will have a hard time accepting my decision if I don't."

"You've thought about your future a lot, haven't you?"

"Hard not to do when you sit in a chair with nowhere to go."

"Then I will give you this advice. Free will is not always free, and the choices we make have consequences beyond what we can see at the time we make them. However, you must still choose what you know and feel is right, right here, right now." Kay nodded, her look very mature for a teenager. "Your father has grown much through his mistakes. Don't be so sure."

Kay nodded, and Sam rose. She watched Stacy walk over to Kay, glad Kay had someone completely human to relate to. A shiver ran down Sam's spine, and she wondered why. She closed her eyes sensing a change in Hunter. Good or bad?

She opened them and hurried over to him. "How do you feel my friend?" She clasped Hunter's hand and could almost feel his cells repairing themselves.

"Better." He clenched his jaw and squeezed Tori's hand hard. "The pain is manageable. This cure won't be fun." He paused and swallowed. "You might want to put a warning label on it."

Sam breathed a huge sigh of relief. Tori started crying. Cord lifted his shoulders and leaned back, letting go of the tension inside. The cure worked.

A couple of hours later with some fresh blood inside, Hunter was ready to get up. He stood, planted his feet as if ready to face an army, and began flexing his fingers and his arm as if to say he needed to fight. "I seem to be missing my sword."

Tori threw her arms around him, laughing and crying at the same time, and Hunter kissed the top of her head as he banded his arms around her.

"I'm going to need a couple of specimens. Just to make sure you're all vampire again," Cord said, the relief in his gaze palpable.

Hunter smiled. "I am. I am."

"We used nearly an entire bag of plasma to introduce the cells into Hunter's bloodstream," Cord added. "We're not going to have that luxury with any of the rogues we're fighting. "The best I can come up with is maybe one hundred microliters and a large gauge needle, so it doesn't take long to inject. I don't think we'll have time for more."

"We can try concentrating the cells now that we know they work," Stacy suggested. She caught Sam's gaze and smiled.

"Do the best you can," she advised.

She shared a look with Hunter, knowing he felt the danger with her. But surprise filled her as she looked at Cord, almost as if he could see the picture in her mind. Were they so attuned now that she couldn't hide her deepest fear?

"He's coming."

Cord walked over without saying a word and pulled her into his arms. Sam ignored the surprised stares. She simply listened to his heartbeat, wondering if this would be the last time she heard the sound.

Chapter Twenty-Six

EVERYONE LEFT THE LAB. THEY ALL NEEDED SPACE, TIME TO SHARE A last kiss. No one, not even Sam, knew the future.

Cord wouldn't let her go, and Sam listened to the steady beat of his heart knowing she belonged in his arms. The Mother never gave her an easy path to tread. And if she allowed her mind to race as fast as her heart, Sam would ask the purpose their union. To make her choice that much harder to bear?

"I don't want to let you go," Cord whispered.

To keep said organ from splitting into tiny pieces, Sam answered, "Are you sure? Kay's staring at us."

"She'll get used to it."

"She will?" Mothering instincts weren't her forte.

Cord drew back, and Sam stared up at him. "I don't have time for a sandy beach, blue-green water, Tikki torches, and champagne. But I—"

Sam placed a finger on his lips. "Don't. Please. Once said, they can never be taken back."

He frowned. "Why would I want to?"

"Because Antu is coming. Once the battle begins, I won't be returning."

"Yeah," he replied. "You've told me." His jaw clenched and his gaze shuttered. He breathed deeply, and she felt his body soften. "Any chance I can get you to reconsider?"

"You know the answer is no."

"Then you leave me no choice." He looked down at her, and she recognized what rested in his gaze. "I love you, Samira-Anai-SeBat. I love the queen, and I love the woman. I love the protector, and I love the squirmy thing melting under my touch."

"Squirmy thing?" She drew her chin into her neck and widened her eyes. "I do not squirm."

He bit his lip, and his shoulders shook. But Sam didn't think his implication funny. She'd built a wall around her heart foreseeing this very moment only to find the wall already cracking.

"And no," he continued. "I'm not some figment from your past, simply the flesh and blood, arrogant-assed scientist."

Fight or flight took over, and flight won. "Your daughter is really staring at us now."

"She's not the one who wants to love you for the rest of whatever eternity we have. I am."

Sam pushed at his chest. He simply tightened his grip. "I've been a queen far too long to know how to love any other way."

"Liar. I've held you in my arms. Samira, not the queen. I think you know all too well, but you don't want to open yourself up long enough to admit it. Don't be a coward."

"I've never been frightened of anything in my life," she snapped, trying to fight her way out of his grasp. His grin made her words a lie the moment they passed her lips. "All right. Antu scares me. And small places like the elevator."

His grin faded into a hollow shadow of the half smile she'd come to know and enjoy, and she stopped fighting. "I don't expect you to dismiss five thousand years of obligation."

"Obligation?" Wounded by the word she bit out, "So you really think saving the entire vampire race is an obligation? If you do, then you know nothing about me, and you know nothing about love."

He grimaced. "Do the needs of the many always have to outweigh the one?"

Sam sighed, the truth a pain in her guts. "I'm sorry. They do."

"What if I begged you to stay?"

Pleased and horrified, Sam took the 'queen' road. "Such an act is beneath you."

He made a face. "Don't be so sure."

"Cord. Please. Our memories are perfect. Let them remain this way." She pushed, and he finally let go. "I need you with me, by my side."

He huffed and shrugged. "Of course, you do."

The elevator doors opened. Stacy walked out of the elevator with Chaz right behind her. "We're gathering plasma right now. As soon as Tori and I thought there might be a chance the cure might work, we made extra plates, but I'll make some more. We'll probably need them."

"Can I help?"

Kay? Cord's daughter? Sam turned to stare. Kay had dressed and pulled her hair back in a ponytail. She'd risen, a little shaky, but remained on her feet by the bed. "Do you feel well enough?"

"Yes."

Cord walked over to his daughter, his gaze asking the same question. Then he hugged her hard. Inside her mind she heard Kay add, *"She's okay. You've hooked up with worse."*

Sam should have been insulted, and she wondered why she wasn't.

"Have I?"

Sam watched the girl nod. Cord looked put out for a moment then said, "Guess I have."

She turned to her friend. "Stacy, you and Kay will remain here. Once you've finished gathering the plasma, the rest of the donation center must close."

"Consider it done."

Sam pulled out her key to the prison and walked over to Stacy. "I am going to take Bahir and Miklos out of jail now. Chaz, you'll stay here, please?" He nodded. "Good. Cord?"

Cord kissed Kay and walk toward Sam. "As you requested. By your side."

HUNTER ALREADY WAITED FOR THEM AT THE PRISON ALONG WITH Mercy and two guards. "He is coming," Sam said. "But you both had knowledge of this part of his plan. What else, I wonder, does he have up his sleeve?"

"My lady. I beg of you. The thirst."

"Are you too proud to drink from a bag, Bahir?"

"Perhaps proud is not the correct word," he answered.

"And Miklos didn't agree?"

"I did not," the vampire leader said.

"Poor Bahir. So faithful, delighting in the scraps your master gives you. How do you like those scraps now?"

"The taste, my lady. The taste. So harsh. So cold."

"I'd have thought you'd be used to such an environment." She shrugged. "I guess not."

"I am ever your servant."

"Very well. I am returning you both to your master." Miklos frowned and drew his shoulders back, not accepting the mantle her words carried. "He can do with you what he wants."

"No tricks?" Miklos asked.

"None." She motioned to Hunter to open the door. "One moment. Trust is a fragile commodity. Must I put you both in shackles?"

Bahir looked insulted, and Miklos narrowed his gaze. "I give you my word I will not try to escape, my lady," Bahir said. Miklos didn't answer but he did nod.

"And you promise not to feed until you return to your master?"

Again, both men nodded.

Hunter opened the cell. Since the stairway was narrow and curved at one point, they all had to ascend in single file. Sam led the way with Bahir behind her, then Cord and Hunter flanking Miklos. Mercy followed to make sure no one tried to escape.

Sam reached the rock landing that led back to the banks of refrigerators and turned to push Miklos in front of her. Bahir came up behind her and faster than any one of them ever expected, pulled out a knife, and made to stab her with the blade. Where had he gotten the knife? Cord moved faster than she thought possible, putting himself between her and Miklos and taking the blade meant to hurt her.

Miklos ran, and Bahir tried to follow. Hunter caught the ancient vampire and lifted him off his feet by the throat. She'd never seen Hunter so angry before. Hunter shook Bahir like a rag doll, squeezing until she heard the snap of Bahir's neck. Then Mercy cut off his head.

So much for loyalty.

Sam looked down at Cord, and the world turned over in her chest. "The protein. Get some protein."

Mercy ran off to do as she asked. She looked over, but Hunter and the other soldiers were already gone, looking for Miklos. Then she bent down, sat, lifted Cord's head, and settled it in her lap. "Thank you."

Sam wanted to lick the wound to close the skin and stop the bleeding, but she understood the protein would do a better job. Besides, the bleeding had already slowed.

"I told you. Sometimes the needs of the one…" he coughed.

Sam shook her head, urging him to stay still. "Don't try to talk."

By The Mother and The Father! Would there never be an end?

Mercy ran back with Tori right behind her. Tori used a syringe and carefully placed a drop inside the wound and as that tissue healed worked her way to the outermost skin. She used three more drops to finish the process.

Cord said, "I'm all right. I can feel it working. Painful but I'm healing."

Sam looked deep inside his gaze. The words couldn't be spoken out loud. She hoped he would understand. Her heart belonged to him now as did her soul.

What a waste. They'd never be able to share their lives together. War knocked on the doorstep. Sam had no choice but to answer.

Chapter Twenty-Seven

SAM COULDN'T BE FOUND ANYWHERE. TORI HAD FINISHED MAKING THE syringes, and Stacy and Kay were locked inside the jail cell for their own protection. Cord felt a little lightheaded and his side hurt, but he was ready to fight. He walked out of the lab determined to prove Sam and her prophesy wrong.

"So newborn, you have decided to fall in love with her. Not a good idea."

"Better than the one you've come up with."

"Perhaps." Cord recognized the man beneath the golden crown, holding a jeweled scepter in his hand, his robe black with red lettering that seemed familiar. "This ending was inevitable."

"I don't know. You could've simply taken what you wanted. I couldn't have stopped you."

"I am my Father."

"A pity."

Nuya's face, so like his own, filled his head. "I needed to kill you again."

Cord laughed softly. "You didn't then, you haven't now. Guess you're not perfect after all."

Cord watched Antu's grip tighten on the scepter. "Nuya was weak." Did he hear doubt in Antu's voice? "He thought with his heart."

"And I think with my head." Cord would have smirked but goading the, yes he *was just a man, wouldn't be a good idea.* "Bahir is dead. I'm still alive. Science. It'll get you every time."

Antu cocked his head. "Not all plans succeed as they are drawn."

"True. But The Mother and The Father left behind a gift. I have a cure. We're going to neutralize your army."

Antu shrugged as if he couldn't care less. "Armies come and armies go. You are insignificant. They are tools."

"And I thought I was arrogant." Cord smiled, reading the concern in his gaze. "She's coming for you."

"She will die."

"Not if I have anything to say about it."

"You?" Antu guffawed. "You are a flea. An annoying flea."

"And I still bite hard enough to hurt. Which is why you wanted me dead and were willing to sacrifice Bahir to do it."

"Not exactly," the vampire retorted, shaking his head.

"Gotcha," Cord replied. "You want her, you'll always want her, to suffer."

"There aren't enough eons in the universe to satisfy my vengeance."

With a huff, Cord answered, "He who lives by the sword, dies by the sword."

Antu laughed. "How does it feel to share her heart with a ghost? Crowded?"

"Just fine, not that you'd understand." Cord recognized goading when he saw it. "You've always been too vain for your own good."

"And you're too weak. All of you."

"We'll see."

Cord shook his head and blinked a couple of times. The hallway to his room inside the mansion came into view slowly. Along with Hunter's face. "Are you all right?"

"You heard?"

Hunter nodded. "He's trying to get you to make a mistake."

"Not me," Cord countered. "Sam. He wants her face to face for the finale."

"Then we need to hurry. Antu brought Miklos' men. He's lied to them and told them we hold their leader hostage and want to over-throw the Council."

Cord ran to his room and grabbed the knife and holster Chaz had given him. He came out to find Hunter wielding a wicked looking

Roman short sword in his hand. "Use that sword," Cord told him. "And Antu will know you're at full strength."

Respect filled Hunter's gaze as he answered, "I can fake it until the time comes. Besides, you need protection. Your death would merely be an added benefit."

They sprinted down a set of stairs, through another hallway, and into the cafeteria where they met up with Mercy. "The woods," she said. They all ran past the patio and toward the forested area of the property. "The north field," Mercy added.

They skirted the tennis court and sped through the opening in the woods Mercy indicated. Not far in, Cord smelled blood. His mouth watered, and his insides clenched. He looked over to find Hunter staring with concern. "I'll be all right."

Chaz joined them as they ran through the woods. Skidding to a halt once they reached a large clearing, Cord watched vampire fight vampire, brother against brother. The sight sickened him. So unnecessary. Such a waste. His gut hollowed leaving nothing but emptiness.

Hunter simply got angry. He smashed his sword against a tree and the sound rang through the air. Cord watched Hunter's face tighten and his jaw clench. "Stop!" Hunter yelled. "I said HOLD!"

The fighting slowed, and Cord realized Sam wasn't there. "We protect, we do not kill each other," Hunter shouted. "Is your loyalty so blind you cannot see you're being used?"

"You want war. You want to overthrow The Council," a vampire called out.

The fighting began to slow. "Not me," Hunter cried. "The high priest Antu. He wants this war. He wants you all to bow to him and serve him."

"We serve no one," another vampire called out.

Soon the clash and ring of swords faded into the distance. But like a forest fire, one spark could cause the flames to erupt again.

"Then why do you fight?" Hunter asked.

No one answered. Good. They were thinking. "Antu doesn't care about you. And your leader?" Cord spat on the ground. "He makes promises he cannot keep, and you believe them. Why?"

Again, no one answered.

"Antu is my maker," Hunter continued. There was a rustle in the silence, a shifting of weight by some of the combatants. Not many knew. "But I refuse to serve him. I spent my entire human life in the service of evil and evil men. I will do so no longer."

"And what of you?" Cord asked, turning in a circle to survey them all. "I spent my entire human life in the service of mankind. Now I will spend my next life in your service. Will you do the same?" Cord watched carefully. At least he had their attention. "The men you trust don't care about you. Especially Miklos. He's betrayed your trust for his own gain."

All of a sudden, Cord sensed Sam approach with Miklos. She walked into the clearing, and they all saw that Miklos neither limped nor used a cane. An angry murmur ran through the crowd.

Hearing the discord, Miklos seemed to switch gears. "Would you deny me the freedom from the pain that has plagued me for an eternity?"

Cord felt a shift in sentiment as some heads nodded in sympathy. He asked, "At what cost?"

"Cost?" Miklos repeated, looking down his nose at Cord.

"Their freedom."

Haughty and entitled Miklos cocked his head and stared at Cord. "They are my soldiers."

"Are they?"

Silence. Good. Better than good. More than some of them were thinking now.

Miklos discerned how to play a crowd and play them well. "You have sworn your allegiance to me, have you not? Have I not served you? Kept you safe? Given you all blood and shelter?"

More nods than Cord cared to acknowledge. "Allegiance is one thing, being used for personal gain quite another." Cord turned in a circle again. "He promised you would fight for Antu. In return, Antu healed his leg. So who exactly, do you serve?"

Many shook their heads, and the feeling running through the crowd of soldiers filled with tension, not all of it good.

"You swore you would fight for me!" Miklos cried.

Silence filled the air, and Cord could hear the wind rustle through the treetops. The smell of blood was everywhere, heady and fragrant. Hearts pounded from exertion and anger, perhaps even fear. The dawn approached, and no one moved.

"Out of his own mouth! In his own arrogance!" Cord continued. "All of you are things, not people to him. You are weapons ordered to fight on his whim. What kind of leader asks this of his people? A leader asks his people to fight to protect. What is Miklos asking all of you to do?"

When no one said anything, Cord answered for them. "Die."

THE ROGUES CAME AT THEM FROM EVERYWHERE. ONE MOMENT THEY were talking in the clearing, the next? They were facing an out of control, mad-hungry horde. Cord had just enough time to pull out the syringes in his pocket. Hunter stood by his side, feinting and parrying until Cord could deliver a cure. And another cure. And another.

When Cord ran out of syringes, he scrambled over to one of Sam's fallen fighters and searched until he found more. The rogues began to falter and fall, writhing on the ground in pain as the cure began to work.

Once Miklos' soldiers saw what he and Mercy, Chaz and Vanessa, and Hunter's men were doing, trying to save, trying to protect and not kill, they began moving as one unit, herding the rogues into the center of the clearing. Many broke free to feed off the fallen, and they lost their heads because of their uncontrollable thirst.

Hunter remained with him, and Cord kept trying to find more syringes to administer. He looked up once from his task to find Sam, and for a moment he watched her fight, in awe of her skill.

Soon though, he reached the inevitable. He ran out of the cure. But the tide of the battle had turned. Soldiers were able to work as one to subdue and destroy the remaining rogues. Hunter protected him, but Cord also needed to protect Hunter, not that he was a master fighter. Far from it. But he was able to guard Hunter's back. And though he felt sad that these rogues had to die, they had no choice but to destroy them.

And Sam? She worked in tandem with Vanessa now, their skill with sword and knife a sight to behold. When the last of the rogues fled, Mercy directed teams to follow.

Tori arrived with units of blood and IVs for the wounded, and Cord helped administer them. But Cord couldn't help thinking of all the waste. War, any war, only left people dead.

Once the wounded were cared for and the dead gathered, Mercy directed her soldiers to help take the wounded back to the mansion. Hunter went with them while Mercy and some of Miklos' warriors spread out around the perimeter of the compound in case of another attack.

The dead would be buried for now.

"Hunter, Sam's gone. So is Miklos. She's going to Antu. My guess is to offer Miklos as some kind of peace offering. I have to leave. If something happens to me, take care of Kayla. She trusts Tori and Stacy and looks up to you. She thinks Chaz is cool. Keep her safe for me. Tell her I love her. When she's old enough, try to make her understand I didn't leave her."

Cord ran out of the clearing. He followed her scent once the odor of blood stopped permeating the air. He wasn't surprised to find the trail led back to her cabin.

Someone had cleared an area in front of the cabin and small porch. Sam stood on the porch with Miklos pinned against the railing and a knife pressed against his throat.

Her eyes widened when she saw Cord, then shuttered.

"Sam. Please. You're not a murderer." She kept her thoughts out of his reach.

"You're right. We fought. I won."

"Let him go."

She lifted her gaze to the trees beyond the cabin. "Come out brother. Take this piece of offal back. I don't want him."

Antu answered, his deep voice almost melodic. "Seems we are of like minds. I couldn't get the prize I really wanted."

Kayla!

"What an idea!" Antu continued, walking out to the edge of the trees. "To lock the humans up in the jail to protect them. I'm incredibly impressed, young one. I might be able to bend titanium bars a bit but certainly not enough to get inside. And blowing the bars out of the rock wall might have created projectiles or a landslide which would have hurt the one I sought. Well done."

Dear God. Would the nonsense ever end? "Another game? Is that it?"

"Another choice. Another impossible choice. For those are the ones that truly titillate the psyche. I do love them so. I cannot tell you, describe to you, the pleasure in watching beings writhe. The power is intoxicating. What should I do? What should I do?"

Cord found Antu's falsetto annoying. More annoying than the vampire himself. "Problem is, like any addiction, the length of time the pleasure lasts keeps getting shorter and shorter."

"Yes, well, that is why we have to play more games. You do understand, don't you? I am helpless. I answer to a higher power."

"You answer to your own miserable desires, nothing more," Cord shot back.

"Enough!" Sam shouted. "Stop drawing out the inevitable. Either you take Miklos back or I kill him."

Antu shrugged and threw up his hand with nonchalant insouciance. "Kill him. I don't care."

"What?" Miklos roared. The elder vampire struggled in Sam's grasp as outrage darkened both his cheeks. "You promised me."

"What?" Antu shot back. "What, exactly, did I promise? I gave you the one thing you desired above all else, freedom from pain. I cured your leg, but in death, pain is also irrelevant, is it not?"

Sam's shoulder slumped. Her grip loosened, and Miklos shrugged away easily. "I tried to warn you," she told the elder vampire.

Miklos ended up stumbling down the steps into the clearing in front of the porch. He straightened. What a blow for such a proud man.

"Betrayer. *Dolos.*" Miklos spat on the ground. "You even shame *Apate*, the goddess of deception. You call yourself a king? You think of yourself as the benevolent ruler? You don't deserve the ground I walk on. Come and fight like a man."

Sam threw him her sword, and Miklos tipped his head in thanks. Antu charged out from the edge of the woods almost faster than Cord could see. Miklos countered a killing stroke just in the nick of time. Still, the scent of blood filled the air from a small cut on Miklos' neck.

"Is this the best you can do?" Miklos spat on the ground again. "You couldn't stand up to my best fighter."

"Miklos. Have a care," Sam called out in warning. "He's toying with you. He wants me, not you."

Still trying to protect. Cord couldn't believe his ears. His heart swelled inside his chest. Sam was magnificent.

"Too late," Miklos replied.

Cord had to give the elder vampire credit. He saw no fear in the man's stance and heard nothing more than righteous indignation in Miklos' voice.

Antu played the game for all his worth, digging his sword blade into the ground and letting Miklos attack, then at the last second, picking it up and parrying the blow. Miklos would feint then swing from the opposite direction, Antu would evade and regroup. Steel rang on steel and at one point, Antu even stuck his tongue between his teeth, completely engrossed in their fight.

But Antu was indeed stronger and the better fighter. Miklos planted his now healed leg and twisted, swinging his sword behind him to protect, but the blade arrived a hair late. Antu slashed him behind the knees leaving them with cut tendons so Miklos could not rise.

Miklos fell to the ground, screaming in pain.

"Brother," Sam begged. "Please do not do this."

Miklos lifted up onto his hands and knees. He couldn't stand but he rose so he could sit back on his heels. "Finish it."

Cord cried out. "NO!"

Too late. Antu took Miklos' head with a single stroke.

Chapter Twenty-Eight

SAM WALKED SLOWLY TOWARD THE FALLEN BODY. ANGER PULSED through her veins with every contraction of her heart but as that muscle expanded to push the fluid of her life once again, all she felt was remorse.

Choices. Damn them. Damn them all to hell. She wanted to tear off the mantle of leadership she wore and stomp on it until there was nothing left. With her next breath, she wanted to fall on her knees and lovingly pick up the pieces and cradle them to her chest while she begged forgiveness.

Antu stared at her with a slight smirk on his lips. He lifted a single brow. The thrones had to become one.

Cord. Solid. True. A rock in a sea nearly out of control. He'd followed her. She would always carry this knowledge inside her heart. "I must go. The time has come."

"Stay." She felt his fingers curl around her arm and tighten to stop her. He pulled, swinging her around to face him. "He'll break you first. Don't ask me to sit by and watch him break you."

"He'll try, which will take a long time, a very long time."

No, it won't.

She wouldn't, couldn't spare Antu an ounce of thought until she absolutely had to. She looked up into Cord's eyes and lost herself within him. "Once I'm sure you're all safe and going to stay that way, I'll challenge him."

Challenge me? Really?

"And you simply expect me to watch?" Cord bit out.

"Yes. For the sake of your daughter and the rest of the vampires in this world? YES!"

Sam broke out of his grasp. She flashed over to her sword lying next to Miklos' body. Faster than Cord would ever be able to see, she swung her elbow into his jaw and brought the handle of her sword down on the back of his neck. He fell forward, surprise filling his insides, pain swamping his head. He moaned, then he dropped his head to the ground.

ANTU CLAPPED, THE SOUND REVERBERATING THROUGH THE TREES. "Sister."

"Brother."

Sam gripped the hilt of her sword tight. "The place never mattered," she began. "You've waited a long time to create the perfect end to the perfect beginning."

"Beginning?" He seemed surprised by the word. "Was there hope in your heart for a return to the old days?" Both of his brows lifted high into his forehead. "After what you did?"

"After what *I* did?" Sam scoffed. "You still can't see you were wrong."

They circled one another, Sam looking for the slightest weakness, Antu believing he had none.

"There can only be one now. One throne. One ruler. I am The Father. I will be king."

Had he not seen the vision? Could his vision be different from hers?

Sam decided to reply to his words to try and find out. "To rule?" He stared at her, suspicious of the question. "How?"

Antu stuck his chin out, but his gaze remained cautious. "With benevolence. With a stern hand when necessary. As we did before."

"And then what? Every vampire? Every human? Kneeling to King Antu? See the future as it will be. Year after year, century upon century, millennia upon millennia. No one left to fight. No purpose remaining. Peace, but no harmony. Because of something you can't see and will never see. The destruction of free will. Then what? What will be left?"

"I will move them. I will mold them. I will bend them."

"And break them? Continue," she commanded. "See the future you wish to make."

"I know the future. They will fight to be free. As punishment, I will set them against each other."

"Again. Continue. You will make them fight until none remain. Can't you see? Your outcome never changes. No matter what variables exist, no one is left. You defeat your own desire. What you seek will destroy you in the end. Why will you not change your path?"

Sam watched Antu frown. "Why do you ask? You will be long dead."

"My death is my fate no matter what I do. So is yours. We are not immortal. So the importance of my death is what matters. If I die trying to stop your insanity, then I will not die in vain."

Antu puffed out his chest and actually smiled. "You cannot defeat me."

Sam always thought Antu drowned in the sin of pride and arrogance. But to be completely blind to the truth? Did someone's hand guide them both now?

If so, Sam needed to finish what she'd started.

Born of The Mother, Sam had never truly accepted The Father into her heart. She'd never truly understood the ways of the warrior, preferring compassion to steel. Now, she realized, the time had come to embrace both sides. She pictured the scorpions side by side, The Father black with his red stripe, The Mother red with black on her back, and she watched the two meld. Power surged through her body.

In this, at least, Sam understood. The feeling drug-like, heady and gone way too quickly. Was this the power Antu sought?

His eyes widened, then his gaze narrowed. "You feel it too, don't you?" he asked.

"Yes."

He looked—he looked jealous. "Intoxicating, isn't it?"

A terrible sadness filled her. "No. Though I understand now. What you seek was meant as a gift, given once, to remain inside. Your entire existence has been to find this feeling again. But you can't. It is never the same, never enough."

"That power is mine by right!" Antu cried as he gathered himself. "And when I subdue every living creature on this planet, The Father will bestow it upon me again."

Her heart broke for him, for the man who gave her sunsets, the warrior who fought to protect. Antu no longer bore any resemblance to this man. "The Father gave you ten times, one hundred times what I felt, didn't he? So you could destroy the Temple."

Sam watched his face light up with the memory. "You will never know. You could never know. The absolute purity flowing through my body. I was invincible. I am invincible."

Thousands upon thousands of times worse than the call of the blood. How cruel. And yet, so necessary. Antu would never have succeeded without The Father's help.

"Did you also know The Mother saved my life that day? She helped me escape with Lia."

Lia stood guard in her chamber, her sword drawn and ready to fight. Samira strapped on her armor, ready to protect Lia. Neither of them expected a panel inside the wall to move or her mentor to motion for them to follow.

"Of course, I know."

"The Mother gave Mensah the plan to put a false panel into my room. We were almost at the grove when your soldiers caught up with us. He turned to stand and fight. Mensah, the scholar, Mensah the teacher, who probably never wielded a sword in his life. He forced me to leave. He told me I had to live. He told me there was more at stake than just his life. He gave his life for me that day, and now I know why."

"You know nothing."

Sam laughed. "I don't?"

Antu stilled, the light in his eyes dimming. "What do you mean?"

"You poor fool. I pity you. All this time thinking you were safe from the whims of The Father, that as his prodigy, no, as his son, you were invulnerable."

"What are you talking about?"

"The tomb. The plans. The passages, the places where moving a single rock would cause a cave-in. Who do you think gave me those plans?"

Antu frowned and didn't answer right away. "He would never betray me."

Incredulous Sam asked, "As you could never betray Bahir? Miklos? Where do you think the spite and the jealousy come from? The Father gave you these emotions so you would want to destroy the temple."

Antu began to pace. "I don't believe you."

"What his ultimate purpose was, I'll never truly know. I've always believed the destruction necessary, that there could only be the image of one Mother and one Father on this earth, and that creating more than one would eventually lead toward annihilation. Now I'm not sure. The reason may simply have been jealousy. I don't think it matters anymore. Even after all these millennia, you still exist for one purpose."

He asked even though every fiber of her being told her he didn't want to. "And what is that?"

"Destruction."

"Impossible."

Sam lifted a single brow. "Why? What does a child, who is no longer a child, do with a toy? Set it aside. Bury it. Even destroy it." With a sinking heart, Sam realized Antu would never, ever, believe her. "Brother, listen to me. Hear my words. We don't belong here. We never did."

"But we are here."

"Yes, and we must move on, we have to move on. We must find a way to coexist." Sam stilled. "Or your path becomes the only path. Creating new vampires simply to have them fight and die so you can make more until the day you too, go rogue."

He stiffened, scorn dripping from his voice. "Never."

"Why do you keep denying the truth? You are already in the toy box, Antu! You continue to wear blinders. They are done with us. They've gone somewhere else to create their mischief. But we still have one thing. We still have free will. We can choose not to follow their path. We can choose our own."

Filled with anger, Antu roared, "And do what?" Sam watched his entire body shake. "Become subservient? Be their caretakers? Debase myself to a human?"

Such sadness. So painful. Sam nearly doubled over in anguish. "You never let her in. Always respectful, always eager to please, but your heart had already closed. You will never understand because you cannot accept The Mother. This is why you could never love me, why you were distant and cold, even when you held me in your arms. Can you not try? Open your heart. Let her in."

Antu refused to speak. Silence stretched out. Sam wasn't even sure he considered her words. She already understood his answer. Every muscle in his body clenched, his back straightened, and his fist clutched the hilt of his sword.

"I cannot."

With those two words, Antu sealed their fate.

Samira sank into the gift The Father bestowed. Pure power flowed through her veins. But while Antu could do nothing more than drown, Sam swam past the euphoria and watched as she and Antu battled each other for eternity.

Her stomach hollowed with the truth. At one with both The Mother and The Father, she saw their choice. Either they fought each other through the galaxies, or they coexisted under an uneasy truce.

Sam fell to her knees. "Great Mother and Father, I submit to your will for their sake, for every being on this planet. If this is your decision, so be it."

Antu looked to one side, then the other. He looked up and down. "What's happening?" he asked, fear in his tone.

"We become The Mother and The Father. Not in their image but worse, in their truth. We exist now only to thwart the plans and devices of the other. We are the queen and king on an empty chess board. Every move you make, I will counter. Neither of us will win."

"You cannot do this!" Antu cried, raising his face to the heavens. "I have worked too hard, waited too long."

Sam rose to her feet. "The Father doesn't care. This is why The Mother allowed you to destroy the Temple. There can only be the two of us, keeping each other in check, one seeming to win for a time but never in reality."

The ultimate sacrifice. No submission, no destruction, simply a counterbalance. No matter how hard Antu tried, Sam would always be given a way, a means to thwart him. No matter how hard she tried to protect the people, Antu would always be waiting in the wings with his plans, subjugating vampires and humans to his will and his whim.

For a split fraction of a second, fear hollowed her insides. And then she remembered Mensah's answer when she asked her teacher why he'd chosen her. "Because of your strength, little one."

Sam lifted her chin. She rose to her full height. "You cannot destroy me."

The Father's power surged again through her veins.

"Of course, I can."

Antu lifted his sword, still red with Miklos' blood, and charged. He thrust, she evaded with ease. He sliced sideways to cut off her head and Sam ducked, reminded of the way things looked in slow motion on television. Antu advanced, she defended or countered. Finally, he stopped, chest heaving, his gaze filled with confusion and yes, fear.

Tears filled her eyes, her pain not only for herself but for him, and for the first time since her human life, Sam felt wetness on her cheeks. Another gift from The Mother?

"We are now the endless cycle. You will scheme and destroy. You will seek revenge. I will thwart your schemes and protect those you wish to destroy. I will counter your revenge. For how long? I don't know. You will become craftier and more vicious. I will become more secretive and devious. We will become The Mother and The Father."

Antu slashed again. By instinct, by whatever power they'd given her, she felt the blow coming and evaded his stroke once again.

"I will rain suffering and destruction on everyone you care about," he promised.

His words tore her insides to shreds. How she hated him in this moment. But again, she would always answer. "I will protect them as much as I am able, then they will be born anew for that is also part of the gift."

He slashed again, swinging his sword faster than the eye could see. And this time, Sam didn't try to evade, she simple countered before his blade bit her neck. "We are endless, Antu. We will continue like this forever. Don't you see? We were the ultimate sacrifice. You obeyed without question, and I questioned everything."

She sighed, already weary of the task. "They had the choice. They could have left our planet. But they were so hungry, and once they tasted our blood, such nectar to their starvation, they simply couldn't leave. Not until they were sated, not until they had enough to keep them alive for the next part of their journey."

Were they wrong, she wondered? Was survival at any cost wrong? Sam didn't know. "You have a choice. I beg of you. Please. Stop this insanity now."

Antu leaped at her. "Never."

Chapter Twenty-Nine

CORD COULD FEEL THE PAIN IN HIS HEAD BUT FROM A DISTANCE, AS IF he were in one place and the pain another. He opened his eyes, registering the scrape of the ground beneath his cheek. Lifting his head, he watched a ballet unfold. Antu would attack, and Sam would parry, almost as if the moves were choreographed.

He rose to his knees. The horizon refused to settle, weaving this way and the other, and his stomach turned over. Cord swallowed and lifted up to one knee not knowing what to do. How could he interfere without Sam getting hurt? Besides, she seemed to be holding her own just fine.

Then Antu roared out a word Cord couldn't quite make out. Antu locked Sam in his arms, and Cord watched in abject horror as Antu's incisors grew to an unbelievable length, and he bit down into her neck.

Strength surged through his body. If given the chance, Antu would drain Sam dry, and such an act could never be allowed. He rose to his feet and jumped, pouncing on Antu's back. He tried with all his strength to pry Antu of Sam. When he couldn't, Cord did the only thing he could think of. He bit down on Antu's neck.

Made from The Mother, drunk on The Father, Cord would never

be able to explain the sensation of power coursing through his veins. Antu tried to throw him off, but Cord clung to his back and would not allow Antu his freedom—unless he let go of Sam.

Cord drew in deep draughts of blood. He sucked until he couldn't, breathed, and then sucked again. His heart didn't just pound, didn't just thud, it was as if the poor organ could shake the very foundations of the world.

Cord felt Antu's indecision, so he kept on drawing Antu's blood into his body. Life flooded Cord's being. As soon as they became joined, Cord understood the balance Sam talked about. Without both The Mother and The Father, they were all doomed.

Thought crashed upon thought. Antu couldn't die, but if he remained alive, how could vampires continue? Antu wanted to kill them all.

Cord reached out with one arm. He slid his wrist against Sam's lips. *Drink, my love. Complete the circle. Let me be the conduit that saves us all.*

The instant Sam bit down, Cord recognized the center. He started to describe it as the universe, but that word wasn't exactly correct. The center of oneself became a truer definition. So he stepped into the center of himself and like the float, he found calm and peace and strength.

With each draw on his wrist, he felt Sam do the same. Together they met on a plane deeper than the metaphysical, a place he would never be able to describe. Another dimension? He would never know.

Outside their sphere, Antu became this maelstrom, sort of like the Tasmanian Devil cartoon character. He had no purpose, no direction. He was all fury and fire and pure destruction.

"Brother. You cannot continue. Let go of the storm."

Amazed, Cord realized she still cared for him. Then he corrected his thoughts. She still cared for everyone.

Lightning flared, and the air shook with rumbles of thunder. A sudden, great Crack! made Cord jump.

I am The Father!

In unison, Sam and Cord replied, "No, you're not."

The storm around them grew in intensity as Sam continued. *"The*

Father was stern, but just. He used power but did not become drunk upon it. Change your path."

"Or die," Cord finished.

Antu drew the storm inside himself. Cord looked over at Sam. She wouldn't harm Antu. Cord let go of her and faced Antu, using the eye, the float, to center his being.

Antu charged. Power burst all around him, but Cord felt nothing. Lightning raged. Thunder boomed. Antu charged again with the same result.

"We can go on like this for an eternity, Antu," Cord said. "And I will remain here to fight you until years become eons if this is what you choose."

"No!" Sam cried. "Fighting for an eternity is my destiny, not yours."

"How touching," Antu mocked. "Both of you wanting to battle me. Both of you thinking I am your destiny."

Cord filled Antu's mind with the never-ending loop of hurling bolt after bolt of lightning and having Cord absorb every one. As he did, Cord felt a sense of peace descend.

"Fear not, my love. I will always be with you," Cord told her

"No. I won't let you sacrifice yourself," Sam replied.

All of a sudden, Sam frowned and then her eyes widened. "Together."

Yes, of course. "Together."

She walked up to him and lifted her gaze, melting inside him. He looked down and opened his being, melting inside of her. He bent his head. Their lips touched.

Slowly, they drew Antu's essence into themselves. Antu had forgotten that love was at their core, always and forever. And though they had a different way of showing it, the balance between The Mother and The Father wasn't some kind of physical tangent. The balance was love. In spite of their faults, The Mother and The Father shared a deep and abiding love, and Antu had missed it completely.

Cord broke the chain first. He drew the last draught of Antu's blood into his body. Sam broke the chain next and opened her eyes as she withdrew her incisors from his wrist. Cord jumped off Antu's back just as the man fell to the ground.

"By The Father," he whispered.

"And The Mother," she answered.

"He's in the eye now. The float. He's at peace."

"Yes." She sighed, a long shuddering breath. "I must take his head."

"Are you sure?"

She smiled. "Mensah told me I was destined for great things. I never understood what he meant until now."

Hunter and Tori, Chaz and Stacy, Kay, Mercy, and Vanessa, all came running into the clearing. Kay yelled, "Dad! Dad!"

Each one of them stopped to stare at the body on the ground. "Is he dead?" Stacy asked.

"He lives yet he does not," Sam answered. "But he is at peace now."

Kay simply threw herself into his arms. "Thank God you're okay."

"What happened?" Tori asked.

"Cord has taken the essence of The Father from Antu. He cannot harm anyone again, but it would be unfair to let his soul remain bound to this earth. Antu was a tyrant, but he was also a king. We will light a pyre tonight for him and all those who have died."

Cord turned to Hunter. "Seems we don't need a scientific cure anymore. The cure has been both The Mother and The Father as Sam has always said. We are both joined now. We are both Mother and Father. We are both the cure."

Hunter laughed, a hearty, head-thrown-back laugh. "Good. Because I never told you. I hate needles."

AFTER THE REMNANTS OF THE BATTLE WERE REMOVED, AFTER SOLDIERS took Antu's body away, after the people he'd come to know and love had come and gone, only Kay and Sam remained. Sam walked into her cottage, and he had no need to read her mind to know she wanted to give him some space with his daughter.

"I thought I lost you," Kay told Cord, her voice wavering. However, she didn't cry, simply let the tears build in her eyes.

Wonder filled him. He would never get used to this feeling of being at one with, well, everything. "Can you feel the connection between us? I mean, I'm connected to every being on this planet now. But can you sense—?"

"That you would never be lost?" she interrupted. "Yes. Yes, I can."

He walked up onto the porch with her and leaned against the railing. "Whatever you decide to do will be fine with me."

"You mean, the enhanced mitochondria?" she asked, picking at the wood of the railing.

Cord couldn't help but smile. "Tori told you, eh?"

"Yes." Kay lifted her gaze. "I like her. She's honest and genuine."

"I like her, too." He threw his daughter a look. "Is this your way of changing the subject?"

"What? No, not at all. I'm just not sure what I'll be. Will I be like Tori? Like you?"

"I don't know exactly. But a good guess is that Tori's more vampire, and you'll be more human. With some vampiric enhancements."

She considered his words and then burst out, "Way cool."

Cord frowned. "I don't think so."

"Yeah, secrecy, blah, blah, blah."

"Your life is not a joke. Do you understand? Serious. Please." He swallowed hard. Seemed being at one with the universe still didn't help negate the fear of being a parent. "You won't be able to tell anyone. Ever. Or your life may be forfeit. Vampires have rules a for a reason."

She sobered immediately. "Gotcha."

"And I don't ever want you to be frightened of me, of what I am. Do you understand?"

"I'm not," she protested.

Cord lifted the corner of his mouth. "Vampires have a saying. There is the blood and can only ever be the blood. But, well, because of circumstances, I'm not a newbie anymore."

"I understand, Dad. And it's okay, you know."

"Yes. Better than not being around, eh?"

"Much better." She nodded. "For both of us."

Cord looked down into her eyes, Allie's eyes, and he realized they would be all right. "This isn't exactly the way I'd planned to save your life. And now I've gone and gotten you mixed up in stuff that should be in a movie theater. I hope you don't mind."

She shrugged. "Can we rebuild the stables?"

"Sure. I was even thinking of doing some remodeling. Removing the ramps and perhaps adding a master suite."

Kay's eyes widened. She tilted her head. Eventually, she smiled. "I'm down with that. I like Sam"

"To be honest, I think she's more frightened of you than you'll ever be of her."

I can hear your entire conversation. Cord bit back a grin.

"Would it be all right to work with Tori?" Kay continued. "I mean, I'm home schooled and tutored way beyond high school." She paused to gauge his reaction. "She's patient and a good teacher."

"All right. No objections."

Kay nodded as if coming to a decision. "I think I'd like to be a doctor. So many people took care of me in the hospital, then at home. I'd kind of like to pay it forward."

"Does this mean you don't want to go back to school?"

He caught glimpses of the cruelty she had endured, and his fingers curled into fists. "Some of the kids were mean. Others were awesome. I know who my friends are."

"If Tori says you can finish your studies with her, then so be it. I have access to wealth I never expected. When you're ready, and Tori agrees, we'll talk colleges. Okay?"

Kay nodded, flashing him a brilliant smile, and with teenaged impetuousness, hugged him hard. Letting go, she said, "I love you, Dad."

"I love you too."

A few minutes later, Chaz and Stacy walked into the clearing. "We can guide her back to the mansion if you'd like," Chaz offered.

Cord nodded. "Thanks. I have some things I need to discuss with Sam. We'll be there in a little while."

Stacy grinned, long enough to get an elbow in the ribs from her husband. They walked away with Stacy placing an arm about Kay's shoulders. Once they were gone, Sam came out of the cottage to stand next to Cord. He slipped behind her and wrapped her in his arms.

"Kay's beautiful," Sam told him. "And you were right. I think I'm more frightened of her than she will ever be of me."

"Maybe. But before we go there, I need to try to understand what happened to us."

Chapter Thirty

BECAUSE SHE UNDERSTOOD THE MOTHER AND THE FATHER FOR SO much longer, Sam had more insight into both of them. "This is one where your science isn't going to help you."

"I kind of figured." He looked a bit bewildered but ready to accept her explanation. "We were joined in a place almost like another dimension."

She thought about the word for a moment. "Yes."

"Okay. But I'm still processing."

Sam laughed. "Because you exist on logic. And?"

"I think we were able to join 'energies.'"

"All life is energy if you wish to use the term," she agreed.

"I feel like I'm part of you, but I'm not. I feel like I'm a part of them, but I'm not. I can hear them all. I can feel them all. I can see them all."

"Yes."

"And not just vampires. Humans too."

Sam loved the awe in his voice. He appreciated that which Antu dismissed.

"You've had this ability?" he asked. "All this time?"

"Not as strong. More like a background."

He thought about her answer for a moment. "You know, things are starting to make sense."

She laughed. "Still trying to force logic into the equation."

He laughed with her. "There's this incredible connection now. So much more vast."

"Beyond global."

"Indeed." He wrapped his arms around her. "I'm not up for sitting on some kind of throne. I hope you don't mind."

She didn't. "I think the vision was quite clear. No more thrones."

"Good." He stared off into space for a moment. "There's a lot more I can do with the mitochondria and vampire cells. Research. Adaptation. Cures for other diseases. No one will know where they came from."

"For Kay?"

"If she wants them. Her choice. But no, for everyone."

Sam felt the pieces falling into place. "She's beautiful, you know."

He smiled with a father's pride. "Can you imagine? I still can't believe it. She wants to work with Tori and become a doctor." He feathered a thumb down Sam's cheek. "She could use a mother too."

"Me?"

He nodded.

"The idea scares me more than facing Antu. I'm overbearing, demanding, impatient, short-sighted."

He kept on nodding. "And you have enough heart to love the world and then some."

Pleased, Sam squeezed the hands covering her waist. "We're going to have other duties. People will be people."

She could hear his disappointment as he answered, "Guess I'm going to have to learn how to share."

"Sometimes."

Sam opened herself for a moment. She could feel them all. In her mind she could see Tori and Stacy, even Kayla, tending to the wounded, and she could feel the respect and gratitude flowing from the soldiers they helped. Vanessa sat in a room sharpening her knife, ready to hunt. Chaz planned for the same hunt knowing he'd have to keep Vanessa in check, for not all the rogues had been cured and all of them would have to be found. If too far gone, they would have to be destroyed. Mostly, he waited for the time when he could be alone with his mate.

Sam felt Mercy and the mantle of leadership the vampiress wore so well as she tended to the dead. Inside her heart, Sam found Hunter, the fierce leader, her true brother, standing on the patio surveying his home. He smiled, for there could be no words between them. The danger, for now, had passed. They were safe. Until the next time.

Cord's finger tilted her chin upwards. He leaned over her shoulder and kissed her lips. Their love was the cure, the lasting cure.

"Will it always be like this between us?" he asked.

Sam shivered. "By The Mother, I hope so."

"So do I."

Cord lifted her in his arms. She looped her arms around his neck. He pushed open her door with his foot and kicked it closed with his heel. He let her legs go once they were inside, and her feet touched the floor.

She curled her hand around his neck and swirled her fingertip down his cheek. She projected and he stilled, for she created a memory for him to drown in.

They were sitting in the middle of a tent with a small fire burning inside a rock circle. The scent of the desert filled her nostrils, and Sam inhaled deeply. Outside were the last stripes of pink of the setting sun. Horses stamped, impatient for their dinner. Meat roasted over a pit, making her mouth water. The light breeze beaded her skin.

"Is this real?"

"As real as you wish it to be."

She smiled as he looked down to find not jeans and a shirt but a robe of soft wool, black with red lettering. She glanced down to find herself in a similar robe but of red with black lettering. He sat up against a pile of large pillows and next to him on a table rested a goblet of fine wine.

She gave him the wine first, and he sipped, still cautious according to his nature. She turned the cup and drank from the place his lips had touched. His gaze warmed. She parted the robe over his chest.

His body had become bronzed by the sun, his nipples dark and begging for attention. Biting her lip, she pulled back.

She could hear faint music in the distance, and she began to sway, following the movements of a dance taught in childhood. She twisted and turned, leaning in with a dare for him to touch, skittering away when he tried.

He smiled and drank from the cup again and leaned back. His robe opened wider, and she could see the prize awaiting her, lengthening with yearning for her touch. She stopped dancing and stood before him, taking the edges of his robe and draping it over his cock.

He sucked in a huge breath. "I hope you're not going to waste——"

"You may only touch."

She leaned forward to let him play with her breasts, sinking into the shivery warmth of his touch. Then she pulled back and danced some more, whirling faster and faster until she didn't know which end was up.

She stopped, and the room spun for a second. His gaze darkened with desire, and he shucked his robe. Sam crawled up the pillows to straddle his hips, the tip of his erection glistening in the firelight. Bending down, she worshipped him, lathing her tongue all over.

He hissed in a breath and grabbed at her head. She smiled, and he lifted her up to bite and suck her breasts. Her head swam. Her heart raced. The drum beat loud in her ears. She pushed him back.

With the utmost care, Sam pushed herself down on his cock. She took in the head, swallowing hard as her core opened to accept penetration. Cord growled, and Sam laughed. But she wouldn't let him deeper inside until she could control the movement. He fell back on the bed, and she could feel his fingers fist the folds of his robe, now strewn around their bodies.

He bit his lip, splitting it with a growing incisor. Blood welled, and Sam lapped at his lip. She sank down and opened her hips until no space remained between their bodies.

She moaned and leaned over to kiss his lips. His mouth covered hers, and their tongues mated as they were mated for whatever eternity remained.

His cock swelled, and Sam smiled inside. Someday, they might make love long and slow, but tonight was about sharing and loving and ecstasy. So she lifted her hips and rode him. His hands wrapped around her hips. But at the last moment, he rolled her so he was on top and plunged into her body. He spread kisses all over her face and neck, his incisors scraping against her skin. Faster and faster, harder and harder, she met each thrust until they both exploded in an incredible bright white light.

When Sam returned to reality, they were naked on her bed in her little cottage that suddenly seemed too small.

He smiled down at her. "I think we're going to have to enjoy this gift more often, don't you?"

"Indeed."

"I hope a plain old bedroom doesn't get stale."

She laughed. "We will never be—stale."

"I could use a bigger bed."

"You have your home. I have Sanctuary. We will bring new life to both races."

He laughed as well. "I guess the needs of the few outweigh the needs of the many now."

"We are the few. We are the many. We are all. We are none. This is what I've been trying to tell you."

Able to finally smile, Cord said, "Consider the lesson complete."

Epilogue

CORD WATCHED KAY WALK TOWARD HIM IN HER GOWN. HIS BREATH caught in his throat, and his heart seemed to swell out of his chest. Since the bond between Tori and his daughter only continued to grow, Tori had asked Kay to be part of the wedding party. She would be a bridesmaid and lead the procession down the aisle.

"You clean up nice," Kay said, patting the lapel of his tuxedo.

Stunned, he let his pride shine in his gaze. "You look beautiful."

"Who looks beautiful?"

Sam stepped into the hallway. Cord's jaw dropped. The simple powder-blue, Grecian-styled gown left less to the imagination than he cared to admit on his daughter and more than he wanted on his love.

"Dad? Earth to Dad."

He shook his head. "I must be the luckiest man in the world. You both look stunning."

Kay frowned, biting her lip. "Do you think Nick will think so?"

Nicholas Costanic, the new stablehand he'd hired, and a very smart young man. Smart enough, Cord hoped, to understand the boundaries surrounding his daughter. Certainly, smart enough to have earned one of the scholarships he planned on donating to Princeton, possibly smart enough to work for CoRRStar someday.

"Yes, he will."

Kay lifted up on her toes and kissed him on the cheek, then hurried ahead of them as she was first in line.

"There will be twenty vampires keeping an eye on her. And him. Relax," Sam said with a huge grin on her face. "She knows what she's doing and what she wants."

"Keep reminding me, okay?"

He placed Sam's hand in the crook of his arm and walked down the hallway to where Kay waited. A few minutes later, music played and Kay walked down the aisle. Hunter stood waiting at the altar, and Cord watched him shift his weight from side to side with a soft smile.

They'd transformed the patio with strings of lights in the trees and bushes, and torches flickering in the soft breeze. Flowers had been placed everywhere without a thought to being frugal, their fragrance soft but heady. The evening shined bright and clear, the sky filled with stars, but a touch chilly, so space heaters helped keep the guests comfortable.

Cord walked down the aisle, then let go of Sam to stand next to Hunter and Chaz. Hunter rolled his neck beneath the shirt of his tuxedo, another indication of his nerves. Seemed the human gladiator and vampire leader had finally met something he actually feared.

Hunter stilled, and Cord looked up. He wondered if his friend would ever breathe again. Tori wore a simple white gown in the Grecian style with lace sleeves, thin straps, and a 'V' neck that plunged low between her breasts. Her hair sat atop her head, held together with a thin snaking band of silver, and two whisps of hair lined her cheeks. She looked—perfect.

The ceremony began, and as Tori and Hunter spoke their vows, Cord knew the future was theirs to mold. Or perhaps parts were preordained? Pictures filled his mind. Tori paced inside a hospital, holding a baby girl in her arms, and strong, stern Hunter followed, looking completely helpless. A young boy of about six or seven years stood with tears dripping down his cheeks, lost and alone, until Stacy kneeled and pulled him into her arms. Chaz kept apologizing for they'd been too late. There would always be rogues to deal with. Kay, strong and beautiful, wore a cap and gown as she walked with her fellow graduates to receive her diploma, sharing a special smile with her beau, Nick.

Cord came back to the present just in time to hear the words, "You may kiss the bride."

As they walked back down the aisle, Cord asked Sam, "Do you want a wedding? We can have one if you'd like. And a honeymoon. Perhaps somewhere on a private Caribbean Island or something like that?"

She considered the offer for a long moment. "No, no wedding necessary. We are bound beyond life. But I definitely like the idea of the private island."

They'd transformed the cafeteria into a banquet hall with drapes of cloth, screens, sconces, and flowers. Centerpieces graced each table, and the sideboard had been turned into a huge buffet.

In keeping with current traditions, the wedding party and then the bride and groom were introduced.

"They belong together," Sam commented as Tori and Hunter danced their first dance.

"Easy for you to say. I was the one who had to take him for dance lessons."

Sam laughed and poured them each a glass of wine.

"Did you know we would win?"

She sobered. "There were many choices and many paths and numerous possibilities. I hoped."

Cord finally understood. Needs, choices, many, few, none of it mattered when they followed the flow of love. "Very reassuring."

Dancers crowded the small dance floor. Cord watched Sam jump up and down and twist and turn with abandon until she stopped, stood before him, and tugged on his hand to join her.

"No way."

She showed him what the future held for him after the wedding, and he shook his head, lost before he could get out a word of protest. He followed, thinking, *choices. Right. Destiny was more like it.*

Thank you for reading! Did you enjoy? Please add your review because nothing helps an author more and encourages readers to take a chance on a book than a review.

Also be sure to sign up for the City Owl Press newsletter to receive notice of all book releases!

And find more from Linda J. Parisi at www.lindajparisi.com

Until then read more paranormal books like COYOTE CALLING from City Owl Author, Heather McCorkle. Turn the page for a sneak peek!

Sneak Peek of Coyote Calling

BY HEATHER MCCORKLE

A brand new werewolf was close to losing their shit. I felt it deep in my bones. The swollen, nearly full moon peeked out of a cloud-strewn night sky as if to warn me of the deadline. Tomorrow I would be out of time. My not-so-trusty guide-raven Gripp cronked directions at me from the sky, but there was no way he could be right. He kept leading me back home. Chances were he was just hungry and tired of flying. I didn't blame him.

Exhausted and ravenous, I trudged to the edge of the forest that backed up to the cheap motel I called home. I stopped next to the bush I'd hidden my clothes in. Walling off the part of me most affected by the moon, I thought about how I wanted to be human. For a split second, my furred body heated and vibrated. My atoms flowed from wolf form into that of a human, smooth and fast as hot syrup onto pancakes. Damn I was hungry. I stretched, getting comfortable in my woman's skin once again. Chilly April air took the edge off heat from walking all night down to a tolerable level. As a werewolf—or *varúlfur*, as I'd learned we were called—I didn't get cold very easily, but I did overheat.

Shrouded in darkness, I soaked the cold in for several moments before reaching for my clothes. Fleece pajama shorts and a black tank top with a built-in shelf bra for the girls made for quick dressing. It might be inappropriate for traipsing around the woods at night, but I was a big believer in a girl being able to wear whatever the hell she wanted, since guys got to do it.

Slipping on my bargain store flip-flops, I started across the ten acres of knee-high golden grass lying between me and the apartment complex. Overhead, Gripp cronked excitedly as he flew ahead.

Halfway through the grass, I smelled something strange on the breeze. Not typical motel stank, or anything bad exactly. It smelled like an animal, canine, but I couldn't place it any better than that. Someone's dog, probably. I shook it off. Dreaming of a big steak and my thrift store recliner, not necessarily in that order, I trudged the rest of the way like a sleepwalker.

A small rest and snack, and I'd get back to searching. Giving up wasn't an option. If I didn't find this person by moonrise tomorrow, their first shift would trigger, and they could go insane. I felt their despair, desperation, and impending madness like an ache deep in my soul. Something else felt off about them, about their power, but I couldn't put a claw on what. This whole *leitar*—seeker—thing hadn't come with a manual—a few ancient diaries, but no manual. The most recent of those damn things was three hundred years old and in Icelandic. My Icelandic was coming along, but I was nowhere near ready to read it. Even if I had been, my history professor boyfriend, whose first language was Icelandic, could barely understand it. He described it as trying to read Shakespeare.

Gripp and I would eventually find the newly bitten werewolf. I had no doubts. We were closing in on them. The thrum deep in my bones told me so. But the ache in my stomach reminded me I had needs as well.

The closer I got to the two-story apartments, the more my stomach churned. I couldn't tell if it was hunger or something else. My exhaustion was too extreme. Gripp perched on the metal railing of the walkway to my second-story unit. What I could only describe as excited clucking issued from his vibrating throat. My bird made some seriously strange noises, particularly when he was hungry. And he knew I had leftover ground beef inside for him.

It took three tries to fumble my keys out of my pocket when I reached the parking lot. The stench of garbage overwhelmed me as I grew closer to my building. The dumpster lay not thirty feet from my door—part of the reason it was the cheapest apartment in the building—and garbage day was tomorrow. I held my nose and fought a gag reflex as I rushed past it to get to my door. I froze in place when I realized the door was unlocked.

Management knew better than to go anywhere near my room. The day I'd signed the month-to-month lease on this dump, I made it clear to them their services would not be needed. A glimpse of fang had been all the convincing they needed. It didn't risk exposing us. The majority of people convinced themselves later they hadn't seen what they thought they had, and the rest would dismiss me as a freak of nature. My boyfriend, Ty, didn't have a key. We were working on personal space and him respecting my need for independence. He wouldn't violate my privacy like this.

It had to be my roommate. Barely a minute over eighteen, Candice wasn't exactly the picture of responsibility. But she was supposed to be waiting tables at her new job tonight.

The sound of breathing and a heartbeat came from inside. Once again, I felt that strange power. This time it emanated from inside my apartment. Definitely not Candice. Chills of trepidation shot through me, banishing the exhaustion. My fingernails lengthened and hardened into claws, and a double set of fangs extended from my top and bottom canine teeth. Before I lost my temper and stormed into danger, I took a deep breath and stepped back. A moment after, I gathered enough control to retract my claws and fangs and take my phone from my pocket.

I shot off a quick text to Ty: *Someone is in my hotel room.*

My stomach roiled again, but I realized this time it wasn't hunger. It never had been. A troubled newly bitten near madness stood on the other side of that door. I knew it deep in my Cherokee Swedish bones. The canine scent came from my motel room, but it wasn't my own or Candice's. Hell, it wasn't even wolf. Without thinking, I opened the door.

A beige and gray canine with a slender frame and ears too big for its head sat in the small space between the desk and bed. It stood, back arched, hair up along it. Lips curled back from its teeth and it growled at me. Gripp cronked at it as if to tell me, "I told you it was here."

On instinct, I bared my fangs and stepped toward it. Angry yips punctuated its growls. Pissed at the intrusion and aggression, I let loose a growl of my own that made its sound pathetic.

"Shift!" I commanded with the full force of my power behind the words. That power shot into the coyote like an arrow, lodged itself deep within, and pulled at the human buried inside. It was painful and invasive, but I had learned it was often the only way. Most newbies who had inadvertently shifted couldn't shift back of their own will. What I didn't want to think about at the moment was how that meant they were sometimes beyond saving—sometimes being the key word.

The coyote shook violently before it blurred and flowed like water splashing out of a container. A moment later a naked woman crouched in the canine's place, body hidden mostly behind a blanket of long, tangled, black locks. The beautiful hue of her skin, angles of her face, shape of her nose, and set of her eyes marked her as Navajo. Chills raced through my body as I kicked the door closed behind me. Tears filled her mahogany eyes when she looked up at me and beseeched, "Help me."

Don't stop now. Keep reading with your copy of COYOTE CALLING from City Owl Author, Heather McCorkle.

And find more from Linda J. Parisi at www.lindajparisi.com

Want more paranormal? Check out COYOTE CALLING from City Owl Author, Heather McCorkle, available now! And find more from Linda J. Parisi at www.lindajparisi.com

---

The children of Fenrir are rising whether werewolf seeker Sonya Michaelson likes it or not.

Sonya's hot college professor boyfriend wants nothing more than for her to move in with him and settle down where he can keep her safe. But Sonya is no damsel in distress, let alone someone's lap dog, even if he is a Viking descended werewolf hot as Thor. She has werewolves tangoing with madness to save, and a new mystery to solve when a coyote shifter shows up on her doorstep. Navajo women are going missing—skinwalkers to be precise. What's worse, someone is turning them into coyote shifters, stripping them of their skinwalker powers.

But before she even has a chance to dig into the mystery, she and her best bud, reaper Ayra Valdisdöttir, are summoned before the Caninus Council to answer for their part in an event that risked exposing their kind to the mundane world. Dancing with council politics quickly take a back burner when Sonya realizes her mother has gone missing— and the reason seems to be directly tied to the abducted skinwalkers.

The appearance of an estranged relative she's never met along with a warning of more to come—people with their own agenda that she shouldn't trust—may be the curve ball that topples Sonya's Atlas-sized load of problems. If she doesn't find a way to hold it together, fend off the council's denizens, and solve the mystery of the missing women, several people will die—herself included.

Please sign up for the City Owl Press newsletter for chances to win special subscriber-only contests and giveaways as well as receiving information on upcoming releases and special excerpts.

All reviews are **welcome** and **appreciated**. Please consider leaving one on your favorite social media and book buying sites.

For books in the world of romance and speculative fiction that embody Innovation, Creativity, and Affordability, check out City Owl Press at www.cityowlpress.com.

Acknowledgments

Once again, my editor Tee Tate pulled the very best writing out of my fingertips. The pleasure and treasure of working with you has been all mine.

Once again, my agent extraordinaire, Eva Scalzo, has been with me through thick and thin. I can't thank you enough.

Once again, my CP Christine Clemetson, jumped in without hesitation to help me get this book in on time. Thank you for all of your help.

Without my publisher, City Owl Press, I would never have had the opportunity to bring my vampires to life. An author can only envision what he/she thinks will be a finished product. This book far exceeded any expectations I could have had.

Last but not least, my support network (you all know who you are), has kept me going through an unimaginable time. I don't know what I would have done without your love, your caring, your prayers and positive energy. Thank You.

About the Author

As a major in biochemistry with a minor in English literature, LINDA J. PARISI has always tried to mesh her love of science with her love of the written word. A clinical research scientist by day and NJRW Golden Leaf winner, N.N. Light's Book Heaven 2021 Paranormal Romance Award winner, and the 2022 HOLT Medallion winner for Speculative Fiction by night, she creates unforgettable characters and puts them in untenable situations, much to their dismay. Choices always matter and love conquers all, so a happy-ever-after is a must. Linda is a member of the Board of Liberty States Fiction Writers. She has served on the boards of other writing organizations, and loves to teach the craft of writing at workshops and conferences. She lives in New Jersey with her husband John, son Chris, daughter-in-law Sara, and Audi and Archer, a pair of pooches who had her at *woof!*

www.lindajparisi.com

About the Publisher

City Owl Press is a cutting edge indie publishing company, bringing the world of romance and speculative fiction to discerning readers.

Escape Your World. Get Lost in Ours!

www.cityowlpress.com

facebook.com/YourCityOwlPress

twitter.com/cityowlpress

instagram.com/cityowlbooks

pinterest.com/cityowlpress

Made in the USA
Middletown, DE
13 September 2022